JULIA ISLAND
A Novel

James Charles Harwood

Julia Island: A Novel

Address all inquiries to:
James Harwood
19320 Orange Ave.
Sonoma, Ca 95476
(707) 321-0764
jamescharwood@me.com

ISBN: 978-1-7374852-0-9
Library of Congress Control Number: 2021913867

Editor: Tyler Tichelaar, Superior Book Productions
Cover Design and Interior Layout: Larry Alexander, Superior Book Productions
Cover Image: Alamy
Author Photo: Pete Sheret

Every attempt has been made to source properly all quotes.

To Amy, love of my life

Acknowledgments

To Amy, who introduced me to the
magical wilderness of the Upper Peninsula.

To Gary Zukav, who introduced me to the
world of Quantum Physics.

To Marcus Luttrell, who described
the realities of desert combat.

To Matt Bissonnette for details on
Operation Neptune Spear.

To Darryl Richards, who encouraged me
to go ahead with my book.

Contents

BOOK ONE

Chapter 1
Hiawatha, Child of Nature

H IAWATHA AWOKE TO A BLAZING orange sunrise through the
bedroom window. His guardian eagle watched him rise and felt
free to spread his wings and lift into the northern wind. Hiawatha had
been blessed with this arrangement since his birth.

He had been born to Jonnye Heywood, a flower child, and sired
by an unknown father, whose identity Hiawatha had invented in his
dreams. He was certain he was the son of Gitche Hay-oh-Went'-Ta,
half of the Spirit World, and that this was the source of his remarkable
power.

The birthing ceremony had not been unusual for the time. Jonnye
had convened her circle of spirit-questing friends in a makeshift sweat
lodge in a remote part of her family's vast property. They welcomed Hiawatha into our world of three dimensions. All the requisite parapher-
nalia was gathered: drums, rattles, chimes (hash pipes). The chanting
continued well after the surprisingly quick and effortless birth, where-
upon the little tribe was invited to dine on the placenta as a source of
strength and enlightenment. This ritual was never consummated, due
to the distraction of Hiawatha himself, who was born with his brown
eyes wide open and a beatific smile, which he bestowed upon each of
the transfixed attendants.

And so began this singular life, set firmly in a bastion of inherited
Gilded Age privilege, and connected solidly to the invisible further dimensions predicted by quantum mechanics and relativity. And above
it all, outside the wigwam, perched Mikiziw, the eagle, set to observe
and assist his young charge throughout the next several decades.

For twenty years, except once, Hiawatha never left the confines of the Chippewa Club, founded in 1889 by the most powerful and influential industrialists of their day. Its original denizens were Scottish, Victorian, and Presbyterian. Its current members were diluted in heritage and in purpose. Hiawatha was the extreme example of how far afield the membership could diverge in a few short generations. Born precocious, set free and naked by his mother at an early age, he set about memorizing the hundreds of square miles of the property, returning to the family cabin most evenings. He swam the great Red Pine Lake chain from end to end at the age of ten. He climbed Mt. Argon at age twelve and worshiped at the dolmen of his ancestors before any of the European descendants even knew what it was. He seemed to be installed with a memory chip for the Ojibwa language, which no one ever taught him. His fellowship with the creatures of the property was fraternal. And so, growing stronger and more independent, he established a network of trails and water routes whereby he could quickly and easily transport himself throughout his domain.

At the same time, his Caucasian status was accelerated by a series of circumstances that would have been hard to predict. Jonnye continued her spiritual quest, ranging farther away and for longer periods, accompanied by a rapidly evolving procession of companions. Finally, word came of her untimely death from a drug overdose in Morocco. Hiawatha, according to the bylaws of the club, assumed her full membership at the age of thirteen.

In Jonnye's absence, Hiawatha's maternal grandfather, Great Daddy McMillion, confined to the family cabin by a series of strokes, became his mentor on the intellectual plane. Unable to speak or otherwise communicate with his large family of five children and their eight offspring, Great Daddy's great joy became the telepathic streaming of information with Hiawatha. Silently, seated on the veranda of the giant log cabin, built in the tradition of the Adirondack Great Camps, they covered philosophy, ancient history, mathematics, Latin and Greek. Hiawatha's education was classic, traditional, and formal. Great Daddy's unexpected benefit was a spiritual enlightenment more profound than he could ever have imagined. Of course, none of these developments were perceived by the extended McMillion family, who struggled to explain the bond between the two, sitting quietly and in perfect contentment, wrapped in Hudson Bay blankets on their Adirondack deck chairs, staring silently across the mouth of the Jack Pine River, and farther across the infinite expanse of Gitche Gumi, the Shining Big Sea Water.

If his relationship with his grandfather was puzzling, Hiawatha's mysterious and vast body of knowledge was astonishing. It seemed to arrive from nowhere. On the rare occasions when he expressed himself, it was shocking. An auspicious occasion might warrant a quote from Caesar Augustus. Adjidamo, the red squirrel, might be treated to a Shakespearean sonnet. Hiawatha was comfortable with trigonometry.

Later in life, the sonnets were to be reserved for Kelley Green, who shared the same hippy heritage and Club privilege. Kelley was a summer resident, brought by her parents for long vacations from Chicago. A child of dilettante artisans, she hadn't blushed when Hiawatha smiled in amusement at her ironic name. Her response was "Oh, I'm the lucky one. They named my sister Keep America."

And so their relationship, founded on common ground and nourished by humor, matured into an abiding mutual regard. Kelley was thoughtful, dainty, creative, and perceptive, and nearly as tuned in to her surroundings as Hiawatha was.

Kelley worshiped Hiawatha at a distance for years before he seemed to take notice. He had noticed all along, of course, his inscrutable Chippewa demeanor belying his interest. So, their relationship enjoyed the bedrock of knowing and loving each other long before the spasm of puberty accelerated their attraction. Each September, Kelley returned to Chicago and school. Hiawatha, owing to the influence and power of Great Daddy, was spared public school education. He might have been the first totally homeschooled child in the Upper Peninsula of Michigan, certainly the only transcendentally educated one.

Each fall, Hiawatha returned alone to his solo existence in the forest. He honed his skills in the art of birch bark craftsmanship. He created Christmas presents of jewelry from picture jasper, agate, and float copper. He went to the cave of Makwa, the bear, and rested his head on its great chest. Listening to the slowing beat of the bear's heart, he softly hummed lullabies and slipped into the Dream World.

Dressed in the hides of Mahingan, the wolf, Hiawatha ventured out on nights of the full moon and answered the yapping and singing of his cousin, Wiisagi-ma'iigan, the coyote. These were sublime moments of rhythm and peace, and served to give Hiawatha the calmness and assuredness he would depend upon later in times of crisis.

Fall also brought the grouse hunters. All the membership loved to hunt with Hiawatha. He was a marvel on the skeet field, shooting perfect 25s with regularity. He was a master trick shot artist with his little .410 gauge Parker, and he never used a larger gauge gun, just to keep it fair. He always knew where the birds were, naturally, and communicated directly with the Animosh, the dogs, on whether to flush them or not, depending on the politics of the situation and the attitude of the hunters. Later, in November, came the deer hunters who appreciated his stalking talents, and who relied on him to recommend which specimens to take.

In a hundred years, the Chippewa Club had progressed from a shooting and fishing club with emphasis on killing anything on the property, to an enlightened establishment of conservation-minded people, proud of their stewardship of the land. The club was held up as an example of the positive aspect of private ownership in the right hands. As for Hiawatha, he was neither fish nor fowl. In season, he hunted and fished for recreation with his lifelong friends, his fellow members. When the membership went home for the winter, he reverted to his native roots. He set snares, tanned hides, ice-fished for trout, and gill-netted the white suckers in the spring, just after ice out. He dried the mushrooms he had gathered in season, and froze the blueberries that the ancestors of his Ojibwa people had been harvesting at the mouth of the Jack Pine River for ten thousand years. In the dead of winter, when the rest of the members were home practicing law, medicine, or finance, he tied flies, tanned hides, jerked meat, and split wood. When the trout fishermen returned in May for the steelhead, Hiawatha was their man. He could tie a marabou fly right on the bank of the stream and never even put down his rod. And he knew every pool and piece of pocket water in the entire eighteen miles of the Brook Trout River, and which fish were probably in it.

In the first fifty years of the club's history, guides were hired from the local population in the town of Little Bay. Descendants of voyageurs, landlookers, trappers, and timbermen, they served the elite with all the skills of the woodsman. A hunting or fishing member, a family of picnickers, or a fine lady out for a float in one of the many Adirondack boats would have the services of a porter, oarsman, fire lighter, cook, and guard. Their skills were myriad. Their hygiene was not. The favorite saying of Wally Leppinen was "If it's been through short hairs, it's clean." Those days were now past too, and the modern membership fended for itself in the wild, unless they were with Hiawatha.

With the exception of the Greens, most families now used their memberships for a week or two during the summer. Some came every other year or less. Few really knew anything about the place, their time being spent on the sailboat races, the tennis and croquet courts, and the cocktail party circuit that ran continuously during the months of July and August. The same passage of time that had changed the ethic of the outdoorsmen had affected the sensibilities of the casual membership. Many were absolute adherents to the Green movement and all its dogma. The apolitical were of the tree-hugging variety. They were chipmunk and pinecone ecologists. Few had actual reasons for their convictions. Fewer still had a grasp of the science supporting or undermining the "consensus" of the coming Ice Age. The overriding fact was that almost no members had the time or inclination in their lives to verify scientific fact, or familiarize themselves with the vast and complex physical characteristics of the property they collectively owned. The irony was that Kelley Green was decidedly not a "Green."

One day during high season, when Hiawatha was entering his teenage years, a group arrived from suburban Enchanted Pointe on the family yacht. This was not a regular occurrence, but these were very young and accomplished emigrants from Silicon Valley. Their money was their own, and there was a lot of it. The young family and their guests moored off the shore in Lake Superior, just beyond a rough surf.

Gitche Gumi is a moody body of water, and today's mood was foul. As the young mother turned to help her daughter into the dingy, one of those quick and deadly moments arrived. The son was gone!

Hiawatha, watching from the shore, hit the water instantly, and was by the boat, diving for the body before the rest of the party fully realized the situation. One of the guests, a tanned and slender blonde, was still sipping her cocktail and asking what was wrong. In an instant, the boy was up, out of the water, spitting and screaming in Hiawatha's hands. Nobody ever forgot that moment. In those few seconds, perception, reaction, and instinct were invaluable. Hiawatha realized that despite all the talents and advantages of this brilliant group of computer geniuses, his talent was the one that mattered.

The weeping wife and mother, the shivering and bawling child, the husband, ashen with shock and fear, and the shaken, dumbstruck guests all seemed diminished and helpless to him. He suddenly saw himself as a dominant, capable, intuitive adult, and as he accepted the tearful hugs and grateful admiration of the group, he resolved to be helpful to others for the remainder of his life.

The program for child care at the Chippewa Club was time honored. It was called Niijaanis, and it was lavishly financed and overseen by a credentialed teacher on summer vacation. Each child was supervised by his own "keeper," who was usually a vacationing student. The program was essentially a summer camp within the confines of the club's vast holdings. In addition to ambitious outings involving week-long hikes to remote campsites via trails, boats, and canoes, there was a localized program for younger kids involving arts and crafts, tennis, sailing, and a chorale that performed for the adults at vespers on Sunday nights. Some years there was even an off-duty circus clown. Swimming lessons recognized achievement with the usual progression of fish names, starting with minnow. Hiawatha entered as a shark, the highest level, as a four year old. Kelley was also a very young shark, and her secret ambition was to head Niijaanis some day. When she shared her dream, Hiawatha reacted in his typical style. "Let's start now."

As a full member, Hiawatha could show up anywhere he wanted, and so that night, they decided to "moonkill" a campsite. Moonkilling was an age-old tradition among older kids at the club. They would sneak up on the little ones' campsites for the purpose of ingeniously terrifying them all, hopefully the keepers too. Tonight, the roles would change. The eldest group of older teens was encamped at Odyssey Beach, several miles down long, narrow Magic Lake. The night was perfectly calm and brightly moonlit. Hiawatha and Kelley adorned themselves in his finest Ojibwa regalia, and they set out in his hand-built birch canoe, he in his Mahingan wolf skins and war bonnet, carrying his tomahawk, and she in her deerskin and beads. There was no sneaking or spooking. They just came into full view on the lake, directly down the moonbeam reflection on the water. Murmured conversations punctuated by bursts of laughter and song echoed along the shoreline from Odyssey Beach; then dead silence as the brave and squaw were sighted. As the birch canoe made landfall, the brave alighted and sprung onto the rocks in front of the campfire, the shadows accentuating the war paint on his face and creating an impression of righteous indignation. Hiawatha spoke in a deep rhythmic voice in Ojibwa, its guttural syllables accentuated by the inflective nature of the language. The words resounded as he stood above them all, arms folded across his chest, each syllable more threatening and violent. Then, finally, brandishing the war axe, it was "Go now! You go now!" And they did! They went now, and they did it very quickly and without speaking a word. Tumbling into their boats with a tremendous clattering of oars, desperately finding their oar locks, they all went just as they were, in various stages of dress, leaving all their belongings in the camp. They rowed the two miles to their landing spot, and walked the rest of the way to the cabin compound pursued by the animal calls that everybody knew were really signals from one band of the pursuing Ojibwa warriors to another, coming from all directions. Sometimes in front, then behind, and off to the side. Kelley had a wonderful gift for coyote song, but the rest was ironically all genuine. The Bad River pack of timber wolves helped, along with Great Horned Owl and Lynx. It was great fun, and very convincing.

The next morning in the Niijaanis cabin, as the telling and retelling was in progress, Hiawatha and Kelley Green appeared in the doorway in war paint. The pandemonium was instant and prolonged. The little kids squealed their delight. The middle schoolers rolled on the floor with stomach cramps from laughter, and the teenagers smiled shyly and punched each other, deciding who had been more freaked out. Kelley and Hiawatha were now the leaders of the Niijaanis program. The teacher stayed on and accomplished administrative tasks, but the clown left. That night, it was Ojibwa tales by the campfire told by Kelley, who knew them all by heart. Great Horned Owl attended in a nearby tree, and the Bad River pack sang from up on the ridge of the Dinner Roll.

So the two continued with Niijaanis, for many years. Their method was total immersion in the land and its cultures, and the children loved it. The emphasis moved from Ping-Pong and Chinese checkers to botany and anthropology. The materials changed from plastic lanyard material to birch bark and braided cedar twine. They got a binocular dissecting microscope, used, donated by the Giacomo Medical Center in the nearest big city of Joliette. All of the overlooked belly flowers came to life. Myriad mosses and sedges with their elegant sexual parts were revealed. Gray smears of mold were transformed into microscopic cities. The armor plating of the ant lion brought exclamations of wonder. Then an eight-inch refractor arrived by parcel post for viewing Jupiter, Saturn, and the Aurora Borealis. They packed it in its special case all the way to the top of Mt. Argon, the highest point in Michigan, for the convergence of Jupiter and the moon. The sensational revelation of the planet's nine moons made astronomy students of the Thayer brothers. Always destined for great accomplishments in academia, their curiosity was whet by that moment, and they both became eminent in the field.

The great benefit to Kelley was her new role as mentor to Keep America and their kid brother Forrest. Keep America was younger, blonder, more reflective and reserved, and she observed her big sister with a studied intensity. Forrest (a family surname) attached himself to Hiawatha like a lamprey any time he could find the opportunity, and often needed to be pried off his lap at the end of a session.

Kelley developed a wildlife photography course whose emphasis was on stealth and patience, Ojibwa traits. Wonderful photos came forth. First, there were the black-and-white night photos of animals captured by trip wire. The kids tended to their setups like voyageurs to their trap lines. The results were unexpected and startling. Amazingly, the slight delay between flash and shutter created almost perfectly posed subjects every time. The herd of white-tailed deer, all looking into the lens at once. The surprised thieving raccoon, complete with mask. The pair of otters with trout draped in their jaws. All these were carefully contained in elaborate birch and hemlock frames. The parents were astounded, and snapped them up like hungry dogs. Then the most sensational and famous of the trip-wire black and whites was produced. It was a startled young Percival Ford who had let himself out through an elaborate escape mechanism down from the second floor of the family cabin for a night of adventure. He had been getting away with it for months, but this night, he was as helpless as any of the creatures. Caught in the act, and immortalized.

Then came the color photography. The vast landscapes from the natural vista points throughout the property. The lime green of new deciduous growth in springtime. The closeups of myriad temperate zone orchids. The fast exposures of tumbling water on the Brook Trout River. They were all sensational, and many became postcards for the local chamber of commerce and the board of tourism. It didn't stop there. A parent produced a Super 8 movie camera, and it was exploited immediately. The challenge became to capture obscure and esoteric plants in motion without the use of artificial light or magnification. They worked in teams, holding a mirror just so, to exploit natural sunlight, and create time-lapse photography sequences of growing plants. Keep America was steady and insightful; Forrest was an adept mirror handler.

One day, a yelp emitted from the dark room, where Kelley was developing the past night's trip-wire pictures. She bolted from the room with a 9 x 12, dripping solution and trembling at the end of her fingers. It was Wawashke, the White Deer of Chippewa legend. He'd not been seen alive since 1912, when Cyrus Rolls had shot and mounted him in the foyer of his Adirondack-style cabin. Mounted on the floor, that is, a full body mount of the likes seen in museum dioramas. The corpus was still right there for the world to see, with its tattered hide and patchy hair. Back then, all the Chippewa began sighting his apparition at once, and an oral history commenced, or rather continued as a localized extension of the ancient legend of unrequited love. Hiawatha knew him, of course. They were best of friends, and Wawashke had bestowed much wisdom over the years, but there was a code of silence between the two. It was really just common courtesy not to broadcast a prominent figure of the Spirit World throughout the cynical realm of three dimensions. Not even Kelley knew of his continued existence. Maybe this was a double, or his descendant. But no, there was no doubt. This deer was translucent! Hiawatha wondered why Wawashke would choose to reveal himself this way. Almost no one had perceived of him within club property. Hiawatha was surely alone among the membership in this regard. There he was, though, in the moonlight amplified by the flash, with Magic Stream Falls illuminated in the background. Hiawatha determined that a visit was in order.

As Dibik, the moon, crested Mt. Argon, Hiawatha set forth across Red Pine Lake to the south shore and its small boathouse. Tying his birch canoe and stowing the paddle in the rafters as protection from Gaag, the porcupine, he continued on foot along the Magic Stream trail, first the meandering part, then the rushing, tumbling gorge with its giant boulders and toppling trees. Imperceptibly, the sound slowly changed from thrumming to thundering. Then, rounding the final rockslide and crossing the narrow wooden bridge, he beheld the pool and its moonbeam. There, in its perpetual mood of persistence, was Magic Stream Falls, pounding the rocks below. And just below its billowing white fan stood Wawashke, drinking in its magical potion. His great head rose and he fluttered his ears in greeting. Emerging from the pool and climbing the steep bank, Wawashke led the way. He and Hiawatha followed the wide, shallow stream above the falls, its benign calm belying the tumult below. Soon they emerged on the sandy beach near Magic Lake boathouse, where another of Hiawatha's birch canoes hung in its sling of cedar twine. As Wawashke entered the water, his translucence was amplified in a magical mixture of moonlight and shimmering water, which spread out behind him in a fan of silver and white. It was as if he were trailing the jeweled train of a European queen, with Hiawatha in his birch canoe pulled along behind. Across the silver lake and under the effervescence of the starlit sky, they swam and floated to the western shore and its short portage to Lake Aniani.

They crossed the pretty little lake with its eagle tree and rocky outcroppings. Emerging again on the rocky point at its western end, they made their way farther, toward the camp of the Crusoe family.

Hiawatha began to sense the purpose of this trip. Over the many years of the Chippewa Club, a well-funded account had always existed for the sole purpose of acquiring land and expanding the holdings under its control. Through it all, the Crusoes were steadfast, and retained their small parcel of 640 acres within the club's boundaries. Their culture was at odds with the modern sensibilities of the membership, the staff, and Hiawatha himself—in fact, of modern society in general. In Virginia, they would have been hillbillies. They were direct descendants of voyageurs, who seemed never to have varied from the old ways, except to enthusiastically embrace modern weaponry. They lived on the property year round, and exploited every inch of it, barely short of exhausting all its resources. Hiawatha detested their use of bear traps. They fished the rivers for the endangered Coaster Brook Trout with pitchforks and lanterns during spawning season, and they were shameless baiters of deer. They also poached club property, but they were cunning, and seldom apprehended. Hiawatha had the power to arrest now, being recently deputized by the Department of Fish and Game for law enforcement within club boundaries.

Descending the last half mile at the foot of Mt. Argon, Wawashke and Hiawatha reached a meadow just outside the Crusoe section, on club property, and there it was, a giant pile of corn with a mixture of apples and cabbage from the garden. Surrounding the bait were a series of trip-wired rifles, locked and loaded. Wawashke stood for a moment, then looked upward toward the stars and vanished in a shower of white sparks. Hiawatha made his way home the way they had come, ready for tomorrow's confrontation.

In the morning, Hiawatha retrieved the warrant from the fax machine, donned his khaki DFG uniform and badge, strapped on his stainless steel Colt .44 Magnum, and drove in his Jeep to the Crusoe place. His bearing was very intimidating. He had grown tall and muscular, with the chiseled features of his Ojibwa ancestors. During childhood, he had worn a regular boy's haircut, but since his new role at Niijaanis, he had grown it, and either Kelley or Keep America had kept it braided for him, Indian style. On his way out of the compound, Mahingan, the wolf, emerged from the forest, and jumped into the passenger seat.

Jacques Crusoe was outside when he arrived, standing in front of the filthy ramshackle hut that housed the entire family. The hut bristled with hundreds upon hundreds of antlers, which obliterated the miserable tarpaper siding and cast a shadow in the morning sun with a likeness of Gaag, the porcupine. Jacques' grandson, Etienne, eyed Mahingan with a mixture of awe and curiosity. Jacques eyed him with unease. He eyed Hiawatha with defiance. Both officers of the law, the deputy and the recently deputized, alighted from the Jeep and approached.

Mikiziw circled above.

Hiawatha had pondered this situation during the little time that had remained last night. There was not too much the Crusoes had to lose. In their minds, the land was theirs, free and clear since 1688. Previous generations of Crusoes had welcomed prosecution and sentencing, with its promise of a warm bed and three meals a day. To Jacques, though, family was everything. Despite his family's abject situation and their crude means of subsistence, pride in his heritage and his concept of honor was all he really had. Hiawatha sensed a weak spot. As Etienne stroked the rough coat of Mahingan, and attempted an offering of friendship, Hiawatha amiably invited Jacques out of earshot.

"I was out at your bait station last night, Jacques. We've been over this before, man to man. This time you put it on my property."

"Oui." He spat a foul stream of tobacco juice to his side.

"But now it's different. I've been deputized, and I have a warrant for your arrest here in my pocket. Do you want me to take you in at gunpoint and in cuffs with Etienne here watching, or are you going to go up there and clean that mess up?"

Shame is a powerful emotion. As his complexion flared and then blanched, Jacques turned and looked over his shoulder at the picture of innocence, and the hint of a tear brimmed. Right then, Hiawatha knew this offense was Jacques' last.

He and Jacques kept their little secret. Jacques became compliant, even familiar over the years, and began to set an example, not always very high, but an improvement. He felt a sense of pride to be the acquaintance of such a strong and righteous man. Hiawatha had that effect on many people. One year, he even reported poachers. He came in person to the patrol office with a long section of gill net someone had been using to clean the brown trout out of Loon Lake. The poachers were apprehended and used as an example, receiving severe sentences. Jacques started shooting bear for his stew instead of letting the creatures suffer in the leg clamp. Wawashke was satisfied that the appalling slaughter of his kin was ameliorated, and that something akin to the balance of nature had been achieved.

The other great development arising from the Crusoe confrontation was Bonnie, the scruffy little Border Collie chained out in front of the filthy ramshackle hut. Jacques apparently used her as an alarm dog, and she earned little for her efforts. Chained out night and day, throughout the seasons, never brushed or combed, she was tossed what few scraps remained from the family table to supplement her gruel of boiled deer parts. None of this damped her enthusiasm for her pinched little life. She kept a happy demeanor, and seemed to live on hope alone, wagging and smiling at everyone. She longed for a romp in the forest, but was considered worthless as a hunter. Jacques thought he needed stronger, more prey-driven hounds for his endeavors of tracking and shooting, and his bird hunting up to now had made use of nets and bait, not gun and dog. Little did he know the stout heart that beat beneath that ragged and tangled breast.

As Hiawatha turned to leave the squalid encampment, Mahingan refused to budge. He had been through the canine protocol of stiff-legged sniffing, and determined that this little collie was a unique and substantial spirit. Hiawatha agreed telepathically, and simply walked over to the chained animal, bent down, and released her. She exploded in a cloud of dirt and turf. Sending up a rooster tail four-feet high, she launched herself into the back of the Jeep from an unlikely distance, and established herself as mascot to the Niijaanis band of paleface Ojibwa.

Jacques stood agape, as if slapped with a glove, his tobacco juice leaking down the stained chin. Then his countenance reflected resignation, and finally a hint of acknowledgment.

Halfway back to the compound, Mahingan leapt out into the forest and entered the domain of his Timber Wolf pack.

Bonnie entered the Niijaanis cabin with a buoyant, prancing gait, and the kids surrounded her, lavishing her with the attention she deeply craved. She expressed her heartfelt gratitude with slathering kisses for one and all. They set about putting her coat and claws in order. Soaped up and triple-rinsed, she submitted to an aggressive brushing that took the better part of an hour and produced a basketball-sized clump of fur. The matted dreadlocks of her belly and nether parts had to be shorn with paper shears. Hiawatha nipped the claws, grown curled into her pads, with bolt cutters, then filed them down with a rasp. The chafed and raw parts of her neck were dressed with iodine, leaving the impression of a soft burgundy collar. Then began the delousing. A coffee cup filled with soapy water served as depository for all ticks, great and small. Later would come a systemic repellant and worming medicine.

Fit and pretty, she was presented with a fine meal of beef stew and potatoes before joining the happy band on a short, five-mile hike to the Rock Fort, halfway up Mt. Argon, affording a vast prospect of the forest and lakes below, and Gitche Gumi sparkling in the distance. A powwow was held with feather garments, rattles, and drums. The boys performed Snake Dance and Sneak Up Dance. The girls, life givers, did the Shawl Dance. Bonnie was decorated with powdered paint and bestowed with a feather necklace. Arrows were shot in a distance contest with Hiawatha setting the standard (out of sight).

Mikiziw circled above.

Upon return, Bonnie's nest was made up for her, under the crafts table, next to the kiln, piled high with discarded goose-down pillows. Then they all went home to their family cabins for dinner, prayers, and sweet dreams of a fluffy little collie bounding ahead through the forest, always looking back to check on the welfare of her human pack.

Hiawatha and Kelley finished straightening up. As he sat recording some of his thoughts and plans in the journal, Hiawatha felt the firm pressing of Bonnie against his calf. As he crossed the room to switch off the lights, he felt her sweep past him in the doorway. She sat outside, gazing directly into his eyes, Border Collie style.

"You're not going home without me, are you?" her eyes asked.

So they crossed the compound, the three of them, across the main club bridge, down the rustic boardwalk with its pink strand of Gitche Gumi sand. Past the warmly lit cabins looming in the night, they crossed the Trappist Bridge and headed for the cabin Hiawatha had renamed Wakaigan. They stopped at his door, Kelley and Hiawatha embracing each other with their gaze, before Kelley continued on to Green Cabin where Keep America and Forrest waited for their dinner and prayers, and Hiawatha and Bonnie went inside Wakaigan.

Over time, Great Daddy regained a great deal of influence over Hiawatha's life though the brilliant and adamant expression in his eyes. The lines of communication with the family opened again. Much in the style of Muhammad Ali in his Parkinson's years, Great Daddy left it to the opposite party to guess his opinion, which he affirmed with his gaze. Later, the whole family learned to communicate using the only remaining voluntary muscle control left to him. He could contract the abductor pollicis of his right hand, and thus make himself understood through a sort of Morse code arrangement, like Stephen Hawking. The grandchildren and great-grandchildren delighted in expanding his vocabulary.

Time had come for Great Daddy to return to the city, where he would be close to proper medical facilities and cared for by the full staff retained at the family compound in Enchanted Pointe. It was a poignant farewell with all the employees of the Chippewa Club in attendance. Trail tenders, patrol officers, cooks, carpenters, mechanics, maids, secretaries, and handymen were all mustered by the general manager for the sendoff. It would be his last, and everybody knew it.

He had been brought up to the club after his strokes ten years ago. The consensus in the family was that the Chippewa Club offered a peaceful and spiritual place to pass from our world of three dimensions. That was before his deterioration turned into thriving health, of a sort, before the rediscovery of his sparkling intelligence and newfound spiritual wisdom.

Great Daddy wanted to be back at the hub of his empire. To feel the pulse of the auto company he had run for so many decades. To make his will known regarding the letter and spirit of his many charitable foundations, and to expand them exponentially since his telepathic epiphany with Hiawatha. And so the ambulance pulled away, out of the compound, and Great Daddy McMillion, grandson of the founder of the Chippewa Club, and the most dynamic and effective president in its one-hundred-year history, was gone forever (in his physical state).

Three years later, when he finally passed over into the Spirit World, Great Daddy had divested himself of nearly all his worldly possessions. Through a combination of primogeniture and consensus, Hiawatha Heywood retained his full membership and became sole owner of the Adirondack cabin, Wakaigan. He was eighteen.

Chapter 2
Hiawatha, Executioner

Above the mantelpiece in Great Daddy's library hung the head mount of Missabe, father of Mons, Hiawatha's great moose friend. It was the largest moose trophy ever collected in the history of the world, and the Smithsonian Institution had made endless overtures to Great Daddy in an effort to acquire it. The old man's unwillingness to part with the mount was an unexplained mystery, belying his generosity and philanthropic nature.

With Great Daddy gone, Hiawatha was the only person in the world who knew the truth.

It was he himself who had shot the unofficial world record moose at the age of eight.

It had been a prescient event, which verified the patriarch's suspicion of his grandson's prodigious power and sensitivity.

On an Indian Summer day, Hiawatha had been alone on one of his epic journeys throughout the vast Ojibwa wilderness.

The weather was bright and warm, and the boy lay supine, dreaming under the white landscape of alto cumulus marching in Rorschach across a powder-blue backdrop.

Lying there absorbed in his fantasies, he became aware of a visitor, large and ponderous, approaching through the aspen grove with a halting gait. It was Missabe, and he was in a pathetic state.

At the end of his time in this world of three dimensions, Missabe was in a state of torment. Racked with the pain of bot fly infestation, and riddled with parasites throughout his massive body, he had reached the point where his dental abscesses made grazing impossible.

Missabe was wasted to a shadow, and he approached Hiawatha for some kindness and nurturing.

The boy rose and cupped the warm and humid muzzle. He whispered sweet praises into the flame-shaped ears. He told Missabe what a great and important life he had led, how famous he was in the human world, and how cunning he was to have avoided the human hunters for so long a time.

The natural hunters, though, would now be forced to do their duty and provide for their own sustenance. Maingan, the wild wolf pack, would pull him down slowly, and tear him to bits. Death in the wilderness is never kind.

The young Hiawatha said, " Come; I will send you to the Spirit World."

Missabe offered his great palmate antler. (There were none to compare in all the world.) He hoisted the young brave upon his withers, and they made off in the direction of Great Daddy's cabin, Wakaigan.

At the West End Farm, where an experiment had been attempted at subsistence many years back, Hiawatha alighted and gave the sign "Wait!"

Missabe knelt and rested in the long volunteer ryegrass, bathed in the warmth of an autumn sun.

Mikiziw circled above.

Hiawatha ran and walked the two miles to Wakaigan. He entered through a side door, sneaking through the secret passage into the library.

The gun case held all manner of firearms, including Great Daddy's famous Remington 30.06. The little brave took it down, found the proper cartridge box, and loaded one round into the chamber.

Rather than retrace his steps, Hiawatha took the stealthy route back to the meadow where Missabe lay. It being high season, he had to avoid discovery by hiking or hunting members. An eight-year-old boy trekking through the forest with a 30.06 was not correct behavior even in a place like this.

Hiawatha approached the meadow straight ahead, and as he emerged from the edge of the forest, the great Missabe rose with Herculean effort, stumbled at first, and then tried again, slowly gaining his full height, and a semblance of his former grandeur.

Hiawatha held the weapon at parade rest and waited. Soon, a melancholy chant began to emanate from his small lungs. The litany of an ancient spiritual soliloquy passed through him from a mysterious source, and as he recited, each syllable was committed permanently to his memory, the sacred gift of his forebears, Chief Hole in the Day and One Called from a Distance.

Hiawatha shot from a freestanding posture, unbelievable as that may seem considering his size. The roar of the rifle rang in his ears, and the echo reverberated throughout the forest for an eternity. The recoil sent him backward several steps and landed him in a seated position. Missabe remained in his dignified regal posture for a full thirty seconds before collapsing sideways, a ruby-colored bead appearing slowly between his eyes.

Hiawatha cycled the bolt and recovered the shell casing, warm in his hand. He kept low and listened for footsteps or disturbance along the pathway.

No sound.

Mikiziw circled above.

Staying low, Hiawatha made his way in stages, pausing to test the air with his exceptional nose, and listen for the slightest hint of human presence. In a few minutes, he was home and in the tack room with the Nitro Solvent, cleaning rod, and cotton patches.

He cleaned the rifle as he had been taught, but instead of secretly replacing it in the proper place, he walked calmly through the library and out onto the veranda, where Great Daddy reclined in his deck chair, swaddled in a Hudson Bay blanket.

This was no time for transcendental communication. He had some explaining to do in plain English.

"Great Daddy, I owe you a cartridge."

"I had to do a kind killing."

"Here's your rifle cleaned up perfect."

He explained everything—the debilitation, the request, the execution, and the spiritual support of the forebears.

And Great Daddy responded!

"Go get Oscar, boss of the guides, and tell him to parcel out the meat. Tell him to cape out the trophy and take it to Le Veques for mounting. If he wants to know the details, send him to me." Then he added, "Hiawatha, you did the right thing."

And so, the trophy was always assumed to be Great Daddy's last and greatest hunting feat. The lore was established early, about his raising himself from a weakened state and venturing out for one last inspired and successful hunt.

The tale was told over and over by the McMillion clan, and who was to doubt it? There was the mount itself over the fireplace. There was the famous Remington 30.06, in the case. And the spent shell on the shelf.

Chapter 3
Hiawatha's Betrothal

I T WAS THE HEIGHT OF the season, and time for the two main events at the Chippewa Club, the Annual Meeting and Jack Pine River Day. The latter was a raucous melee dominated by the Niijaanis, with canoe races, mud pie fights, and outrageous costumes, culminating in a gigantic bonfire on the beach, campfire songs, and s'mores for the tribe. The parents relaxed, reclining in their Adirondack chairs and nursing their brandy-spiked coffees before drifting away in twos and threes for bridge, poker, and more libation in the Club House.

This year's finale was another unforgettable event. Toward the end of the night, as the flames began to dwindle, revealing a purple-vaulted sky shot through with the brilliance of Tchibekana, the Milky Way. Hiawatha fulfilled his promise to bring a special guest. Entering the glow of the firepit from down the beach, with the starlight as its pale illumination, came a shadowy figure nearly ten feet high. Approaching the group, the silhouette sharpened into three distinct figures: Hiawatha and Kelley, in their fine Ojibwa regalia, were mounted astride Mons, the moose. Hiawatha was adorned in his ceremonial Chippewa headdress of bear fur and a lone eagle feather. Over his shoulder hung a bandolier of sewant, and around his waist his wide storyteller's belt of wampum. Kelley was in her deerskin garment of beaded leather and bejeweled with float copper and feathers.

And so the most dangerous beast of the forest entered the circle and knelt, first his forelegs, then his hindquarters, as the brave and maiden slid down to the sands of Gitche Gumi. The great bellows of Mons' lungs produced powerful jets of breath, which stirred eddies of pink sand beneath his chin, and the great palmate antlers cast dancing shadows across the firepit. Here he lay, comfortable and serene, under the influence of Hiawatha's calm assertiveness.

Soon the pipe hawk was produced with its tobacco bowl opposite the steel axe blade. A token puff was taken by one and all, the young Niijaanis gagging and spitting, to prepare the minds for storytelling. As the tale began, the sky began to lighten in the north, and faint dancing rods of green-blue light began to traverse the horizon. And as it progressed, the rods grew together, mixing with the particulate matter of the atmosphere, and creating pulsating tones, first yellow, then gold, first orange, then red, finally blending with the purple background of the sky in a blinding crescendo of florescence, and all against a background of the effervescent silver starlight of Tchibekana, the Milky Way.

Mikiziw circled above.

Across the Jack Pine River, atop Wakaigan, Great Horned Owl witnessed from afar the glowing fire, the circled campers, the brave and maiden, the palmate antlers the size of tabletops, the billowing smoke, the adamant pulsating crescendo of mysterious Northern light, the vault of shimmering stars, and the beating of the tom toms keeping time to it all.

Hiawatha stripped off his wampum belt and began the tale of the ghost of White Deer. He told of the love of a young brave for his chosen maiden. He told of the impossible price exacted by the maiden's father, the hide of the white deer. He told of the steadfast hunt, the perfect shot, and the continual wandering of the White Deer, never falling, always wandering, an arrow through his heart. He told of the unrequited love of the Ojibwa maiden, grown old, continually waiting for her warrior to return.

Then Hiawatha broke the secret of Wawashke, and told everyone of their friendship and of the mighty deer's apparition, of his wandering and caretaking of his herd, and of his love for the Chippewa Club and its members. He told of the blessing that Wawashke had bestowed on him, Hiawatha, for a long happy useful life with a beautiful Ojibwa maiden at his side. Kelley's heart sank. And Hiawatha told of how this special night, with the colors in the sky, the vast vault of starlight, the conglomeration of friends, the special guest, the pulsing Northern Lights, was the chosen night for Hiawatha's betrothal. He told of Wawashke's promise of the legendary princess, and her inevitable appearance here, tonight in this very place. Kelley's shoulders began to shake with grief. And as Hiawatha spoke, and the last glow of the campfire was waning, a beautiful plume of smoke arose, changing into the shape of a lovely Ojibwa maiden, wafting above the embers, in her deerskin garment of beaded leather, adorned with float copper and feathers. The fire extinguished. A light breeze blew, and the apparition traveled slowly across the starlit firepit, enveloping Kelley, and becoming one with her. Hiawatha rose to one knee and asked her hand in marriage, while the tears of joy streamed down the cheeks of his beautiful Ojibwa maiden. They all stood, silenced by the solemn magical proceedings. Above, in the purple-vaulted sky, a sparkling blue meteor streaked across Tchibekana and burst into the shape of multi-pronged antlers. Now the vibrant dancing sky intensified with one final burst like a sunset, only to the north, and then relaxed into a long thin reflection of the great Gitche Gumi, the Shining Big Sea Water, shimmering golden above the surface of hammered silver. Mons arose with his brave and maiden mounted tandem, she in front, he embracing from behind, and they rode off down the beach of pink sand toward the forest trail, Green Cabin, and Wakaigan.

The Niijaanis doused, double-doused, and triple-doused the embers before they all drifted home for prayers and bedtime.

The next morning, when Kelley arose and went to the mirror, she was greeted by a much darker visage, with black shiny hair and dark brown eyes, with braids held by rawhide strips and a necklace of silver beads. Across the foot of her bed was a new dress of deerskin, completely covered in the finest white wampum, and trimmed with the feathers of loon, kingfisher, and merganser. Her parents were shocked. Keep America and Forrest were thrilled.

Imagine, their sister, a real Ojibwa Princess!

The transformation of Kelley to Kamali (Spirit Guide) was explained by different people in different ways. Those who never knew Kelley at all took her for what she was, Kamali, an Ojibwa girl, a friend of Hiawatha. Casual acquaintances familiar with Kelley thought she used makeup, for the sake of the children's program. Good friends and her parents didn't know what to think. A strange metamorphosis coinciding with late puberty? The tardy occurrence of some weird atavistic quirk? A disease? Once the medical exams revealed perfect health, the subject was dropped, and Kamali was accepted as a previously unknown phenomenon. Only those in attendance at the encampment on the beach on that special night were in possession of the truth.

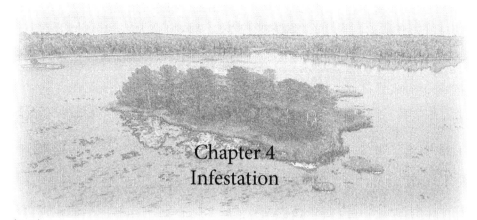

Chapter 4
Infestation

The Annual Meeting was always a source of entertainment for Hiawatha. Hundreds of members attended from all parts of the country, many for their only visit of the year. It was an irreverent spoof, a parody of a serious social endeavor. People showed up in period costume, or intentionally garish outfits. There were funny, frivolous motions from the floor regarding the consistency of the chocolate chip cookies, or what trophy would be offered for the annual tennis tournament, Forest Thrills. There were comical disputes over the size of fish logged into the register. Boisterous and garrulous jousting ensued between friends:

"I move a point of order!"

"I think we can reject that notion out of hand!"

And from the throng: "Hear, hear!"

Then came a substantive discourse involving the condition of the trails, the repair and maintenance of boats, and the state of the fishery. All the committee chairs gave their reports ranging from Land and Forest, Skeet and Trap, Conservation, Charitable Giving, Sailing, The Farm, and Niijaanis.

So, for the first time, Hiawatha was expected to report on his children's program, which he did. He accounted for money spent on equipment and materials, programs added, programs dropped, behavioral problems (there were none), and finally, the budget. Everything was in order, and the president singled him out with special recognition for shouldering responsibility and enriching the children's program as a selfless and charitable act. A serious and prolonged round of applause followed. The only query from the floor came from a member who was confused about the new Chippewa girl, Kamali, and what it cost to retain her. "No problem, she's a volunteer," was Hiawatha's only response.

So, the silly, jocular discourse followed to its usual conclusion. The sounding of the gavel signified another successful resolution of issues, and the membership left, secure in the knowledge that its tremendous endowment provided a unique luxury—that they remained encapsulated within a primeval enchanted world of frivolity and innocence. The meeting was adjourned with a feeling of comfort and satisfaction that the status quo was guaranteed by the very size and financial power of the place.

In fact, the situation was quite different, and the Chippewa Club, insensitive to its vulnerability, was about to come under withering attack from several separate and unrelated entities over a sustained period of time.

Mikiziw told of the first crisis. He came screaming down from aloft and blasted over Hiawatha's head in a maneuver usually reserved for murder, then went up and away, toward the west. Again and again, he dove and rose before setting forth to the top of Mt. Argon. Hiawatha spent his afternoon gaining elevation on the mountain trail. Halfway up, Mons arrived, and bending slightly to offer the great palmate antler, he swept Hiawatha up and onto his withers. They arrived at the dolmen on the summit in the waning light of the summer evening.

A strange moaning and grinding sound emitted from the forest to the west. Hiawatha trained his army surplus field glasses on the expanse below, searching for the source of the weird cacophony. His magnified sight revealed a hideous monstrosity. What appeared to the naked eye as a heaving pile of yellow maggots was a team of earth-moving and logging vehicles, carving a wide swath through the primeval forest in the valley below.

Hiawatha was not an anti-logging environmentalist, much less an activist. He had worked with a hoedad and dibble bar himself, as a kid, helping to restore several thousand acres of red and white pine and hemlock, lost to fire in the Burnt Mountain sector of the club. He understood the value of timber as a natural resource, and sustainable harvesting practice as the responsible method to achieve a balance between man and nature. He had friends in the forest products industry at all levels, from the fallers and buckers who passed their evenings at the Lumberman Saloon, shooting pool and darts, to the slingers and graders he played horseshoes with at the Lightning Bay pits. He knew management people all the way up to Shultzenberg himself, who owned a famous newspaper company, and controlled millions of acres of pulpwood forests all over the world. Shultzy came for grouse season every October as a guest. He was a dead shot, and he always asked to go out with Hiawatha.

As in any industry, there were conscientious and ethical corporate cultures and there were those made up of unscrupulous cheating liars. Most operations fell somewhere in between. This logging operation looked like it was near the bottom.

All cutting on club property—and many sections had been harvested over the past hundred years—was selective. Forest management consultants had been retained in modern times to define a long-term plan whereby the many resources could be converted into cash. The proceeds were used for acquiring land, paying taxes and other expenses, buying mineral rights, and generally easing the burden of membership. Many important "legacy trees" would be left behind to seed their surroundings with new trees of their same DNA. Large old burlwood and birdseye maples, near the end of their lives, were taken for their high market value. Young midsized trees were left behind to continue growing and reproducing. No land within the view of Mt. Argon had ever been treated like what Hiawatha saw today. It was an indiscriminate clear-cutting the likes of which are seen in pulpwood forests where all the trees are planted by man with the intention to harvest them all at the optimum time, like corn. And it was directly adjacent to the boundary line, on a neighbor's property.

Hiawatha dismounted and slapped the flank of his giant steed. Mons quivered his hide, and turning, penetrated the forest, rattling through the aspen with his great palmate antlers as he went. Once alone again, Hiawatha set and kindled a small fire, boiled water from his canteen, and made a meal of the wild rice and venison jerky he always kept in his sporran pouch.

He sat facing the ancient dolmen of his Ojibwa people as the small flames cast dancing shadows against the granite walls of his rock-lined shelter. He began the soft ritual chant, entering the meditative dream state he used to consult with the forefathers. He paid homage to One Called from a Distance and listened telepathically to his sage advice. He called for Chief Hole in the Day and communed with his spirit. He chanted the ritual prayers of his people and waited for the inevitable moonset to provide him with the cover of complete darkness in the starless, overcast night.

As the fire dwindled, Hiawatha doused and re-doused the glowing embers. He tested the night air with flaring nostrils and set forth. These were his most favorable conditions for stealth. A light rain fell, dampening the ground and holding the scents that he used for navigation. His deer-hide moccasins lent him the feel of the trail. In this state of being, his sense of smell was amplified well beyond the human, to that of the keenest canine, and his hearing was acute. Now the night was black as a cave. Perfect.

Through the thickest of nights Hiawatha crept. By the scent of past steps he navigated the trails of his youth. Past the pungent mushroom colonies and the fiddlehead ferns, among the red pines, white pines, hemlocks, and Norways, each with its distinct aroma. He felt the rasp of thimbleberries as he passed. Noted the scat of his forest friends in their favorite haunts. Heard the pup cries in the age old cave of Mahingan, the wolf, and her brood. Minded the rushing waters in their proper places. Felt the mist of the falls and the puff of prevailing wind in the valley of the Chive River. All of this was as familiar as the hallways of the great Adirondack Cabin. He crept to the modular office of the logging crew, set upon its cinderblock foundation and glowing with incandescent light. Crawling underneath, he bedded down and afforded himself an insider's perspective of the motivations and habits of this new, insidious entity.

Hiawatha got to know them pretty well in this short, troglodytic period. Their story emerged quickly and easily. It was a resort development company, caught up in the search for ever-more remote and exotic destinations for their golf and spa chain. The financials must have been pretty good because this project was virtually inaccessible. A helipad was planned for shuttling patrons from the Joliette Airport. The idea was to sell memberships to people who could fly in on their own and enjoy world class resort facilities in a place their friends had never heard of. Hiawatha could understand how the dramatic nature of the topography would seem attractive at first, with its sheer rock outcroppings and dramatic vistas of mountain lakes, and the Shining Big Sea Water in the distant north, plus the blinding fall color produced by the northern boreal hardwoods.

But this tract was much more complex than it appeared at first blush. Except for the higher elevations, there was no problem with water. In fact, the buyers had been assured of its plentitude, but therein lay the real problem. At the center of the tract lay a large cranberry bog, usable as a decorative lake, presumably. The bog was fed by a series of springs that amplified the waters of the Chive River. What nobody knew about was the Chive's underground twin, running just below the surface, ten times its size, waiting patiently for the past ten thousand years to suck hundreds of acres, virtually all the usable flat land, down into its gullet.

It was time to prepare the object lesson. Hiawatha was assured by Hole in the Day and One Called from a Distance that the misting rain of the present would become an unrelenting biblical torrent. As fortune would have it, the equipment yard was located at the property's lowest point, adjacent to the bog, where the driving range was to be.

Time to call in the excavators and engineers of the natural world.

Hiawatha crept back across the property line, set up camp at Aniani Lake, built his signal fire, and with his tom tom, summoned his forest friends. They came by the thousands, all the burrowing animals. The gophers, the ground squirrels, all species of rodents were present and accounted for. Woodchucks and rabbits arrived, ready to carve a warren of interwoven tunnels and caves. They went to work directly beneath the Caterpillars, Bobcats, slingers and graders, dump trucks, pickups, and the modular office itself.

Then the engineers arrived. Every beaver in the surrounding area left his lodge and set to work. The result was that inside club property, where the Chive straightened briefly before continuing its course to

Gitche Gumi in the north, there appeared a gigantic beaver dam, the likes of which had never been seen anywhere.

Mikiziw perched on an ancient pine above.

As the water began to rise, the construction crew waited it out in the office, drinking coffee and playing the endless game of Georgia-Pacific Night Shift Rummy. When it didn't relent by the second day, the coffee drinking stopped and the beer arrived. On the fourth day, someone cracked open a bottle of Jack Daniels and turned the country music station way up. The fight happened that night, and the next morning, all the temps were sent home and told to wait for orders. By Friday night, the water was up to the hubs on the pickups, and the foreman made the decision to abandon the camp. It was a good thing because on Sunday morning, the inevitable happened. The sinkhole that started out tipping a crane over on its side grew over a period of seventy-two hours to about three quarters of an acre, taking the entire operation, all sixteen-million dollars worth of it, down into the bowels of the earth, where it would be broken down by nature's various processes over the next twenty-million years.

Monday morning dawned bright and beautiful. Hiawatha and Kelley/Kamali spent the day at the beach with Keep America, Forrest, and Bonnie. Forrest brought his bat and ball, and they played Fungo in the pink sands of Gitche Gumi with Bonnie as outfielder, a duty she cherished and performed with remarkable proficiency.

A few weeks later, an advertisement in *The Wall Street Journal* announced one thousand acres of timberland for sale west of Little Bay, Michigan. Please respond to PO Box 12400, New York, NY 10016. Hiawatha responded, and when the price turned out to be just two hundred dollars per acre, he called the president of the club, Great Daddy's first son, James Russel McMillion.

Hiawatha's Uncle Russ was a tall, athletic, confident figure whose bearing and demeanor exuded the assurance of a privileged upbringing. His Roman profile, set off by horn-rimmed spectacles, lent him a serious presence, which shrouded a dry and ironic sense of humor. He listened carefully to Hiawatha's proposal that the club move quickly with Land and Forest money to acquire the land and mineral rights of the adjacent thousand-acre piece. There were plenty of reasons to move ahead. The price was excellent. The timber could be used to re-pay the cost of acquisition quickly, and it could be harvested selectively, intelligently, maintaining a balance and sustaining the natural aspects of the forest. The resort people were including their harvest of about forty acres of northern hardwood in the deal.

"Well, what about this sinkhole I've been hearing about?"

Hiawatha explained the event people had seen on TV recently. The amateur film taken by one of the resort owners from his airplane had made national news. Somehow, the morning shows got hold of a copy and ran with it. Network news loves nothing better than an ongoing crisis to hold its viewers spellbound, and a sinkhole had just as much potential for continuing drama as a car chase or armed standoff. As it turned out, a mysterious blockage of the Chive River had cleared quickly, and the floodwaters that had caused the dramatic event receded over a period of about twenty-four hours. By the time local stations got their helicopters airborne on Tuesday, the situation had stabilized, and all that was left to see was the crumpled earth with the mast of a large crane protruding at an angle. The story lost momentum, and the networks lost interest.

"I figure it was a one-time event. Those guys from Texas provoked the situation with their big, clear-cut monstrosity. That land is okay for us. Besides, if it starts up again, we have a nice canyon, and maybe there's gold down there."

Uncle Russ had been lukewarm on the whole idea of buying a thousand-acre potential sinkhole until his mercenary mind grasped the potential mining concept.

The whole UP economy had been developed on two fronts: timber and mining. Copper had been exploited by the Ojibwa since aboriginal times, when it could be found laying on the surface in large quantities. It had just "floated up" to the surface over millions of years of glaciation and recession. The Ontonagon Boulder weighed nine thousand pounds. Before the Ojibwa, a mysterious ancient people had pit mined throughout the peninsula. Carbon dating places them between 5000 and 1200 BC. When the Europeans arrived, they brought modern mining techniques, and exploited copper, finding great float pieces as large as fifty tons, just below the surface. Then they burrowed thousands of feet down in search of the metal. When the Ojibwa ceded their thirty-thousand square miles to the US government in 1842, the copper boom began in earnest, and a copper rush commenced, which lasted four years and left most miners destitute.

Iron ore had also been mined profitably since 1850.

But now, the new rumor in the business was of previously over-looked deposits of other metals, nickel, silver, and gold. Eagle River, the giant mining corporation, was actively searching the UP for exploitable ranges.

Russ reacted. "Let's go ahead and make the offer."

So, the following Monday, armed with a cashier's check for full price, Tony Armand of the Land and Forest Committee executed the sales agreement. The deal closed in thirty days.

Chapter 5
Eminent Domain

H IAWATHA'S EXPERIENCE OUTSIDE THE LOCALIZED area of the
Chippewa Club and its immediate surroundings was nil. Isolation
was considered part of the charm of the place, and the attitude of
members and staff toward modern conveniences was dismissive. The
only telephone on the property was at the gatehouse guarding the main
entrance. Any messages were written on memo paper and placed in the
recipient's mailbox. Urgent calls could be relayed by walkie-talkie to
key personnel, patrol, fire department, and the general manager.

Television was frowned on by the Board of Directors, and forbid-
den on club property. Only once in its history was the rule disobeyed.
During the Watergate scandal in 1973, members defiantly smuggled in
sets. The reception was poor with rabbit ears being the only antenna
they dared use, and it was definitely adults only. They removed them
again when the hearings were over. Hiawatha didn't even know they
were there. His first TV show was years later on a trip to Little Bay, ten
miles away, when the Tigers were playing the Yankees on the TV set
in the Lumberman's Saloon. He was twelve years old. The game held
his interest for a few minutes, then he went across the street to pitch
horseshoes with the slingers and graders at the Lightning Bay pits.

The Joliette Mining Journal was delivered weekdays and contained
mostly local Joliette and regional news. Most members had their big
city papers mailed to them during high season, and *The Wall Street
Journal* was sometimes available from June to September.

The two radio stations that offered good reception were the Christian one, with its nonstop evangelism, and Public Radio. Sometimes

Hiawatha tuned in to the classical music program on NPR for the soothing effect it had on Niijaanis at their craft tables. The work seemed to come out better with an infusion of Mozart. You could always hear it wafting from the boat shop, where Gerard Lund practiced his craft to the soothing tones.

The isolated nature of the club was a partial explanation of how the eminent domain case got so far before it was uncovered.

The new occupant of the White House was a messianic former governor, whose self-righteousness was exceeded only by his naïveté. High on his list of pet programs was the expansion of the National Park system, the goal being to make virtually all wilderness area within the US accessible to every citizen. Since his party held both the Presidency and Congress, he was drunk with his nearly complete control of government, and determined to test his powers in the first thousand days of his presidency. So, his most trusted party members were summoned to the Oval Office to collaborate on a congressional blitzkrieg of acquisition. The idea was to begin the land grab with a remote, inexpensive, large parcel of land in a relatively unpopulated and hopefully economically depressed area of the country, so as not to create too much of a fuss at first. Then, having set the precedent, the snowball effect would make each subsequent case easier and less likely to be resisted successfully. Among the first candidates was a very large land holding in a remote area of the Upper Peninsula of Michigan. It was the site of some sort of former hunting club whose membership was unclear, and whose activity was low. Judging from building permits filed in the Powell County land office, there hadn't been an improvement made in seventy-five years. This would be the test case.

A search committee was established by the Department of Interior. The members were selected from a pool of influential Michiganders. A public relations campaign was launched to provide local support. The concept was replacing forestry and mining with the "clean" business of tourism.

When James Russel McMillion got his first phone call from Gerald Stoner, the Department Chief, he thought it might be a tax issue, and girded himself for a battle over how much the increase would be. When he asked about the subject of the proposed meeting, the answer shook him to his core. "Mr. McMillion, we are filing a proposal of eminent domain against the property known as the Chippewa Club. Your land has been identified as the first in a series of national recreational sites, specifically to be used for off-road vehicles and power boating." Uncle Russ felt a surge of bile creeping up his throat. The instant visual image of water skiers and motorcyclists tearing through the pristine lakes and primeval forestlands of his forefathers, and leaving behind their inevitable flotsam, nearly blinded him. A cold, irreconcilable hatred coursed through him like an electrical charge.

Uncle Russ paused to collect his emotions and responded in his most even and mellifluous tone. "Mr. Stoner, I will be represented by counsel."

The malaise of the Chippewa Club was broken like a miraculous awakening from a coma. The reaction was instantaneous and grew exponentially in a matter of hours. All the talents of the membership were stimulated, from the many lawyers and tax experts to legislators, journalists (both broadcast and print), and a more recent phenomenon, activists. A command center was established in the guide house.

This event took actual measure of the club's involvement with the surrounding communities. Up to now, one could argue whether the club was hated as an upper class haven, tolerated as a necessary evil, or respected as a contributor to the wellbeing of the area. Now there was no doubt. The citizens of Little Bay, the Black Dog Plains, and Quarter Point rallied to the cause. People in Joliette lent support. Many of them had been employed by the Chippewa Club as permanent or part-time employees. If not, they knew someone who had been. The pay was always above average. The club looked after its own. The community summer camp was supported by members. The hospital was founded by a member. The club had built the Little Bay Marina and maintained the community park. The general citizenry had the Black Dog Wilderness Area as their playground, and it was plenty ample. Who was going to begrudge the Chippewa Club its fair share, especially when the adversary was the federal government? So, liberty and individual property rights trumped class warfare.

Then Hiawatha went to the Ojibwa tribal council. The Good River band was advised. So was The Black Earth band, The Hundred Lakes band. All sent emissaries to protest the violation of sacred ground. Their native land might be deeded to the White Man, but it was respected and nurtured, with one of their own as a steward—one who possessed the wisdom and judgment of the forefathers. As for Hiawatha himself, he knew this place was a window to the Spirit World. It couldn't stand disruption, and he wouldn't abide it.

The meeting took place in Joliette, the county seat, in a wainscoted room reserved for the Board of Supervisors. The Department of Interior attorneys had not anticipated a greeting from green power activists with their cardboard signs outside the building. They were surprised by the presence of local TV. They didn't expect to run a gauntlet of questions and comments hurled at them in the building's hallways, and they were set completely off balance by the sheer volume of witnesses and spectators assembled in the hall.

The meeting was called to order by Spencer Bancroft Tillinghast, Deputy Director of the National Parks in Michigan. His aloof and condescending demeanor was matched by his sartorial correctness. The button-down Oxford, the loosely affixed bowtie, the nailhead tweed. Opening comments were made by representatives of the various state and local agencies. When they were done droning about non-germane issues, those from the general population were invited to speak. There was a five-minute limit. Hiawatha reserved the last time period. He seated himself within the colorful array of the tribal council. He was attired in his first business suit, bought at Target, gray flannel and conservative. He wore his hair parted in the middle and braided by Keep America. When he rose to speak, his full charismatic character came through as if called upon for an auspicious occasion. His physique was strong and dominant. His bearing was calm and self-assured. His voice was a smooth and effortless baritone, resonant within the dignified walls of the chamber.

He said, "Your Honor, distinguished members of the panel, fellow tribal elders, members of the Chippewa Club, fellow Michigan citizens, I am Hiawatha Heywood, and I was born on the land in question, the land you want to open up to snowmobiles and vending machines, to jet skis and ATVs. I have spent my whole life on this sacred land. This is the second time I've ever been off it. The first time was to the Lumberman's Saloon. I was twelve."

A murmur of laughter rippled through the audience.

"I was with my uncle, and I wanted to see what TV was."

Another ripple.

"Your Honor, my ancestors have been on this land for 10,000 years. They hunted the deer and elk. They seined the whitefish and brook trout. They gathered the blueberries that still grow there today. They made their canoes of the birch bark. They worshiped at their dolmen on Mt. Argon. When the white man came, he had no interest in this place. For 200 years, it went unnoticed, and when the Chippewa Club made their offer, it was through mutual respect and a pledge to be good stewards of the land. In 100 years, they have never wavered from that pledge."

Tillinghast had planned to allow public comment and then ignore it. His experience in these matters was that grass roots resistance was easily circumvented this way. He allowed the most virulent opponents to vent publicly. They were usually satisfied with their five minutes of fame. Half of them were crackpots. Then, the emotions duly aired, he was free to proceed surreptitiously with the less public procedures involved in acquisition. This, however, was a different situation. He had conducted countless public hearings on many different matters. He had encountered every reaction from benign compliance to righteous indignation and even outright violence. Today's situation had a different flavor to it. There was a symbiosis between the various groups, and a certain energy ran through them. It seemed to emanate from the young Chippewa in the center in the Native American group, the one with unusual articulation. He seemed to gather the combined emotions of the separate factions and concentrate it.

Looking out over the crowd, Tillinghast began to doubt the feasibility of his project. There was a strange continuity he had never seen before in hearings like this. The suited and tied business community, the activists with their homemade clothing and exotic hairdos, the tribes, adorned with their feathers and fur, the Club members in their polar fleece vests and mail-order hiking boots, the hundreds of ordinary citizens. They all seemed to direct his attention to Hiawatha. The picture was one of extraordinary resolve. There was a power to this confederacy that transcended its sheer numbers, and the charisma of their leader was palpable.

As Tillinghast surveyed the situation, his mind turned to the list, back in his office in Washington, the one with all the prospective properties suitable for the National Recreation Area in Upper Michigan. He remembered comments from his staff about the lackluster and dissipated membership of the Chippewa Club, and how they were unlikely to offer any sustained resistance to the takeover. That had been the project's charm. Pick an easy target for the first park and set the precedent. The subsequent sites would fall in to place in an orderly fashion.

As Tillinghast ruminated on how to bring matters to conclusion for the evening, he began to notice a strange pulsing sound. First, it seemed to originate from the air conditioning, or perhaps the plumbing pipes were singing with the vibration so often found in these older buildings with steam heat and radiators. It had a resonant quality like that of a firmly struck church bell. It was a harmonic vibration like he had heard once in a Tibetan Buddhist temple, like a vibraphone.

Tillinghast looked the crowd over from right to left, scanning for the source, but it seemed ubiquitous, and it was growing in intensity. The audience was perfectly still. They gazed at him curiously, as if he were an animal at the zoo. The vibrating resonance intensified, and Tillinghast felt a strange disconnection from the entire proceeding, as if he were observing himself and the audience from above. He sought out the Chippewa and found his gaze to be penetrating and beneficent. He couldn't disengage. The energy just kept increasing, and the panel members began to react nervously. One by one, they excused themselves and left. Now it was just Tillinghast and the group. He felt a unique sense of foreboding, as if he were being swept along an involuntary course. His pulse quickened, and he began to feel as if he would swoon. The sound seemed to enter inside his skull and hammered with such intensity that he felt he could no longer hear the outside world. The room went black and his heart raced at an incredible pace.

Slowly, Tillinghast became aware that the episode was abating. He felt as if he had experienced a heart attack or an epileptic seizure. As his sight returned to normal, he expected to be on the floor with a crowd around him.

"Give him room. Let in the EMTs."

But in his clearing field of vision, Tillinghast beheld the same pleasant faces in the audience. Three sharp reports rang out and he heard the sound of his own voice. "This case is closed." He heard a faint crackling, like fatwood in the fireplace. It grew to a persistent and sustained applause and he realized that the radiant and beaming faces in the crowd were celebrating his benevolent act of removing the Chippewa Club from the list of park sites.

If you asked a casual observer for an accounting of the procedures that day, it would go something like this:

"We were all packed tightly in the room. Nobody wanted to be left out of the scene. Most people thought it was our only chance to show how we felt. Hiawatha made a nice short speech, and we waited to hear what the Secretary was going to do. Everybody thought he would go back to Washington and hold meetings and hearings and such, but he just ended it right then and there, for no apparent reason. It seemed like he took a long time making his decision, like he was figuring all the angles, and then he just picked up his gavel and adjourned the meeting. Bang, bang, bang, and he said, 'Case closed,' and that was it.

"It was anticlimactic for some of the activists. They wanted a forum, with all the TV coverage for their issues, you know, the Spotted Owl and all that, but the rest of us were relieved. Some of the businessmen liked the idea of the tourist traffic, but most of us like Little Bay just the way it is. It's a nice place to live, and the club is a good citizen. Their crew responded to the American Legion fire. They came out with a tanker. We'd have lost the building, and it's important to us. The pinochle league and all, you know."

Chapter 6
Blizzard

THE REASON HIAWATHA WAS ALONE on the property most winters was the lack of modern heating in the cabins. Most people stayed away, starting in November, and didn't return until May at the earliest.

Wakaigan was built in 1894 with ten fireplaces. Hiawatha used two. He spent his time in a small sitting room and bedroom, burning northern hardwood and cooking with the hanging pothook and a Dutch oven.

Between periods of rest in the Adirondack cabin, Hiawatha snowshoed the vast property for days at a time, running his snare lines, fishing his ice holes, always thanking his fellow creatures for their lives. You could see forever through the forest with the leaves all down and everything lined with a white snowy backdrop. And the sounds carried so well. You could hear the husky bark of romping otter all the way across Red Pine Lake. The song of the Bad River Pack traveled miles across the snowy canyons on moonlit nights.

The signs of a harsh winter began early in Hiawatha's twenty-first year. September brought unusual color to the northern hardwoods, and brisk flurries blew through quickly. The long summer drought was satiated by a persistent procession of aggressive cold fronts bringing boisterous thunderstorms and torrential downpours. One day, the marine weather channel broadcast a tornado watch in its monotonous computer-generated voice.

By the middle of the month, the lakes were brimming, the falls were roaring, and the mosses and lichen were softened and happy. It was too late for the blueberries, which never had a chance that summer. They and the ferns were in a state that no amount of moisture could help. They would wait for a fresh start in the spring.

Chipmunks and squirrels began their harvest and storage of acorns while they were still green. The waterfowl migration started early and was finished in record time. Makwa, the bear, was nowhere to be seen, and the field mice were invading the cabins of the Chippewa Club by the thousands.

By the first of October, not an insect could be found, and the snow began in earnest. Every day, the snowfall increased, and it all stuck. The first storms were still and lush, with large flakes accumulating softly, leaving a fairyland of moist snow that bent boughs and draped rooflines. Occasionally, the insulated silence was broken by the muffled thud of an overladen tree. As the weeks wore on and the temperature continued to drop, the character of the season changed from a soft and comfortable accumulation to a steady and persistent march of continually harsher conditions.

The weather seemed to take on a personality. What started as relief from the drought and became a playful dusting of the landscape took on a serious and aggressive tone. November intensified with a northeaster that became colder and more forceful with each passing day. Sunshine became a memory as the last of the clinging fall leaves were ripped from their tenuous hold by the steady and unrelenting wind. By December, the windy days were accompanied by a constant diagonal downfall of hard, grainy snow, pelting down and stinging with an icy vengeance. Toward the middle of the month, a slight respite offered no real hope of relief, considering the earliness of the season. The sky did lighten a little, from gunmetal gray to a dull white, and the scudding altocumuli raised their heads from the all-out attack, as if stretching their muscles briefly before really getting down to business.

Now the mood of the season showed its vitriolic streak. As Christmas approached, everything intensified. The wind changed from a whistle to a howl and then to a scream as the Gitche Gumi tossed its head in a froth of fifteen-foot waves. The Big Rock lighthouse, which was forty feet to the top, became encased in a sheath of cloudy white ice and took on the appearance of a gigantic melted wax candle. The gale finally settled in at a groaning sixty miles per hour, and the snow lashed down in waves. The storm's intensity was exacerbated by its duration. Above the forty-fifth parallel, most weather events last a day or two. This was a double-cored, low pressure trough that stalled out over the Great Lakes for a week.

When it was all over, Christmas had come and gone. Most residents of Little Bay had to leave their houses from the second-story windows, and a car top wasn't visible anywhere within fifty miles.

Then the cold set in. New Year's Day dawned bright and still, and matured glaringly. It was perfectly clear. The temperature never made it above twenty below, and after about four in the afternoon, it really started to drop. Anybody with a mercury thermometer found it broken in the morning. Mercury freezes at forty below. Lake Superior set a record for ice accumulation, and eventually, it froze completely over to its center for the first time since 1912. Amasa recorded sixty-one degrees below zero. The next two months were whipsawed with alternating snow and cold. Some of the creatures of the forest dealt with great suffering and mortality. It was worst on the deer, as usual, and a fine year for the wolves. Makwa, the bear, never noticed a thing, his enemy being a warm winter, waking him when there is little forage.

Hiawatha had spent his fall preparing. His larder was packed to the ceiling with grain, pemmican, dried fruit, and nuts. He had all his mushrooms from their separate seasons. The morels from May, the chantarelles from July, the boletus and puffballs, oysters and chicken of the woods from fall. His root cellar held the fruits and vegetables he and Kamali had put up in glass jars that summer. All his tubers were laid in there too. Outside, in his log strongbox, was the meat and fish, frozen solid. Beside it, in the lee, his dogsled stood, buried in ten feet of snow.

Hiawatha spent the winter with Bonnie as his companion. She and his crafts were his way of coping with the growing emptiness he felt in his heart as the days and weeks of Kamali's absence grew into months. This was her senior year in Chicago, and his hope was that she would choose the State College in Joliette for next year. In any event, they planned for a wedding in August, a year after the magical betrothal on the sands of Gitche Gumi.

Christmas was shared with Atchitamo, the little red squirrel Hiawatha found so amusing. The abrasive protectionism normally reserved for Atchitamo's nest had been transferred to the entire Wakaigan cabin. He spent hours scampering from one vast room to another like a watchdog, searching for offensive intruders, and imagining them when they couldn't be found. When the storms came, though, he joined Hiawatha and Bonnie in the redoubt of the sitting room, busying himself with thoughtfully provided nuts and pinecones. These he consumed in great quantities from his command post on the windowsill, compiling a slag heap of shells and husks on the floor below. Bonnie had a fierce time with her primal instincts at first, almost giving in to her most murderous emotions on a couple of occasions. Hiawatha was understanding but firm, and she eventually mastered her urges for this special case, grudgingly. Her relationship with Atchitamo was a tenuous one, as in a truce between warring parties, but Bonnie lived for Hiawatha's words of approval and was steadfast in her obedience.

On New Year's Day, Hiawatha readied himself to set forth on a journey to Little Bay to find out how the general population had fared through the crisis. Making his way through his snow tunnel to the strongbox, he burrowed off at an angle and eventually found the buried dogsled. He ran a clothes pole up to the surface as a reference, and then exited Wakaigan through the upstairs bedroom. Rigging a snatch block from the nearest tree, he was able to dig and pull the crusted sled to the surface over a period of two hours. He spent the next hour provisioning himself for a mercy mission with the medical supplies he always kept in quantity, along with plenty of food. About a third of the way through the packing process, Hiawatha laid his head back and gathered his breath for a long, powerful, and plaintive howl, repeating three times. From far to the south came Mahingan's reply. By the time the sled was loaded, the Bad River Pack had arrived, ready to be tied in the traces and join in the mission. They were treated to large slabs of frozen coho netted the past November and full of nutrition. Mahingan was placed in the lead, then the alpha bitch and her daughter, with the younger males in succession. It was a team of twelve, with Bonnie running free as a scout.

Back in Wakaigan, Hiawatha set out a large cache of cones and nuts for Atchitamo and battened the upstairs window. Then he and Bonnie mounted the sled; he whistled sharply and mushed on out toward the main gate, destined for Little Bay. They negotiated the nine miles in about an hour, due to the rough conditions and falling through soft spots all the time. Bonnie leapt off and paced the team for most of the way, turning back regularly to judge the welfare of the expedition. They coasted in to The Lumberman's Saloon about five-thirty, in the dark.

You could hear the raucous crowd from a quarter mile out. Everybody within snowshoe distance was bellying up and recounting their personal experiences. The snow was matted, and vehicles were starting to appear, having been finally extracted from their tombs of several days. There were the ubiquitous early predecessors to the snowmobile, contrived feats of bailing wire engineering. Stacks of skis and snowshoes were propped along the log walls of the primitive structure as Hiawatha and the team glided up. He staked them out and entered.

Hiawatha released the team from its traces and staked each one separately, with a slab of venison jerky apiece.

He stomped himself free of excess snow and tested the back door to Lumberman's. It gave slightly, so with a couple of kicks to loosen the ice-bound jamb, he set his shoulder to the door and smashed into the din and the glare.

If this had been Dodge City, the ragtime piano music would have stopped short. Everyone went silent. Half the town of Little Bay was in there, waiting out the blizzard. They all turned with startled, wide eyes to behold a strapping mixed-blood Ojibwa clad in animal hide, dusted with a fine powder of fresh snow and belching a fog of sub-zero breath. For a couple of seconds, the silence prevailed. Then Chippewa Chuck announced:

"Hiawatha!"

The tension released instantly, and the crowd roared a welcome. "Get him a drink!" "How are youse?" "Where's your girl?" "How you get here?" Hiawatha accepted a hot chocolate and began bringing himself up to date on the state of the world, at least the little world of Little Bay.

The regulars splayed their elbows at the bar. The Friday night pinochle league was scattered throughout the tables of the dining room, all ages and occupations, the skidders and splitters and great-grandmothers rotating from table to table in round robin fashion.

The mayor and councilmen were off in a corner discussing contingencies in case this weather tightened its grip. There was an accounting of the population and concern about the various trappers, squatters, and hermits in the outlying wilderness.

"Wait a minute!" said Jonny Aho, Chair of the Council. "What about the Mottsons? You know, Mr. Newberry from Detroit sent them out to sit his copper claim last fall on Manitou Island."

"Yeah," said the mayor. "Come to think of it, the harbormaster told me he never saw the provisioning boat they was promised."

"You don't suppose they've been out there all this time, since ice over, with no supplies? It's been almost three months."

"And too far to make it, walking across the ice."

"We better call out the Coast Guard for a chopper," said Oly Olsen.

"I talked with the commander. Ship number one is down for repairs, and two is on loan to Baraga for a mission in Wisconsin."

Hiawatha said, "Well, then, I guess I better harness the team and go help them."

And so, after another hot chocolate and more food for the team, Hiawatha set out from Lumberman's with the canned soup, the jerky, the dried fruit and nuts, and the salted whitefish, bound for Manitou Island ninety-two miles across the ice and forty-two degrees below zero.

> Forth upon the Gitche Gumi,
> On the frozen big sea water,
> With his pack of wolves exulting,
> Not alone went Hiawatha.

When they left the frozen slope of the beach, they struggled across a tumble of ice chunks, tossed and scattered along the littoral like giant shards of broken glass. They emerged onto the vast plain of the frozen and dusted Gitche Gumi, bathed in blue moonlight all the way to the horizon. Hiawatha checked the North Star as his compass and struck out across a vast plain of nothingness, inhabited by no one except the bitter, fierce heart of Bibon Manitou, God of Winter.

The team settled into a steady lope marked by the cadence of twelve sets of lungs expelling clouds of crystalline fog. Hiawatha inwardly thanked his Aleut brother for the pouch of seal blubber he kept by his breast, ready to fill his body with life-bolstering heat when needed.

At their optimum speed, Hiawatha reckoned to arrive at the Mottsons' one-room cabin at about six in the morning, barring the worst luck, which would be soft ice or open water blocking the way, but his year there was to be no problem with a thaw of any kind. The persistent cold had locked the great Gitche Gumi in a total freeze across the entirety of its 150-mile breadth.

After four hours of mushing across the wasteland, the deep magenta line of dawn appeared on the horizon, slowly expanding in width, and lightening to red, then orange, then yellow. Soon, a mass of dark rock began to swell in the distance, and Manitou Island appeared.

Now another hour in a final push and the one-room cabin hove into view, its single chimney devoid of smoke, and no sign of life anywhere.

As Hiawatha approached closer, a pile of debris set away from the cabin became apparent, and from it emerged a leaf-like figure, human in form, and resembling a butterfly before its wings have fully dried. A tiny arm emerged and hailed in a pathetic sign of welcome and gratitude.

It was Angelique Mottson, or what was left of her after three months of starvation and exposure to the most wicked winter in 100 years.

Hiawatha brought the team to a halt and approached the mysterious pile. It proved to be a perfect Indian lodge, built in the Chippewa style of bark and sticks and an occasional stiffened hide.

And now, the shadow of a woman approached and spoke with inclined head in the Chippewa fashion.

"Anamikagewin, Nind anamikage. (I greet you!) Mignetch! Onjita! Wendjita! (Thank You! Thank You! Thank You!)"

And Hiawatha: "Anamikagewin (I greet you), and where is your husband?"

"I am pijigokwe, a woman who has no more a husband."

So there she was, Angelique Mottson, a full-blooded Chippewa, saved by the missionary successors of Father Baraga and married to Charlie Mottson, an Englishman down from Kapuskasing.

The gaunt and withered countenance had one feature that belied her age. The eyes, black as obsidian and burning with a zeal born of deprivation. They bore into you in a disturbing way. It was like looking into the very essence of despair.

And so they entered the lodge, and sat before a bed of coals that barely glowed.

"Oh, that fire," she remembered. "You don't know what company it was. It seemed alive just like a person with you, as if it could almost talk, and many a time, but for its bright and cheerful blaze that put some spirits in me, I think I would have just died."

She accepted the jerky and started right in with a vengeance. Satiating in no time, she leaned forward and began the tale.

"Back last fall, we met Mr. Newberry; I thought he a nice man. He said, 'You a nice couple. Him English, you Chippewa. I need a pair like you to sit my claim out here on Manitou. Come on out. I will stake you.'

"But he never did. Here we were, Charlie and me in this cabin, but no supplies.

"I want to tell you one thing. You can't cheat hunger. You can't fill up that inward craving that gnaws within you like a wolf. We fought like hell. We fished till the net gave out and got so weak we couldn't fix it. We were okay till the canoe floated off. Then we had to forage on this god-forsaken place. He just kept getting weaker, and then he went crazy.

"I came home from getting some bark to eat and he was sharpening his Bowie with a whetstone. He said, 'I'm going to kill a sheep and eat it right now!' And I knew that sheep was me! He was down to 100 pounds, and I kept to my side of the cabin with the splitting axe right beside me for six days. Then he got over it and he was just the same old Charlie again, but that was the end. He wasted after that, and one day he was cold as a stone. I stayed with him for a week. It seemed like company, but then I knew I couldn't stay no more, and I left him right there in his chair. I couldn't put him in the ground if I wanted to, this hard, frozen tundra, so there he is up there for you to see. Blue as ice, and perfectly preserved.

"I couldn't keep a fire for fear of thawing him out, so that's why I built the lodge. So me and my friend the fire could be together.

"I believed there was a Christ, and that he would carry me through, if I prayed to him. But what I feared most was myself.

"Sometimes I was so hungry, so very hungry, and the hunger raged so in my veins that I was tempted, Oh, how terribly I was tempted, to take Charlie and make a soup of him. When that dreadful thought came over me, I wished to die and die quick, rather than suffer any longer.

"Then I would pray; and it always seemed to me after praying hard, something would turn up, or I would think of something that I had not thought of before and have new strength given me to fight on still longer.

"That's when I started with the rabbit snares. I used my nice long hair, wove them, and set them along the rabbit paths. The first one I ate raw, right there on the trail. Ripped the skin open and tore him up. And I couldn't wait for the next one. Two days later, there he was, but I waited and cooked him like a civilized person."[1]

So Hiawatha went on up to the cabin and let himself in, and there he was, old Charlie, sitting there like he wanted to discuss the latest hockey game, blue and translucent. It was as if his spirit had been frozen within this block of ice, to be released at a later date.

They left everything there just as it was. Angelique bolstered herself with several tiny meals of fish and trimmings. Strangely, the nuts went down easiest. She kept popping them into her mouth like M&M's. Those and the parched corn, food of her ancestors.

Hiawatha considered her depleted condition and offered her a bit of the seal blubber as safe measure. She felt the strange warming sensation begin in her belly and course with life-sustaining warmth out through her limbs, all the way to her fingertips.

Aleut magic.

---

1. Inspired by the true story of Angelique and Charles Mott, who were trapped for the winter on Isle Royale. The story has been retold numerous places, first in Ralph Williams' *The Honorable Peter White* (1905), p. 127-30. Angelique's words here are largely taken from original sources.

Next morning, they left with the team freshened and rested, back in its traces. Hiawatha in the traditional musher's position, Angelique bundled and trussed with the food, and fortified with seal blubber. Bonnie out front on the point, and Charlie trailing behind in a little sled, like a lagging friend, tagging along, his spirit embodied within him still, waiting for release in a warmer place.

Hiawatha remembered the old Robert Service poem:

There are strange things done in the midnight sun
  By the men who moil for gold;
The Arctic trails have their secret tales
  That would make your blood run cold;
The Northern Lights have seen queer sights,
  But the queerest they ever did see
Was that night on the marge of Lake Lebarge
  I cremated Sam McGee.

And the last stanza:

And there sat Sam, looking cool and calm, in the heart of the
  furnace roar;
And he wore a smile you could see a mile, and he said: "Please
  close that door.
It's fine in here, but I greatly fear you'll let in the cold and storm—
Since I left Plumtree, down in Tennessee, it's the first time I've
  been warm."

Hiawatha surfed home before a northerly zephyr, and made good time all the way to Little Bay. They struggled back through the tumble of beach ice, Charlie bouncing along in his sleigh, and glided up to Lumberman's for the phone call to the ambulance and the coroner's office. Hiawatha unhooked the little sled and pulled it around to the equipment shed behind the building, and helped Angelique enter her first properly heated building in 105 days.

The little Ojibwa squaw was awkward in her celebrity, and wound up in the back corner table with a bowl of hot porridge and tea.

In thirty minutes, the ambulance crew arrived for the trip to the hospital in Joliette, and the coroner showed up twenty minutes later. He wanted to interview Hiawatha about the "crime scene."

"There will be an autopsy and full investigation, you know. We've got a big push in the office to be very thorough in cases of domestic violence among Native peoples. It's the most common crime on the reservation."

Hiawatha related Angelique's story, and the scene as he recalled it.

Then, "If there's charges to be brought, they ought to be against that Newberry for leaving those poor people to starve the way he did."

So, Angelique left for her long recovery, and survived the investigation.

Newberry was never called for an interview, but the incident left him changed. He left his job in the city and came up to the Good River Reservation to do social work. He substitute-taught in the junior high school, and delivered the Word of God on Sundays, his recurring message being charity and concern for one's fellow man.

Angelique lived a long and happy life as a domestic servant in the city of Joliette. Her strength and determination became legendary. She won the UP Marathon three years in a row, and set the Women's State power lifting record for her age and weight class. It still stands today.

Chapter 7
Preparation

AFTER THE CORONER LEFT FOR Joliette, Hiawatha shushed home to Wakaigan, turned out a vast helping of moose carcass parts to the team, and unfettered them to feast, before they returned to their normal pack life. He put up the sled, reorganized the tack, and then tunneled back into the confines of his vast lodge.

Atchitamo's pile of shells had grown to cover the entire kitchen table, cascading into an alluvium of husks like so much gravel off a dump truck. He had finally retired into a torpid state in his burrow, awaiting the ignition of the giant fireplace and pot-bellied stove.

Hiawatha scraped a peephole in the frost of the giant picture window and beheld the hoary scene of the northern boreal forest in its dormant and elegant snow-sagging state, crystalline and nearly blue.

He began the methodical chore of breathing new life into Wakaigan, cleaning Atchitamo's debris, stoking the fires, shelving the supplies, opening the bins of crafting materials and heaping them where the nutshells had been. Then he settled into a period of solitude and reflection, tempered by hours of studious attention to the reference books and classics of Great Daddy's walnut-paneled library.

After his reading and contemplation, the first and most important project was to design the wedding gown of his lovely Indian princess. He assembled the materials for the task, which would be the crafting job of a lifetime, driven by his devotion and abiding love for the most beautiful woman in the world.

But Bichon Manitou wasn't done yet. He laid on sixty more days of debilitating cold and record snowfall. When the thaw came on April

Fools' Day, it came all at once, with eighty-degree temperatures that unleashed an historic flood. It washed out fifteen bridges, and left the flotsam choking the mouths of all the area's rivers. It moved the mouth of the Jack Pine River one thousand yards down the beach from its usual location in front of Wakaigan. Three of the cabins downstream tipped over and splashed into the river face first, one hundred years of sentimental memorabilia gone in a couple of hours.

Then it got cold again.

The extended winter gave Hiawatha an opportunity to perfect his wedding gown project. He made contact with all the chiefs of the area. He had access to the best crafts and materials of the different tribes, since winter was the traditional time to work this way, and now people wanted to get some cash after a long dry spell.

Some people had gold, and he found some small natural nuggets for accent pieces. Some had quartz crystals that resemble diamonds. He found plenty of wampum beads and the finest of all feathers.

The final result was almost impossible to describe because it was more than the sum of its parts. It glowed and shimmered with its combination of shell, feather, metal, and stones. It took on an energy of its own and promised to convey that energy to Kamali, to complement her radiant beauty.

Kamali had a dress of the softest and finest deerskin, but the leather actually served almost as an undergarment, being completely sequined with beads, gems, shells, wampum, feathers, gold, and silver.

Her tiara was of the finest silver wire, studded with stones of Herkimer diamond and interwoven with gold.

After a month of working sixteen-hour days, Hiawatha was satisfied. He carefully stored the final product in a special handmade cedar footlocker in preparation for the wedding day.

Chapter 8
The Wedding of Hiawatha

P REPARATION OF THE WEDDING BARGE took a week. It was set upon a pair of pontoons like a catamaran, and had a deck of white cedar, the likes of which would be used normally for the finest canoe or Adirondack boat.

In fact, when dismantled, it served that exact purpose.

It was festooned with layers of wild roses and violets, wreaths of cedar and hemlock, birch and aspen. The sides were of birdseye maple and tiger maple, and the poles were golden birch. It was propelled by oarsmen from the Chippewa High School football team, Division D State Champs.

All the flotilla of accompanying vessels were birch bark canoes of the finest quality. There were Ojibwa Longnoses, Fur Trade styles, Abnakis, and Passamaquoddys. And each occupant was finely attired in traditional Ojibwa costume with their bear fur and feather headdresses, medallions and hair pipe breastplates.

Kamali's artisan parents drove her up from Chicago with Keep America and Forrest in the family station wagon. They settled into Green Cabin a week before the event to synchronize with the environment and get into the rhythm of things.

Kamali arrived in a totally transformed state.

Her jet black hair was fine by Native American standards, and it flowed over her shoulders and down to her calves, with a slight golden highlight.

Her eyes were large, dark brown, and sharply defined. They shone with keen intelligence and danced when she laughed.

Her skin was reddish copper in color, but it was the softness and smoothness of her complexion, almost like a baby's, that was so striking.

Her smile was radiant and spontaneous, and showed off the strikingly perfect teeth that had never needed braces.

Her petite figure had developed into a perfect size three, which required some costume adjustment by her artisan mother and friends. The final adjustment yielded a dress of the softest deerskin, measuring 32, 18, 32.

Her diminutive height was augmented a bit by ingenious platform moccasins that were to be used only once during the ceremony, to bring her a little closer to Hiawatha's stature, for the vows.

On the wedding day, the magnificently prepared barge set at the foot of Jack Pine Falls, with the cascade pounding a rhythm behind.

Hiawatha stood centered in his full Ojibwa regalia.

Beaded moccasins with beaver tail soles.

Bear hide leggings with ermine trim.

Trousers of felt, with a belt of the finest sewant.

A magnificent silk blouse with the storytellers' wampum and ceremonial medallions from the French Occupation.

A breastplate of blonde quill, bordered with coral beads.

A special medal in the form of King George of England.

And then, the necklaces of all his forebears.

The great chief's float copper strand.

The gold nuggets of One Called from a Distance.

The Herkimer diamond pendant of Hole in the Day.

The final accent was the traditional Ojibwa headdress of bear fur and eagle feather. Hiawatha wore two feathers in honor of his forebears. Most chiefs wore one.

Seated to his left were the artisan mother and father.

The honored guests were gathered from every corner of Little Bay Society. Every band of Ojibwa was represented. The club membership turned out in its entirety including all staff members. All the forest products community was there in Mackinaw plaid and Carhart overalls. The Crusoes came in tattered denim. The Mayor of Joliette was there in a cutaway and top hat.

They lined the banks of the Jack Pine River and waited for the barge to alight at the wedding site.

As the sun appeared over the birch grove of Maiden's Beach, the beat of tom toms began, and after each measure, a different instrument joined in—guitar, dobro, fiddle, mandolin, bass and cello, then the flutes and winds. Everybody who had musical talent in the area was gathered at the Jack Pine Falls to await the father and the bride.

The two appeared at the head of the Chippewa Trail, and the artisan father presented the most beautiful bride, within and without, in all of Ojibwa history.

And so the barge set forth, and floated the Jack Pine River all the way to the mouth, with Hiawatha and his beautiful princess, the artisan parents, Keep America and Forrest, all propelled by the Division D State Champs, and guarded by a flotilla of birch bark canoes.

And the rest of the wedding party trailed along past the Coffee Banks, under the Chrissy and Trappist Bridges, and onto the sand spit of the Great Gitche Gumi, where the two chiefs awaited in their corporeal disguises.

The great barge rounded the last curve and straightened toward the Club Bridge and the main compound. A light breeze carried the sound of the wedding chant, led by One Called from a Distance, and performed by anyone with knowledge of Ojibwa. Slowing at the docks, in honor of the waiting staff of maintenance, carpenters, guides, cooks, fire, and patrol, the procession was struck by another gentle gust, which loosed the wild rose petals from their garlands and produced a shower of natural confetti over the bride, clinging to her hair and spangling her shoulders with sequins.

As they made landfall and the party alighted, the Niijaanis struck up a soprano and treble chorus. They began with medieval music, and changed to baroque. Then they broke into their own creation, especially arranged for the event. The effect was resonant and harmonic.

When they finished the Ojibwa wedding chant, along with the chiefs, everyone went silent. Chief Hole in the Day offered the prayer. He turned to Mudjekeewis, the God of the West, He who painted himself Black; to Kabibonokka, the God of the North, He who painted himself White; to Wabun, the God of the East, He who painted himself

Yellow; and to Shawondasee, the God of the South, He who painted himself Red; and asked each his blessing.

Chief One Called from a Distance turned to Gitche Manitou, the God Above, He who painted himself Blue, and asked for the blessings of happiness and productiveness, for children, and a fruitful existence.

Hiawatha and Kamali approached the images of One Called from a Distance and Hole in the Day.

A Niijaanis maiden rushed up to fit the platform moccasins.

And they recited the Ojibwa wedding prayer:

> *Now you will feel no rain,*
> *For each of you will be shelter to the other.*
> *Now you will feel no cold,*
> *For each of you will be warmth to the other.*
> *Now you will feel no more loneliness,*
> *For each of you will be a constant companion to the other.*
> *Now you are two bodies,*
> *But there is only one life ahead of you.*
> *Go now to your dwelling place,*
> *To enter your days of togetherness.*

It was that simple, but the energy and emotion of the assembled throng was released at that moment in celebration of a long-awaited milestone. The cheer that erupted was spontaneous and extended. Tears flowed and everyone embraced.

The sight of the radiant couple, supported by all the segments of the local community, the tribes, the citizens, the families, the staff, and the members, was sublime.

Cameras came out. A tall cake was produced. The wedding party of hundreds proceeded en masse to the Club House for wine, cake, song, and dancing.

Mingling among the revelers were two special guests from the Spirit World, Hiawatha's best friends from his childhood imagination, Chibiabos and Kwasind. Nobody in the crowd would discern they weren't human, their holograms being so perfect as to escape detection. They stayed at arm's length from the others to prevent being penetrated by any solid objects. They carefully avoided the embarrassment of being walked through by any of the terrestrials. They were also mysteriously missing from any of the wedding photos.

Chibiabos, the musician, took the stage, brave as man and soft as woman, pliant as a wand of willow, stately as a deer with antlers, and when he sang:

> *All the many sounds of nature*
> *Borrowed sweetness from his singing;*
> *All the hearts of men were softened*
> *By the pathos of his music*
> *For he sang of peace and freedom*
> *Sang of beauty, love and longing*
> *Sang of death and life undying*
> *In the Islands of the Blessed*
> *In the kingdom of Ponemah*
> *In the land of the Hereafter.*[2]

Kwasind, the strongman and acrobat, performed his amazing feats, crushing rock, heaving whole tree trunks like Scottish cabers, leaping and tumbling with blinding speed and agility.

Then, in a final series of back flips, he launched himself in a backward double somersault, and dove into the image of Chibiabos. And the crowd gasped as they both disappeared!

"Wow, did you see that? Where did they go?"

"It's a trap door in the stage."

"Nah, it's a gauze curtain they hang; they shine the lights just so, and you can't see them behind there."

"Watch, they'll come out and take their bow."

"Once I saw Siegfried & Roy."

"David Copperfield."

"Houdini!"

But Kwasind and Chibiabos never came out. People talked about it for years. Everybody had it all figured out in a different way.

Kamali knew instinctively, and watched the hint of amusement pass across her husband's face as he looked skyward at a pair of faintly distinguishable comets streaking back toward their proper places.

---

2. From *The Song of Hiawatha*, "VI. Hiawatha's Friends" by Henry Wadsworth Longfellow.

Hiawatha and Kamali presided for a brief few minutes more. Then the announcement was made, and they were accompanied to the dock at the main compound for their short canoe ride to Wakaigan, and the beginning of their lives together as husband and wife.

Chapter 9
The Honeymoon of Kamali

HIAWATHA SAT IN THE WAR canoe amidships, his arms enveloping Kamali from behind. They were propelled by the two strongest members of the Chippewa Indians, Division D State Champs. The quarterback, Russell Buffalo and the star tight end, Stuart Buffalo.

As the sun began settling upon the horizon far behind the boreal forest, down the impossibly long strand of pink Gitche Gumi sand, the wedding couple alighted on the boardwalk and entered, hand in hand, into the vast confines of the great Wakaigan Lodge.

As the oaken door closed behind her and she entered the fragrant and magical Creative Room, where Hiawatha spent his time weaving and tying his spiritual crafts, Kamali felt a strange emotion rising within her that transformed her quiet and reserved demeanor, and she felt an assertiveness and power that she never dreamed she would possess.

She turned and cast her gaze upon the countenance of Hiawatha, son of Gitche Hay o Wen Ta. The only man she had ever looked upon with lust in her mind.

She had held him up as the example of manhood before she really even fully understood the concept of it. He was just there, always there, as the balance to her feminine sensibility.

I am she and he is he.

He had been her absolute idol since she had first noticed a bare-breasted, copper-toned Indian brave, rippling with muscular power, and brimming with good nature and kindness, bending to care for the neediest and weakest of his fellow citizens.

Now here they were, together as man and wife, within the vast confines.

She tilted her incredible face with its feather, gold and Herkimer diamond tiara, and fixed the Great Hiawatha with a devilish gaze that made his knees go weak.

Her exquisite hand moved to her brow and swept the headdress off onto the floor.

She took his soft, powerful hand in hers, and guided him through the long hall, past the armory and the library, and into the softness and welcome of the master (now mistress) bedroom.

Hiawatha had taken great care to prepare the wedding night suite.

With the same detail he had exercised on the wedding gown, he had dressed the bed with the finest Hudson Blanket décor, but with cotton and silk instead of wool. With feathers and fur and everything soft and pliant.

Candles of fragrant balsam flooded the room with pulsing rhythm. Dream catchers hung above. Small chimes driven by candlepower filled the room with delicate sound.

Kamali began with the headdress of bearskin and feathers. She reached to the top of his head and carefully lifted the sacred crown. Next, she removed his necklaces, one at a time.

The Herkimer pendant.

The float copper strand.

The gold nuggets.

Then she started on the breastplate, and finished with the moccasins, so that he stood in front of her in all his naked, incredibly powerful state, pulsating with emotion.

When she began disrobing, it was as if she had rehearsed it for her whole life. (She hadn't.)

And then she was before him in her indescribably breathtaking beauty, unveiled and revealed, with a stray rose petal upon the exquisite softness of her shoulder.

And they stood together, entering a completely unique and transcendental world.

As she looked up, she found herself under the entrancing gaze of her heroic man, and felt herself weaken, as he had weakened only moments before. She drank in his powerful kindness and compassion. She swooned beneath the inevitable dominance of his sexuality.

As he looked down, he thanked all the gods for the gift of so exquisite a wife. The delicate frame of her body. The luminescence of her skin. The breasts. The fine hair of her sexual parts. The fragrance of her breath. The intelligence of her gaze. Her submissive charm.

Their passion, which had been incubating for so many years, exploded into an indulgence that neither one had ever imagined. It was as if they had become the embodiment of a great movement of orchestral music.

Kamali began with a feather, and the temptation and passion slowly built during an excruciating period of prelude, developing into wilder and more reckless abandonment, and culminating in a crescendo of ecstasy that continued to build upon itself until they were left spent and torpid, in a sweat-bathed tangle of bedclothes.

Kamali awoke, enveloped in the tender strength of her lover's arms.

And then it started again, after their strength had rejuvenated.

And again after that.

And that explains Kamali's lifelong fondness for Stravinsky's *The Rite of Spring*, with its pulsating tension, building toward a culminating cacophony. She never heard it without reliving the experience of that first night with the love of her life.

Man and wife, brave and princess, now King and Queen of their Gateway to the Spirit World.

And father and mother to the one who would take his first breath exactly nine months later, Hayowenta Heywood.

When Hiawatha and Kamali arose from the disheveled mess of their Wedding Night, they made their way to the Empire of Adjidamo in the kitchen. They made powerful tea, and planned for a honeymoon voyage throughout their domain.

The trek lasted a week.

They packed up provisions and started out together down the Cyrus Trail. Bonnie pranced out in front, followed by Kamali, under the watchful gaze of her protector and provider. Hiawatha tested the air and harkened to the whispers of the boreal forest with his superhuman senses.

Mikiziw circled above.

They hiked across the White Pine Forest to the boathouse at Jack Pine Lake. Then, rowing across to Magic River and hiking up to the falls, they stripped down and inundated themselves in the sacred rejuvenating waters, and resumed the ritual of consummating their vows.

Reviving, they made their way to the Magic Lake boathouse and set out for Odyssey Beach in Hiawatha's birch canoe, *Exulting*.

The afternoon softened as they set forth, with the sun deepening orange and the water a pale yellow. The lake mirrored a formation of altocumulus marching very slowly, imperceptibly, from west to east. All this was cast against a backdrop of stationary buttermilk high up in the sky and reflected in the water below.

Viewed by Mikiziw, they appeared as a pair of chevrons etched upon the water, constantly growing. The small one in front was tipped by the black and white head of Bonnie. The larger was carved by the birch canoe *Exulting*, and its two oarsmen, Hiawatha in the bow for power, and Kamali steering true in the stern.

They made landfall as the setting sun cast its golden beams heavenward, like the fingers of some giant hand making its offering to Gitche Manitou.

They found the camp in fine North Woods condition. A stack of firewood, left in the tradition of the woodsman. The axe, sharpened, oiled, wrapped, and in its proper place. The screened bunkhouse, clean and orderly. And the utensils, hung on nails, ready for the next meal.

Bonnie shook herself out, sending forth an explosion of spray, and went to check the perimeter.

Mikiziw wheeled above, folded himself into a stoop, and accelerated at ballistic rate toward the water. Throwing himself into a murderous dive, he hit at a shallow angle, sending up a gigantic water bow before him.

He emerged with a nice rainbow trout for two, which he dropped on the beach before the man and wife.

They cooked dinner over the stone firepit and languished in its glow for an hour afterwards.

Then they bedded down for another strenuous night.

Bonnie kept guard and respected their private zone, keeping keen vigil in the moonlight.

After another consummation, the couple wrapped themselves together and entered the Dream World.

Bonnie looked back over her shoulder and watched them depart upward, two silver and translucent figures, propelled toward the billowing moonlight clouds. Then she resumed her duty guarding the bodies below.

They slipped the surly bonds of Earth.

They chased the shouting wind along, where never lark nor even eagle flew.

And touched the face of Gitche Manitou.[3]

Sunrise brought the shrieking of Ojawane, the Jay. He raised the honeymoon couple from their slumber, and welcomed them back to their earthbound existence. They packed up their stuff at noon and laid a fresh pile of firewood for the next occupants. Then they set forth to Dooley Point and its camp overlooking Magic Lake. From its rocky point at the narrows, it offered a prospect both north and south across a glassy and perfectly calm surface dotted here and there with the rings of rising trout.

They spent the third night at Tupper Point, and the fourth at Estling.

At the extreme south end of the lake, forming the border of the vast Chippewa Club, was the Spruce River. It was home to myriad brook trout of legendary size and willfulness. In fact, the Spruce fit the legal definition of an "attractive nuisance," tempting poachers from afar in search of an unbelievable trophy for their wall at home. The presence of these trespassers was unhealthy and dangerous for the river and forest. A family had recently been found encamped along the bank, their firepit left smoldering and unattended, and their coolers filled to the brim with trout of all sizes. On the day of their arrest, the game warden counted 172 fish, some of them rotting on the ground.

Today, the Spruce was back at peace and alive with brook trout fry, teeming and boiling after a hatch of mayflies.

The burrowing owl, Kokoko, perched above and regurgitated castings of hair and bones.

---

3. Inspired by John Gillespie McGee's poem "High Flight."

The bobcat, Essiban, slunk carefully through the aspen in search of rabbits to eat.

Mikiziw dove from above and picked off a little trout for himself with a one-handed stab.

The Hiawatha party passed through silently and swiftly en route to their next encampment. Hiawatha honed his perceptive senses to the max, and smelled for intruders. Bonnie did too, and they determined that the place was back to its normal, natural self after an unusually harsh period of trespassing and exploitation.

Maybe the crackdown by Fish and Game finally scared the persistent poachers off. The fines were stiff, and two of the party got jail time for resisting arrest. It was in the *Joliette Mining Journal* on the front page, above the fold. JOTV ran with the story for three days.

Then they began the return journey past the Picnic Rocks on Lake Aniani, spending the final night on Mt. Argon, where they held their private ceremony at the Dolmen of the Forebears, the earthly gateway to the World of Further Dimensions.

Next morning, they made quick passage through the Denmarks and past the Lake of the Rushes to the pink sand beach of the Gitche Gumi, and down to Wakaigan.

They entered the vast confines through the kitchen door. Kamali spanked Hiawatha's butt as he passed through, and he reached out to grab her, but she was too quick. He almost caught her at the stairway, but she squirted around the banister and up into the mistress suite, shedding her shirt as she plunged through the door and onto their Hudson Bay bed.

"No place like home, huh." She grinned.

"And no time like the present," he answered, unbuckling his trousers.

Chapter 10
The Youth of Hayowenta

ON JULY 31, HIAWATHA AND Kamali celebrated his twenty-second birthday with a feast and a little fireside romance.

They lounged around afterward on the bearskin rug under the massive mantelpiece, gorging on chocolate cake and roasting their skin in the glow of the fire.

Kamali broke the silence.

"Well, I think all your hard work paid off."

"What hard work?" asked Hiawatha. "I haven't done a productive thing since the wedding."

"Oh, you've been productive all right, or reproductive."

She returned his dumb-looking quizzical gaze and a pent-up peal of laughter burst forth.

"Already?" Hiawatha was dumbfounded.

"It isn't so soon if you consider the statistical data. Just multiply romantic interludes by spermatozoa."

"Wow. Wow. I never figured so soon. We better go to the doc and check. Are you sure?"

"Well, we can go to the doc and check if you want, but I've got a baby in me and I know it."

"Oh, wow. Well, when will she come?"

"He will come in the spring. It's a boy."

"How do you know, so soon and all?"

"I just know. Trust me."

Hayowenta showed up on March 21, the vernal equinox. He was born in the Father Baraga Hospital in Joliette, with all the best modern medical care.

They had decided to have their child in a hospital after Kamali's best friend in high school had delivered by natural childbirth with a midwife attending. They stayed in her own home out in the country. Problems came up. The baby was late and big, and the bones had hardened too much. By the time they made it to the hospital and got help, the child had an oxygen deficit and brain damage. Kamali had been furious at the time.

"Here we are in the twentieth century with all this help. Don't these kids read history? Everybody lost mothers and babies in childbirth back then. It steams me."

At the hospital, the Greens were there to welcome Hayowenta. It was too early for them to come up to Green Cabin and stay. It didn't have a furnace and wasn't winterized. The Greens were used to urban comforts, so they didn't warm to the notion of confining themselves to one room and a fireplace, the way the Heywoods did. So they stayed in the Lightning Bay Inn in Little Bay, and ate pizza and pasties for a week, visiting the new family every day.

Keep America was just dazzled by the baby. She became protective and authoritarian, giving advice and opinions on how he should be fed and cared for.

"Don't put that blanket on him like that; it's pink!"

"Here, hold him this way; support his head so he can see!"

"Didn't he just feed a little bit ago? He'll get bloated!"

Forrest was enthralled and stood back with one finger in his mouth, drinking in the wonder of new life in the human form.

Then they all went back to Wakaigan together and helped the new family settle in.

The mistress suite had no fireplace or heat, so the winter and spring living quarters were confined to the small area of the library with its massive fireplace, and the kitchen, which was warmed by the heat of the wood-burning stove. Everybody crammed into the small dining area for three meals a day, with Hayowenta propped up at one end in his handmade Ojibwa papoose.

When the artisan parents' vacation days were up and it was time to make the trip back to the big city, a major scene ensued. Keep America was resolute in her refusal to budge. No amount of cajoling or threat could dislodge her. When the artisan father became forceful, she dropped to her knees and pleaded, the tears pouring down her cheeks and off her jawbone, splattering into two distinct puddles on the floor below.

"But you love school?"

"Not anymore. I'll grow up ignorant; I don't care."

"What about all your friends?"

"They can write, and they can come visit. I have to be with my new nephew."

Kamali stepped in.

"Well, if I'm going to homeschool this boy, I guess I could use some practice."

"Yes! Yes! Yes! And Forrest too! Please; please. I can cook. I can clean. I can change him. I can shovel snow."

"Winter's over."

"Cut wood, then. Clean up Niijaanis. Rake the pathways."

"Rake the pathways? They don't need raking. They're natural from a hundred years of trodding."

"Now you're just teasing me. I hate you. No, I don't."

"Maybe, then. We'll have to talk about it."

So they left her to stew for a day while they pondered the concept. After prayers and bedtime, the four sat before the massive hearth and discussed the issue over powerful tea. The artisan father had brandy from his flask.

In the end, Keep America stayed, and it was a good thing. Kamali supplied the nurturing and the milk. Keep America worked and slaved as she had promised, and the result was greater than the sum of the parts.

The best part was Kamali's daily assignment of schoolwork. They had a treasure trove of academic material. The Niijaanis microscope and telescope were brought down. Great Daddy's library was attacked with a vengeance. Keats and Yates, Euclid and Ptolemy, relativity and quantum mechanics, history of Western civilization, geometry, algebra. Just bits of it, mind you, partially digested and simplified by Ka-mali's methodical mind.

Forrest liked the epic poems and wanted *Evangeline* read to him by the fire, but the all-time special favorite was Longfellow's *Hiawatha*. Kamali meted it out slowly, one chapter per night on Saturdays. That way it lasted twenty-two weeks.

Then there were field trips for botany and zoology once the trails were passable. On one trip, Kamali scooped up a black stain off a stub-born island of residual snow.

"Ugh, what do you want that for?"

"It's not what you think."

"Looks like somebody lost some crankcase oil to me."

Upon microscopic examination, it was revealed as a massive colo-ny of snow fleas, gathering for their annual mating ritual in the spring.

They were pudgy little mite-like things that hopped around with little control over direction or distance.

"See? Life is not always the way you have it figured out."

Initially, Hayowenta tended not to be precocious. He was born a normal boy, fussy at night and demanding in his waking hours. He walked at twelve months and began expressing himself a little later. He was completely tuned into our world of three dimensions, and devel-oped right on schedule.

As Hayowenta gained maturity and began to have preferences, he showed a tolerance for solitude. He spent long hours stacking play-things in orderly piles and then annihilating them with imaginary cannon fire. He observed and mimicked his mother in her daily home-making routine. He helped his father with ordinary tasks without com-plaint. Eventually, he learned to handle rod and gun with proficiency.

The big surprise came when school age approached. Hayowenta was far ahead of his age in all the traditional subjects, and he had got-ten started early on piano. An old upright in the Club House was used for evening vespers on Sunday nights during high season in the sum-mer. He claimed it, and convinced Keep America to show him what she knew from her five years of formal instruction. He was a good stu-dent and actually made the trip down the boardwalk by himself just to put in some practice when time allowed. Keep America found a copy of *Alfred's Basic Piano Library*, and he started working his way through the lesson plans.

Kamali's program of homeschooling was advanced, but well-paced and fun. Since Hayowenta's two fellow students were older, it was natural for him to strive more; plus, they were both very patient and spent long hours bringing him along.

On his fifth birthday, Hayowenta asked for one thing.

"Can I go to school?"

"What did you say?"

"Well, that's what I want for my birthday. I want to be with the other kids at the Little Bay Schoolhouse."

Kamali couldn't believe her ears.

"Where did you hear about any schoolhouse in Little Bay?"

"Onni. He told me it's fun."

"Onni Lehtinen, the gate guard's son?"

"Yeah. Please, can I?"

"Well, what about me and Keep America?"

"You don't have to come; you already know everything."

"No, I mean as your teachers. Don't we do a good enough job?"

"Yeah, you guys are great, but I want to see the rest of the world."

"What will Keep America do? She moved here just because of you, you know."

"Well, yeah, but that was a long time ago. Besides, she can come, too, and Forrest."

So a big family powwow was convened at the kitchen table, and everybody approached the issue from a different perspective. It would have been easy to dismiss the whim of a six year old, but Hayowenta already showed signs of a steadfast and resolute personality. In that way, he was very much like his father.

Keep America was eleven now, and she saw the value in it.

"I say let him go. The schooling's no good, but we can pick up the slack. He might need to have street smarts some day."

Hiawatha started. "Street smarts?"

"Well, you know, the other world out there—the rest of America. How to get along without getting hurt. He might need a job some day, and have to venture out even farther."

And Kamali said, "Look, I'm from Chicago, and he doesn't need any street smarts. That's what we're preparing him for. To get above that stuff."

Forrest added, "I want to go, and I'll watch over him. Nobody touches my Hayowenta. Or makes him feel bad unless he deserves it."

So in the end, as patriarch, Hiawatha made the decision.

"Here's the deal. What we have here is our family values. They're strong, they're permanent, and they're the bedrock of our individual lives. Hayowenta can already tell right from wrong in his heart. He's seen it and lived it for six years. Toss him out there with Forrest as his guardian. He'll swim just fine. And if we see something going wrong, we'll take action. Forrest, you're the point man. We're counting on you, and I know you won't let us down."

So, in the morning, everybody sat down for breakfast and ate in silence. Then they told Hayowenta it was okay and he would be starting at Little Bay in September.

You could just see the satisfaction start in his heart and glow within him.

And everybody knew it was fine.

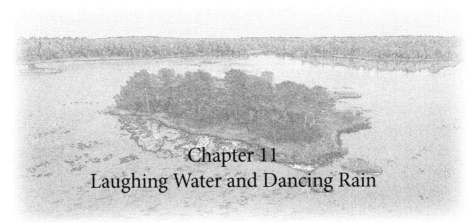

Chapter 11
Laughing Water and Dancing Rain

W HO WOULD HAVE DREAMED THAT the babies would be so far apart?

The next conception almost coincided with Hayowenta's schooling decision. Actually, the girls were conceived a little before that.

Kamali missed a month after she had quit really paying attention. Then she missed a second month.

A gypsy had read her palm in Chicago, on the South Side, when she was a little girl, and it was always going to be just one, and a boy.

But just about the time Kamali started sending Hayowenta off to school every weekday, she sensed it again, and this was big time!

"Hy, I think I'm pregnant!"

"No way! After all this time?"

"Yep. And it's way different this time. I can't tell just how, but it doesn't feel the same."

So, they waited and felt and listened and tuned in to the Spirit Guides, and it was still a mystery. Then they went in for a sonogram and there the twins were, curled up together and ready to go. You could just see they were soul mates the way they acknowledged each other in the womb. It was as if they were already communicating, sharing secrets, and giggling together. They lay face to face, and when the time came, Laughing Water turned toward the opening first, and was followed by Dancing Rain. They showed up in the atmosphere vigorous and enthusiastic, taking their first drink of oxygen and really rocking the room with sound. Their cries were melodic in nature, and the room rang with a perfect harmonic overtone. They were born vocalists and

remained vocalists for the remainder of their years here in our world
of three dimensions.

Keep America was brought in as naming consultant, since she had
personal experience fighting orthodoxy.

"I never minded ridicule; it seems pathetic to me. What a sad
thing. That a kid would take pleasure trying to make somebody feel
bad about her own name."

"And what a great honor to have the names of two famous prin-
cesses."

"But we're of two cultures, and they are one spirit, so let's do both."

So they used Ojibwa for the first, and English for the second, the
harmonizer.

Minihaha and Dancing Rain.

They were known as Minnie and Danci.

"It's so funny, Minnie has haha in her name. Minihaha Heywood!"

So now they were five, plus their aunt and uncle, of course, and
Bonnie, and they set about immersing themselves in their enchanted
world. Everybody went out together, and they spent more time in the
vast expanse of Chippewa than in Wakaigan itself. They encamped for
weeks at a time all over the property. Odyssey Beach for the sense of
tribal unity. Magic Stream Falls for the link to further dimensions..
Dooley Point for the physical prospect of the magnificent Magic Lake.
Mt. Argon for the connection to the forebears and all the points in
between. They built a second birch canoe together to go with *Exulting*.

They all worked on *Damsel* as a team. They searched far and wide
for a tree big enough to supply the bark. When it was found, they felled
it and stripped it and flattened the bark with boulders. Then they had
to find the roots for the ribs, and cut the white cedar for the thwarts
and gunwales. Then they strung the dried gut for wrapping the parts,
and wove the cane seats. They tapped the pine pitch for sealing the
seams and finished the job with a nameplate of copper. *Damsel* was
christened as a second vessel to accommodate the whole family. They
set forth with the parents in each stern, guiding true, and Keep America and Forrest in the bow, for power.

They communed with all the creatures of the boreal forest, and
joined in its rhythm. The children learned to understand and respect

the competitive and harsh nature of life in the forest, as it is throughout our world of three dimensions. They suffered through the torment of manitons, the biting insects. They sweated and toiled climbing the five mountains together, Kamali and Keep America each with a papoose. They bore down hard into the biting headwind of Gitche Manitou, and cut through his frothy combers for miles at a time. They hunted and trapped and netted and fished. They learned to build a proper Ojibwa lodge of stripped aspen and birchbark. They always gave thanks for the gifts of the gods. For the pelts and the meat, for the fiddlehead and purslane, the morel and chantarelle, for the all the myriad gifts of nature.

The boys learned the sweet science of Chippewa Martial Arts, and became able wrestlers and boxers like their mentor, Hiawatha. Self-defense would never be a problem. Hayowenta would later add the study of jiu jitsu and mix in the punching style of Tae Kwan Do.

The girls were beguiling in their mastery of dance and song, particularly of song in the case of the twins.

And as the twins grew and absorbed the love and understanding of their family and its unique perspective from the viewpoint of their special life, they celebrated it with song.

First, they learned and repeated the simple tunes from Forrest's *Alfred's Basic Piano Library*: "Mary had a Little Lamb," and "Somewhere Over The Rainbow."

Over the years, they built upon their repertoire. They started with folk music, then they learned the Ojibwa songs, which they transformed from simple chants to melodic modern versions. Later, they dabbled as singers with the local Black Dog Boys, whose Bluegrass renditions were the premier act around Little Bay. As adults, they would become famous for their own creations, having formally studied music theory and gained advanced degrees from prestigious institutions.

It always seemed as if they were of a single purpose and almost of a single mind. Often Minnie would begin a sentence and Danci would end it. Just like their singing, where Minnie took the lead, Danci harmonized and a ringing harmonic created the "angel's voice" or "third voice" that chimed in on certain notes, like a barbershop quartet, only two.

Minnie and Danci were mirror image twins. Minnie was right-handed and Danci was a lefty. Minnie was right-eye dominant and Danci shot skeet left-eyed even though she was taught right-handed. Their dimples were on opposite sides, and each had a cowlick that whorled in the opposite direction.

This symmetrical tendency made for a nice visual effect when they danced the shawl dance at powwows.

They might have joined Hayowenta in the revolutionary notion of public education, but before they had the option, an event took place that would change the course of their lives forever.

Chapter 12
Conflagration

T HE CHIPPEWA CLUB'S MEMBERSHIP HAD two schools of thought regarding the conservation and protection of its vast holdings. You were either a Hugger or a Cutter.

Discounting the large percentage of completely apathetic and clueless members, the split was essentially 50/50.

The Huggers were of the persuasion that man had no business interfering with the course of nature. The club was a laboratory for the scientific community to study. The only unlogged Northern Boreal Forest remaining in the United States. Preserving it was a responsibility the club owed to posterity, to the legacy of the club, to all of mankind, and to Nature itself.

One rule was that if a tree fell across a trail or road within the vast wilderness, it was to be cut, cleared, and moved aside, left to decompose naturally. (The Cutters considered this rule a perfect example of unreasonable waste.)

The Chippewa Club enjoyed special tax status, as a nature preserve.

"We are guardians of a rare and great treasure, unique and scientifically valuable as well as beautiful and pristine. A singular example of what would have existed had European settlers not invaded and destroyed it for their personal enrichment. Some of these trees are 300 years old. My great-grandfather knew them, and pondered beneath them. I want my great-grandchildren to ponder beneath these same boughs."

The Cutters pointed out that trees have lifespans too, and any tree your great-grandfather hugged was probably about to die.

The club policy was set during the Victorian era. It was quite advanced for its time, and contrarian. The idea was to set aside a percentage of the land their timbermen and landlookers had surveyed and claim it for their own personal use.

The same phenomenon occurred again in the late twentieth century when the technology and internet billionaires began grabbing up millions of acres in the American West for their trout stream and golf course retreats.

In any event, these were the Huggers. "It was created this way by nature. We inherited it and preserved it in its original state. We should work to keep it the same. Original. Pristine. Virgin."

Then there were the Cutters. They saw the land as a resource. They wanted to maintain the vigor of the club as it was intended, as a recreational retreat. They saw the timber as a resource to be managed and harvested reasonably and responsibly to keep the treasury solvent, and the forest healthy. They tended to be the hunters and fishermen, the skeet and trap shooters, the tennis enthusiasts.

The Huggers wanted to restore the original fish in the lakes, mostly ugly and inedible carp, and bony northern pike. The Cutters wanted to keep planting rainbow and brown trout, brook trout, and smallmouth, like the founders had.

Sport fish.

Cutters wanted to selectively harvest sections at long intervals. One section, near the Brook Trout River, was assumed to be pristine wilderness by the Huggers, even though stumps from a hundred years back proved them wrong. The Cutters saw money in the timber for infrastructure.

The fire trucks were dilapidated. The main bridge over the Jack Pine needed replacement. The Club House needed a new roof.

Huggers tended to be content to limp along on a wing and a prayer.

"The trucks will make it another couple of years."

"Park your big SUVs and walk a little. It's good for you."

"Patch the roof."

The debate broke into open warfare the year the breakwater collapsed. There was a big assessment, and some people couldn't afford it (mostly Huggers).

The Cutters' spokesman was Russ McMillion, and he saw an opportunity to prove his point for good.

"Let's get an unbiased opinion. We'll get an expert from the Forest Service."

So the expert came and looked and studied.

At the annual meeting, he gave his report.

"Your forest is dead!"

Gasps from the Huggers.

"Nothing new and vigorous can grow under the canopy of your overly mature forests. Look underneath. Nothing but pine needles, mushrooms, and deadfall. You need management, or Mother Nature will manage it for you, and she uses a very broad brush. Just remember that nature's agent for rejuvenation in this environment is fire, and you are ready for a big one. In my opinion, you can start thinning and cutting and make some money, or you can watch the whole place burn to the ground one of these days. You probably read about all the forest fires we've been having out in the Rockies. It's because of 'hands-off' policies like yours."

Unbelievably, the Huggers were unmoved.

"We need more campfire restrictions."

"No smoking!"

"We'll take up a collection for a new firetruck."

"Solar-powered fire alarms!"

From the Cutters side, snidely: "Ever hear of lightning?"

So they took the vote, and the Huggers won. No change to the long-held preservation policy until more studies could be scheduled. Right now, the budget didn't allow for another study any time soon.

Russ McMillion, under his breath, said, "Ouroboros the dragon devours his own tail."

As luck would have it, the following year was unusually dry. June brought the usual spring rain showers and blustery squalls, but that was about it for the summer. July rainfall was zero. August logged 0.5 inches. The trails crunched beneath hikers' feet, and the mosses and lichen formed a crisp crust on the forest floor. Nobody had ever measured, but the depth of pine needles in the jack pine forest was many feet thick, offering fuel for fast-moving underground fire to spread unseen.

Come October, the mushrooms didn't even come up. Songbirds perched and gasped in the heat. The ferns gave up and wilted early, and the blueberry bushes never turned their brilliant mahogany red. They just went brown and curled up.

The members had a fine time right up to Labor Day.

"What a year, no bugs!"

"We'll have to keep this a secret, or the UP will turn into California, with all the tourists. Sunshine every day, nice warm surf in Lake Superior."

"Mosquitoes? What are you talking about?"

After the members left for the season, Hiawatha led the family on their annual trip to Dooley Point.

Before, the guide service broke camp late in the season. Lately, it was understood that the Heywoods would use it in the waning days, and tear it down for the winter when they were through. Utensils were brought back to the guide house. The tent was collapsed and rolled with its stakes for storage in the boathouse along with the cot, the saw, and axe.

October 12 was another unseasonably warm day. It dawned sultry and still. A south wind wafted gently from the direction of the Spruce River, four miles down the narrow lake. It built slowly and steadily, until they had to secure the tent flaps and tighten the stake lines.

"Daddy, let's have poetry!"

"Let's sing!"

"I can do Snake Dance."

"We'll throw the bones and gamble for chores!"

So, Hiawatha cracked out his harmonica and led the family in traditional folk tunes, bluesy stuff.

But that creeping feeling of foreboding was upon Hiawatha. He and Kamali had been oppressed by it for three months, and it seemed like everything was going to be okay for the year, once fall arrived.

Kamali said, "We're through it, right, Hy? There's never been a big fire this late in the year."

Hiawatha said, "We'll be through it when the temperature drops. Let's pray for snow."

Minnie and Danci said, "Okay. We'll do a snow dance!"

And they invented one, with hand-dancing like Hawaiian Hula and swaying hips.

After a while, the kids got tired, and everybody got on their knees together. They each offered their prayers, kids first, in reverse order of wisdom, and they weren't prayers for things.

"Please help me understand others."

"Please give me strength to withstand a challenge."

"Make me grow up a strong and helpful person."

"Please help me love people more."

And the last and wisest from Hiawatha and Kamali together:

"Please give us the strength to hold our family together in unconditional love and steadfast support no matter what happens to this world of three dimensions."

Everybody kissed and turned in.

That night, of all nights, Hiawatha was not in his best perceptive form.

Maybe it was the distraction of family life, or the thrumming of the tent sides in the wind, or pure exhaustion, but he didn't notice the signs until way too late.

Later, he wondered why, with his superhuman sense of smell, he never perceived the smoke. With an hour head start, they might have made it to Wakaigan in time to save it, or at least some precious contents.

He dreamed of howling wolves, of roaring rapids, of a gigantic landslide down Mt. Argon, and when he awoke, it was Bonnie howling and she was accompanied by a different sound; a groaning, crashing cacophony of destruction.

Hiawatha started awake in a moment of realization, and he didn't even have to look to the south, but he did.

The campground at Dooley is against a rock wall, and the southern horizon is blocked. But above in the sky was a flickering orange reflection.

When he got them aroused and in order, with Kamali as their commander, he ushered everybody to *Exulting* and *Damsel*, calmly and in an orderly fashion.

"Leave everything and come with your mother and me."

They boarded the vessels they had crafted together. They cast forth and entered into the protection of Magic Lake.

When they reached a safe area about a hundred yards out, everybody turned to see the advancing wall of fire.

It was ungodly.

This was by far and away the most powerful display of natural force any one of them would ever see in their eight lifetimes. It was like a dry hurricane, which multiplied the ambient wind velocity by a factor of four. It fed on its own updraft as much as on the unlimited supply of perfect fuel in its many forms stretching for miles ahead, all the way to the Shining Big Sea Water.

The flames reached into the heavens, two hundred feet up, lashing across the night sky like giant incendiary bullwhips.

Keep America heard Willie Nelson, over and over in her head, singing "Ghost Riders in the Sky."

And that's what it was, the great force of Gitche Manitou in his most powerful earthly state, riding wild across the thousands and thousands of acres of the Magical Kingdom, the Gateway to the Spirit World.

Just like the Ghost Riders chasing the Devil's herd, upon their fire-breathing mounts.

An Indian Apocalypse with Gitche Manitou in the center, flanked by Wendigo and Jawawinodin.

And Hiawatha thought to himself, *If we don't think fast and take action, we're all bound for the Spirit World in an ugly, painful way, and it's not time yet.*

Then he told his family, "We've got work to do here in this world of three dimensions, so let's paddle out of Hell."

He picked Julia Island.

Julia was the kind of place everybody wanted to spend a night on once in a lifetime, but nobody ever did.

It sat at the north end of Magic Lake, far from the boathouse, and against the cliffs of Mt. Argon. It was shaped like a peanut shell, with a certain asymmetrical perfection to it. Everything seemed in balance.

They struck out, Hiawatha in *Exulting*, steering true with Forrest in the bow for power. Bonnie and Hayowenta sat amidships.

Kamali followed in *Damsel*, steering true with the twins amidships and Keep America in the bow, for power.

As they turned to their task, the conflagration ramped up and sent new hot wind behind them, whipping the turgid waters and providing helping wind.

Keep America said, "Funny; we're riding the wind of evil."

Kamali replied, "Use your enemy's strength as your own, like jiu jitsu."

They made landfall in twenty minutes flat and set right to work. Kamali took command of the kids.

"Forrest, go find a cedar and cut strips of bark. Make them long ones. Pile them over here, and the girls will braid them for twine.

"Keep America, find a yellow birch and cut bark for buckets; we'll sew them and caulk them with pine pitch.

"Girls, keep your eyes open for sparks and embers. Daddy will stamp them out."

Hiawatha hauled the canoes and cut some boughs for a shelter. When the work was done, they huddled inside and watched the fireworks, their faces illuminated by the flickering orange light.

Here they were, the little band of paleface Ojibwa, reverted to their natural state of survival. A Stone Age clan (except for steel knives, fishhooks, and Daddy's collapsible fly rod) huddled against the elements as their ancestors had done over the past ten thousand years.

They watched Dooley Point as their nylon and polyurethane tent exploded in a blue flash.

The wall of fire was off to both sides of the lake now, and the threat of flying sparks was still high.

"Daddy! There goes one!"

Hiawatha got up to stomp out the falling ember, but it extinguished upon hitting the ground. Inexplicably, this happened all night and throughout the next several days. Julia seemed to absorb the energy from all the sparks and embers, neutralizing them, as if they had entered some sort of black hole.

After a while, they fell asleep one by one, Hiawatha and Kamali trading watches in two-hour increments. They judged time from the red moon shining through the smoky overcast.

In the first hour, Hiawatha spied two bow waves approaching from the west. It was Amik, the beaver and his mate. They were the first of many creatures of the forest to seek shelter at Julia, as if there had been a fire drill and training, like humans do at the schoolhouse. After two days, the island was like Noah's Ark.

Hiawatha rose at dawn and pulled *Exulting* down to the water. Embarking, he reached under the gunwale and retrieved the little ought weight rod, a Hardy Palakona from the 1930s. He searched out his fly wallet, taped under the seat, and looked for terrestrial patterns. A hopper on a number fourteen hook, barbed.

The big ones would be along the shore by now, snapping up the fleeing bugs opportunistically.

Hiawatha's instinct was right and he had two nice fat German browns in ten minutes. Five pounds apiece, which is pretty cute work with an ought weight bamboo.

Breakfast for the clan.

When Hiawatha got back, Kamali had made up a mush of acorn and pinon nuts for the girls. They ate it obediently but not enthusiastically.

Then they dug roots and baked acorn bread.

The second day, Forrest went ashore, found a freshly cooked deer, and cut a roast, giving thanks and offering prayer.

They finished the roasting in the firepit, and offered Indian grace with heads bowed.

Tucked away in the crannies of *Exulting* was a trove of survival gear, which Hiawatha produced as if by sleight of hand.

A titanium and flint firestarter, army surplus.

A folding hatchet and shovel combo, up under the foredeck.

Waterproof matches.

A Leatherman tool.

String and wire on small spools.

A packet of pemmican.

They were progressing into the twentieth century a little more.

Forrest took *Damsel* ashore to see the condition of the trails, or what had been the trails.

"Still pretty hot."

So they waited two more days for the ground to cool before breaking camp for home.

Hiawatha planned out the return route.

"Forrest, how was Magic Stream and the Falls?"

"It seems like the fire jumped it. It looks green down in the canyon. And cooler, with the water and spray."

"Let's go home that way. We can portage where we have to."

So, next morning, after smallmouth bass and acorn mush, they started out for Wakaigan.

Magic Lake boathouse was a smoldering pile of debris with ashes floating on the surface around it.

The land was black and gray.

Nuclear winter.

Ash piled a foot thick everywhere. No need for trails, really. You could see for miles. Every few hundred feet stood a legacy tree large enough to escape total annihilation and with the possibility of survival.

They crested the Falls, and descended into the canyon of Magic Stream, first the vertical part, where the portage was really a chore. Footing was tenuous unburdened, but Forrest and Hiawatha really had their hands full trying it with canoes balanced on their shoulders, yoke or no yoke.

The lower part got easier little by little, and soon they were waterborne and headed for Red Pine Lake.

It was completely covered with a scum of gray ash from shore to shore, and through the narrows into the rest of the chain. Second Red and Third Red would be no different.

They set forth and crossed. Behind them stretched two black mourning ribbons of wake.

The great White Birch Forest was obliterated. Nothing burns like birch. To the west, the horizon was spiked with black carcasses of the largest pines and hardwoods. Hiawatha prayed for some life left within them, or some surviving seeds.

They made their way across to the Red Pine Lake boathouse, which was still smoldering and steaming in the shallows.

First, they tried to continue by water down Red Pine River, but it was choked with fallen tree trunks straddling from one side to the other.

They reversed course and left *Exulting* and *Damsel* on the beach in their sorry blackened state, looking more like two burnt logs than the finely crafted vessels they were.

The last hike was through the Jack Pine Forest, now the Jack Pine Plains, flattened all the way to the horizon. They marched single file with Keep America at the point, and Hiawatha surveying from the rear, minding his little clan.

Bonnie now had the appearance of a long-coated Labrador, totally black. She heard the crashing surf of Gitche Gumi first, and started out ahead for some Superior water to sooth her parched and dusty throat.

They came over the last rise, and Keep America screamed. And then she screamed again.

Stonehenge!

There before them stood seven stone chimneys, the seven fireplaces of the great Wakaigan, standing alone in the ashes. Not even mounded, just a flat carpet of soot, really, with some shards of metal objects here and there.

It was surreal. Here you had seven fireplaces, but the smoke was all rising outside!

They stood there processing information, each in his own way.

Wakaigan had a different history with everyone, and each was feeling the loss differently.

Danci came up. "Oh, Daddy, I forgot to pray for Wakaigan. It's my fault!"

"No, honey, that's not a thing you pray for anyway. Wakaigan was just in the way, that's all."

Kamali sat straight down in the soot and ashes, sending out a black cloud in all directions, and began to weep. The sight of their blissful romantic retreat, the home base for their lifelong commitment together, the place their kids would remember and always come home to.

It shook her to her core.

The tribe had started out with black moccasins and lower legs, but now they were completely covered with a grime so fine it was embedded in their pores like graphite. White eyes rimmed in pink peered out from within.

Minnie said, "Look; Danci is a Tar Baby."

Danci said, "Well, then you're Tar Baby Two!"

Keep America got mad. "It was the damned poachers; I know it. Deer hunters. The slaughtering kind. I feel like hunting them down myself. I think I will."

Hayowenta and Forrest consulted off to the side. Then said, "Hey, we're all still here and nobody's even hurt. We better find the others and see if they need help."

They started down the pink (black) sands of Gitche Gumi toward the Club House and the compound. Every cabin was a smoking hulk, all fifty of them. Gone. The Club House sat smoldering, its American flag, tattered and gray, fluttered above.

Turning inland, they crossed the main bridge, scorched but sound, and approached the former site of the operations department. Because of the large clear area, the buildings remained standing. A big white tent was in the middle of the lot with a Red Cross on it. A forest service helicopter sat in the middle of the lot, and uniformed personnel roamed around with walkie talkies.

The JOTV van was parked to the side with its dish antenna deployed, and Kaarlo Boniak, the news anchor, stood before the Red Cross tent broadcasting to the networks.

A volunteer with an armband noticed the approaching band of Tar People with their Tar Babies.

"Hey, Kaarlo, here's eight more!"

The reporter approached, mike outstretched.

"Tell me, sir, what was it like out there? How do you feel about losing everything but your lives?"

Hiawatha walked straight past him. "Sorry; I'm tending to my family."

Their days of independence were over. They accepted free clothes and were guided to the makeshift temporary showers.

"Men to the right and women to the left, please. When you're done, find yourselves a place in the main tent. Meals will be served at eight, noon, and five."

Hayowenta said, "The overalls are okay, but I don't feel like myself in them."

Keep America muttered, "We're refugees."

Inside, they found themselves a spot in the far corner opposite the main entry. Kamali encamped her clan and Hiawatha headed for the door to go find friends.

"Sir…Sir! I'm sorry. You'll have to stay inside for now. We need to account for everyone. It's dangerous out there."

Hiawatha looked down at the spectacled volunteer with his clip-board.

Hiawatha reached into his vest and pulled out his deputy's badge, gold and heavy. Held it in his palm and fixed a gaze on the young man that caused him to avert his eyes to the side instinctively.

"Oh, I see. I'm sorry. We have orders, you know. It's for everyone's safety."

"I understand. Where's the sheriff?"

"I think he's commanding in the field. I can radio him if you want."

"Okay, tell him Hiawatha is here and wants to talk to him at the tent."

Sheriff Otto Outennen's squad car skidded up sideways. The door was opening before he came to a stop and he hit the ground as if he were stumbling off an escalator.

"Jesus, Hy, we thought you was dead! How's Kammy and the kids? Where the hell wuz you? We sifted through the ashes at the cabin."

"We spent the fire on Julia Island, and fished for a living. Who was here? What are the casualties and how many survived?"

"Well, the management and staff were heroes. A couple of the fire-fighters sustained minor injuries, but it went off well, considering how quick the fire came. Only three member families were here, and two of them jumped in their cars and made it out the front gate as soon as the siren went off. That was the McMullins and the McKormacks. Everybody else retreated to Superior."

"When the fire crew saw there was no chance, they manned every boat they could launch and took everybody out beyond the surf line. The fire burned itself out when it reached the beach. After a couple of hours, they came back in and gathered here in the compound. So, it's the employees and the Derrys. About fifty people here in the tent. Now that you are accounted for, we can find lodging for everybody and start sending people home."

Inside the tent, all the little groups of friends and associates gathered and consulted about the future. Little Bay did not offer much of a job market, so the employees wondered how they would survive once the Club closed down, which they figured would happen pretty quick.

When Hiawatha reentered the tent, he saw that the Derrys and Kamali and the kids were all together and engaged in lively conversation.

Keep America and Forrest were gone to Red Pine Beach to recover *Exulting* and *Damsel*. They portaged them back and set to scrubbing and rinsing them.

"Daddy, we need to put these canoes away. Don't we have a storage shed over there across from the garage?"

Hiawatha thought a minute.

"Well, yeah, I guess we still do. I guess whatever is in there is all our worldly possessions."

The twins jumped up. "Let's go see!"

"Yeah, I want to see our worldly possessions!"

So, they set out and counted the doors of the row houses until they came to number six.

They lifted the bar and pried off the rotted lock, and there was the sum total of everything they owned, except for their new clothes and the canoes.

"Look, a car!"

It was Great Daddy's 1934 Packard Dietrich Convertible.

"It's gotta be worth a fortune!"

"And the trunks! What's in there, gold?"

"No, mostly it's stuff Great Daddy traded from the Chippewas. Wampum, tomahawks and the like. And here's a whole bunch of deer-skin and beads and rawhide."

The twins were ecstatic. "We can make outfits!"

Kamali and Cathryn "Cat" Derry came over to see what the excitement was about. Just as Keep America and Forrest were rolling the gigantic vehicle out into the daylight for the first time in decades.

"Look! Yellow! With white sidewalls. Let's clean her up."

Everybody put a shoulder to the big beast and got her rolling with Hayowenta at the wheel, which was a bad idea since he couldn't reach the brakes and had a hard time with no power steering.

Reaching the garage, they all ran around to the front and brought the Packard to a stop next to the hose bib.

"Fill the tires up more!"

Jerry Kilcox, the mechanic, came out and took a look.

"No, those tires will have to go, and most of the hoses and belts need changing. They're not that hard to find in car collectors' catalogs. Then we need to drain the gas and change the oil and check fluid levels and test the shocks. I can find a battery that will fit."

"Then we have to register it and get Daddy a license."

Keep America stood up on the running board and patted the big open hood panel. "Well, wherever we go, we're traveling in style."

"Where will we go, Daddy? Little Bay? Joliette?"

"I don't know yet, kids; it's too early."

Kamali interrupted. "Listen, Hy; Cat has an idea. She says we should move in with them in their brownstone."

Cat explained, "Our boys are grown and gone, and we have ten bedrooms. The kids could go to public school, and you should find employment pretty easily."

Hiawatha wondered. "Doing what? In New York City?"

The twins had it all figured out. "We can sing and dance. Mommy can sew. Keep America can wait tables."

Keep America slammed her fist down hard on the open fender and winced. "Now just a darned minute. There's lots of stuff I could do. Wait tables? I'll run for office!"

"Yeah, and Forrest is a jock; he could go out for the Yankees."

So, Jerry the mechanic set about putting the Packard in running order, and the family retired to their refugee tent to make plans for the future and set their lives straight. The girls hauled the rawhide trunk over, and they started right out making authentic Ojibwa deer hide garments for each other. The jeans and T-shirts from the Red Cross were starting to bind, psychologically.

Two days later, the Derrys left, and the agreement was binding. The Hiawatha Heywood clan would take up residence at 34 E 62nd St., New York, NY.

It took a couple of more weeks for the car to be rendered serviceable. The clothes were all sewn and adorned, and on November 1, they set forth through the front gate of the Chippewa Club in the 1934 Packard, with the top down, and all dressed in traditional Ojibwa garb. The trunk full of worldly possessions rode snugly on the rear luggage rack, just like in *The Great Gatsby*.

It was shift change, and gate guard Harv turned to his relief.

"Now, there's something you don't see every day!"

Chapter 13
Venturing Forth

T HEY DROVE STRAIGHT THROUGH TO New York City, with Hiawatha, Kamali, and Keep America sharing driver duties.

On their way to the Mackinac Straits, it turned cold, and they had to stop and put the top up. It was amazing how comfortable and warm the old Packard was. The kids curled up in the sumptuous backseat and on the floor, which was vast. It was like a mobile wigwam, and the radio worked.

They listened to '40s music on the NPR station. Tommy Dorsey and Count Basie. Then there was Bluegrass, and after that Country and Western.

In Ohio, it got warm again for a day, so the top came back down. People honked and waved. What a sight!

"Who can they be, and where are they going? They must be celebrities!"

"Look, they have feathers in their hair, and the woman is so amazingly beautiful!"

The Packard loved the open road, and gobbled up the miles effortlessly, just cruising along as if deprived for too long a time.

And every time they stopped for fuel or natural reasons, they created another sideshow.

"Honey, you won't believe what I saw down at the gas station. A little band of Indians all dressed in rawhide, and riding in an old-time convertible!"

"Aw, for Crissake, Homer, can't you just watch football like the rest of the guys?"

After eighteen hours, they pulled up to the brownstone and parked at the curb.

Forrest was unimpressed. "It looks like a normal building to me."

Keep America corrected him. "Beggars can't be choosers, bro; it beats the Packard for legroom."

Hiawatha pressed the doorbell, and they heard a distant resonant chime.

Cat didn't come to the door, a butler did, and he almost slammed it right away. What an apparition, and multiplied by eight. This wasn't possible!

"Hello, I'm Hiawatha; we're the Heywoods, and Mrs. Derry is expecting us."

"Yes, of course; please come in. Mrs. Derry is upstairs in the drawing room. Can I help you with your luggage?"

"Yes, please; there's just the one steamer trunk on the luggage rack in back. Boys, help the gentleman."

Forrest and Bernard, the butler, hefted the trunk while Hayowenta minded the doors.

They entered a marble foyer trimmed in magnificent mahogany. The elevator door opened with a chime. Too small for the whole party and the trunk. The guests all glanced at each other with eyes as big as dinner plates.

An elevator inside your own house?

No way!

They went up in two loads, first Hiawatha and Kamali with Keep America and the twins, then the butler, the boys, and the trunk. And Bonnie.

The doors opened into a room you would expect in Victorian England. A giant fireplace with an imposing portrait above. Overstuffed furniture and chintz everywhere. Fabulous oriental rugs. A Tiffany glass chandelier.

Cat came bounding off the couch in her sweats with her hair tied back.

"Oh, good! Good! Good! You made it! Oh, it's so exciting, and you look fabulous. The outfits! Where are the boys and Bonnie? Sit down. Have coffee. Tell me about the trip.

"Charley is down at the firm, but he'll be relieved. You should have seen him. He's been fussing over your rooms, worrying about the menu, wondering aloud about your likes and dislikes. He's been so lonely without the boys and their gang around. He's going to love this.

"First, let's all have breakfast; you can freshen in the powder room. Then I'll show you what we have figured out for your rooms. Oh, it's the biggest thing for me in such a long time. Imagine, Hiawatha himself and the whole Heywood clan are all in New York City at once!"

After breakfast, Cat showed them their quarters.

Hiawatha and Kamali had a sumptuous bedroom with en suite bath.

Keep America had a two-bedroom suite with a room for herself and one for the twins, and a shared bath.

Forrest and Hayowenta shared a room with a special dog bed for Bonnie.

Cat had ideas already. "Let's all go for a walk in Central Park. The weather is beautiful. Bonnie, you have to be on leash. Sorry, baby."

Dinner that night was a big deal with standing rib roast and trimmings, the magnificent banquet table set for nine with Bonnie demure in the corner.

Just as Cat had said, Charley was delighted to see everybody. He had always worshiped Hiawatha and considered him the most naturally talented and highly principled person he had ever known. That was quite a compliment coming from a twelfth-generation Knickerbocker, and general partner in one of the world's most powerful law firms.

Charley delighted in the kids, and after dessert, when the twins treated him and Cat to their especially composed song of thanks, he started to mist up.

The resonance left a ringing in the great room for several seconds after the final note.

Charley was emotional. "Thank you. Thank you. On that note, I think I'd like to turn in."

Kamali couldn't have agreed more. "Big day tomorrow. We need to find jobs."

When they emerged onto the street in the morning, two pieces of paper were fluttering under the windshield wiper. The first was a parking ticket for $125.

"Holy moly! That much for one ticket? We weren't even driving!"

The second was a note written on the back of a business card from a "Mr. Daniel Triumph, Commercial Real Estate." It read: "Interested in selling this car? Please call my private number on the reverse side."

They had an impromptu powwow on the sidewalk.

Kamali was adamant. "Jump on it, Hy. We need some money right away. It would save trying to auction it. You know, the hassle and the storage and all. Sometimes these things happen for a purpose."

"Okay, why don't you guys go out looking, and I'll try to do a deal here at the brownstone."

Hiawatha found the duplicate title, which Jerry had insisted they get back in Joliette, and picked up the phone.

He was put straight through to Mr. Triumph.

"That's a pretty nice car. Very nice actually, which I'm sure I don't have to tell you. I've actually been looking for that very model for years. There aren't many. Do you have provenance?"

"Well, I'm the second owner. It belonged to my grandfather."

"He must have been a man of means, and of taste. As I said, there weren't many like it. Do you have the title?"

"Yes, it's right here on the desk in front of me."

"I'll be honest with you. It fills a hole in my collection. You could probably get damned respectable money for it properly restored, but every part on it would have to be perfect. Right down to the spark plugs. Reproductions, I mean, not modern. And those tires have to go."

"They're brand new!"

"Doesn't matter; they're not correct. Here's my offer. I'll send a man over to pick up the car with a tow truck, and with instructions to collect the signed title. He'll have a cashier's check for a hundred thousand dollars even, and I'll pay the parking ticket I saw on the windshield this morning."

Hiawatha thought he was going to choke! He covered the receiver and tried to clear his voice and get back his wind. He took three deep breaths.

Silence.

"All right then, a hundred and twenty-five, and that's my final offer, and it's a good one."

Hiawatha hoped his voice wouldn't squeak. "Sold."

"Mr. Charles Smith will be at the door before the close of business today. I presume yours is the brownstone?"

"Yes, yes, it is. Number 34."

"Good. Thank you. Maybe we'll meet some day. I'm leaving for Washington right away."

"Yes, maybe we will. Bon voyage."

Hiawatha replaced the phone in the receiver, and when he stood up, he felt a little dizzy.

"Wow! What a start to life in the big city."

The family came home at six, brimming with excitement and stories.

"Daddy, you should have seen! There's people everywhere, and some of them sing and dance just like us; well, not just like us, but people give them money for it!"

Keep America verified. "Minnie and Danci tried for a while, and a guy dropped five bucks right in the hat! I swear it's true."

"He did, Daddy, and that was after about three minutes. Not even the whole song."

Hayowenta was a little worried. "Hey, Dad, where's the car? Did you find a garage? I hope nobody stole it."

"It's okay. I found a buyer today. He just came by with the check. That's one possession we don't have to worry about taking care of."

"Sold already? How much?"

"We'll talk about that some other time."

Hiawatha and Kamali talked about it in bed that night.

"Hy, did you make a good deal on the Packard? I'm having seller's remorse."

"I think I did, being the first customer and all, plus he paid the parking ticket."

Kamali winced in the dark. "Okay, so how much?"

"A hundred and twenty-five thousand."

"What…? How much…? You're kidding!"

Kamali snapped on the light to see if he had that impish smile. She looked into his eyes, and it was true.

"Holy smokes, let's get clothes for the kids."

"First, let's get a bank account."

"Okay, first thing tomorrow."

Chapter 14
Encampment

Eventually, they found their place for doing business. They set up a nice camp in the East Village, right near the Peruvian flute players. Lots of ethnic people were selling their wares and playing music. They made a habit of showing up almost every day, including weekends (especially weekends), and they had the "full deal."

Hiawatha sat and crafted stuff for tourists to buy. First, he made his things too nice, and Kamali told him so.

"Hy, you're spending too much in materials, and look! They don't even buy the good stuff. It's too expensive. Stick to the little pouches. Put a fetish in it and bless it for them. Blessings come cheap."

"Yeah, but is that okay? It seems like selling air!"

"Not if it's a real blessing, and I know yours are. If you get a bad vibe, just don't bless it. You've got the spider senses!"

Kamali cooked fry bread and sold it in little plastic trays. Great profit margin!

Naturally, the twins performed almost nonstop, and they were the main attraction. Their voices were seductive, and then they held the people in with the dances. That way, people bought more stuff.

Keep America struggled at first. She didn't have that much to offer beyond childcare, which was huge, but her pride suffered. Especially when the boys came up with a martial arts show.

They choreographed a great artistic version of Bruce Lee style fighting.

In loincloths—sexy.

It all took place in their little sidewalk space, next to the Peruvians. All these things happening together. They were a force because of their variety and continuity, and energy.

After a while, Keep America came into her own. She modeled the really expensive stuff.

At this point, she had developed a magnificent figure. And she had those deep green eyes, and long blonde hair.

She was a perfect model. Maybe not all that Indian-looking, but she carried it off in a way that appealed to the average Midwestern tourist.

She made it seem like, "Hey, I could wear that, just like her!"

She could spot the affluent ones from a mile away. "Would you like to see our designer line? It's back here behind the screen. Just a few pieces my father makes for Hollywood."

And she could sell. She fixed them with those green eyes and asked, "And what would you like to go with that?"

The Cash Queen. She took great pleasure in counting up the day's revenues.

Then there was the matter of the second trunk, the one with the real museum quality artifacts from Great Daddy's collection that they found in the garage.

"We could sell it to collectors. There's all kinds of galleries that would pay a fortune for that stuff. It's real."

Hiawatha sat them all down. "Let's not get mercenary. Remember the spiritual life. We just got here, and look how we're getting caught up. Keep your dignity. We have a link to the forefathers in those trunks. Just remember, we've been very busy trying to fit in and survive, but in case you haven't noticed, this is a spiritual wasteland. Listen to the people talk. Hear what they care about. These poor people are unfortunate. They don't know the natural world. They don't know God's way. They think of things from their own viewpoint. They think that if bad stuff happens to people, then God is bad. Look at the churches. They're empty, or bums use them as latrines. Listen to their vulgar language and look at the TV. We know better. We're here, and we have to survive, but remember who you are. Who we are."

They took it to heart and started to notice more about the people around them.

Keep America still couldn't keep her mind off of the money. She enjoyed accounting for it, and one day, she asked if she could do the deposits.

Kamali thought it was a great idea, so they turned over the checkbook with a little ceremony. Hiawatha made her kneel and accept financial knighthood, tapping her on each shoulder with the book.

When Keep America went to enter the day's deposit, she couldn't believe her eyes. "Hey, where did all this money come from?"

"The Packard."

"Well, we're rich. What are we even working for?"

"We're not rich, girl. How much do you think that house we live in costs?"

"I dunno."

"Millions and millions, honey. What we have is a little foundation to build on. Let's try not to let it ever get lower than the base value you see right now."

"Well, a little lower at first; we need normal clothes."

"Let's wait a week and see what we get from work. Then we'll shop."

"Okay. Well, if it's our foundation, what's it doing in checking? We need to earn interest, don't we?"

"I suppose your right about that, smarty pants."

They opened a savings account.

The next night, *The New York Times* carried a big story:

BALD EAGLE SIGHTED IN CENTRAL PARK!

Mikiziw circled above.

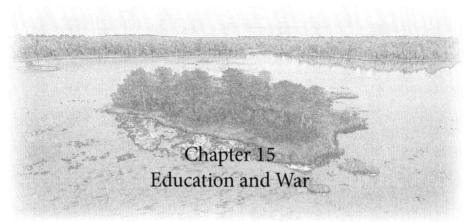

Chapter 15
Education and War

D URING HIS TIME OFF FROM school, Forrest decided to take Tae Kwon Do.

He stopped off at a dojo on the way home, and came home late, having his dinner alone in the kitchen, at about eight at night.

At sixteen, his testosterone had kicked in. He was strong and fit.

He had always been a boy of few words and decisive action, with natural athletic talent. He was a plodder. Not brilliant, but a good student, purely on work ethic and determination. After about a month, he started to place high in his age group. In three months, he was winning tournaments, and the ribbons and trophies began to accumulate.

He went from white belt to blue in record time, and by early spring, he was a red belt.

One day in April, Forrest was in such a hurry that he skipped the elevator and ran three stories up the fire escape to bring home big news.

"Hy! Kam! They hired me to teach! I'm a teacher! They gave me a class of little kids, beginners, you know."

And so Forrest began to supplement the family income with a real minimum wage paycheck for his teaching after school, in addition to spare change from the fighting shows on weekends in the Village.

Still, the money was definitely not coming easily, and they were enjoying a comfortable life only because of the largesse of Chuck and Cat.

Hiawatha and Kamali were grateful, but the whole concept of dependency weighed on them, and they often talked about it in bed at night.

Hiawatha felt a need for independence. "We should get an apartment and fend for ourselves, no matter what we have to give up."

But Kamali and Cat were really growing close, and the Derrys were adamant about their staying. One night, the adults sat around the great room and played whist in front of the fireplace.

Hiawatha decided to test the waters.

"Chuck, how much do you think a three-bedroom apartment might be in Brooklyn?"

Chuck peered over his reading glasses and summoned his most mellifluous courtroom voice.

"Irrelevant, your honor; the subjects are not going anywhere."

Cat laid her fan of cards face down and pounced.

"That's right, and I don't want any arguments. We love you guys. What are a couple of sixty-somethings supposed to do around here without a little action? Bernard was about to quit out of boredom till you showed up, and now he's taking Tae Kwan Do from Forrest in case somebody bad comes to the door. I can't manage life without Keep America's help. Now she's even managing the household budget. Besides, what about the new college expenses on top of everything else." Her hand cupped her mouth involuntarily and her eyes popped wide open.

"Oh, nuts, I blew Keep America's secret. She'll kill me. She wanted to make the announcement herself."

So everybody played dumb later when Keep America came down after prayers and bedtime with a letter in her hand.

"Take a look at this. It's from Columbia. Remember Mrs. Solomon? She's the one who buys all of the good stuff you make, Daddy. Her husband is Dr. Solomon, the math professor, and he asked me to take an experimental test from ETS. I did great, so he said I should apply for a full ride. It came through. I start in September."

Kamali felt her heart swell with pride as she looked at her little sister in her fully blossomed maturity at twenty-four The sister who had become like a daughter, in a way, who called Hiawatha "Daddy" some of the time, and who had helped raise Hayowenta and the twins as her own.

"I still need money for lots of things," said Keep America, "but I have an idea. I've got the whole summer to work on setting up a book-keeping company for other households in the neighborhood. Then, when my workload kicks in at school, Sis can do it. Keep it organized, and I'll take a look every once in a while to make sure it's all correct. What do you think, Sis?"

Cat broke in. "It's brilliant. I know a lot of women who would love to have their household expenses taken care of by a bright young math-ematician. Chuck can bankroll it. Can't you, Chuck?"

"Well, I can do that, and shop it around the firm, too. Maybe there are some wives who would be interested."

And so, Keep America Green Bookkeeping Service was born. It turned out that many of the customers were Sierra Club Members. The environmentalists flocked in like migrating birds. Chuck bank-rolled a modest payroll and some office equipment. It didn't really take very much money. The company was in the black right from the start.

Hayowenta and the twins were entered into neighborhood public school, and Forrest commuted to a high school close to the dojo for his junior and senior years.

At this point, it turned out the boys were better off going to Tae Kwan Do on the weekends. Forrest to teach and Hayowenta to learn. The argument was that they really didn't bring in that much cash from the fighting show. They just served to create excitement and attract people to the group. They agreed to perform just this one more week-end, and that was a lucky thing.

On their last Sunday night as a troupe, they all walked home in their deerskin garments and feather headdresses. It was a great week-end, being a holiday, and the cashbox was full. Keep America figured they had a record take.

The twins scampered about out front, with Keep America survey-ing. Bonnie had to be on her leash, but she was used to it by now. Hi-awatha and Kamali observed from the rear. They cut through Central Park diagonally, as usual, and that proved to be their undoing. Too much of a regular pattern.

Six young men approached from the opposite direction. Sagging trousers, stocking caps pulled down. A chain dangled from the big one's belt. They stared coldly as the two groups passed.

Brooklyn, probably.

The twins recoiled instinctively and melted into the center of the little band. Bonnie snarled quietly.

"Quiet, girl."

Then from behind. "Hey, Tonto! How much money you got tonight?"

Hiawatha felt his calm self-assurance creep in as his adrenaline began to elevate. "Look straight ahead, kids, and keep walking. Girls in the center, men outside."

Hayowenta marked that moment. "Men."

Keep America held the box close in to her center and cursed under her breath. "We had to stay right to the end. Now it's getting nice and dark."

"Hey, Blondie, where you goin' so fast? I need some pussy."

Forrest tensed, and almost turned, but he checked Hiawatha first with a quick glance. Keep going.

Then up ahead, two more, right in the middle of the path. The little one in the leather skullcap. He was the leader.

"Tonto, don't be stupid; all we want is the money."

And from behind, "And the pussy."

From the side, "And a little fresh ass from Junior."

Hiawatha touched Forrest on the shoulder.

"Switch with Hayowenta."

They did. And they tightened the circle (circled the wagons).

The irony wasn't lost on Kamali. "Now here's some karma for you. This must be how the settlers felt."

Hiawatha issued quiet orders. "Keep to your side. Don't turn around till you absolutely have to."

They went for Hayowenta first, of course. Hiawatha anticipated this, and grabbed the first one by the throat. He pulled him in, delivering a sideways head butt that split the bastard's brow and produced a gusher of blood.

The rest of them charged, and a shriek erupted from the center. The girls dropped into a pile with the twins on the bottom, holding on to the cashbox, and Keep America on top.

Kamali stood and fought.

It was all so fast that each one remembered it differently. Hayowenta got in two good kicks before he was overwhelmed. Forrest was in the zone; everything moving in ultra-slow motion as he methodically delivered one perfect shot after another.

When the reinforcement showed up, Hayowenta had his teeth sunk deeply into the throat of his kidnapper, holding on with a wrist-locked grip around his neck. Forrest had two of them out cold on the ground and was dealing with the third. Hiawatha was engaged with the biggest one and had his hands full. The leader moved in with his stiletto and slashed through the deer hide shirt, spilling crimson down the sleeve all the way to the cuff.

As he stepped back to avoid Hiawatha's grasp, an amazing thing happened. An object the size of a medium-sized dog whistled down out of the sky like an artillery shell. It knocked the leader seven steps sideways onto the ground, leaving four deep gashes across the shiny dome where his skullcap had been.

Mikiziw had performed a perfect zoom maneuver, trading airspeed for altitude. He wheeled around on one wing at 300 feet and dove again, folded into his compact and deadly bombshell form. The second pass ripped the knife from Skullcap's grip and left him holding the poor remnant of a hand. The third removed the big one's right ear and about a fourth of his scalp.

"What the fuck *is* that? Some kind of monster?"

"Kongamato!"

Forrest was on the leader in a flash. He applied his favorite submission hold, the guillotine, and yelled, "Get out of here or I break his neck!"

They got out of there.

Hiawatha and Forrest tied Skullcap with rawhide and looked around for the rest of them.

Gone.

A small crowd had gathered. "We sent for police, dialed 911."

A park patrol officer arrived on a bike. He radioed in for an ambulance for Skullcap and Biggun, whom they intercepted a hundred yards to the north, on his way to the emergency room with his ear, hoping for reattachment.

Hiawatha needed stitches for his deltoid, and the deerskin blouse needed a new sleeve.

Forrest's whole outfit was smeared with blood and had to be thrown out. Otherwise, he was okay.

Hayowenta must have caught an elbow. His busted lip was big and tender.

All the girls were fine.

Nobody but the twins slept that night. The adrenaline wouldn't go away.

Keep America counted out the cash, and it was a new record, just as she had figured.

The twins wanted to sleep with Daddy, so they started off in the marital bed, and Kamali switched them later.

Next morning dawned bright and beautiful. Everything seemed better.

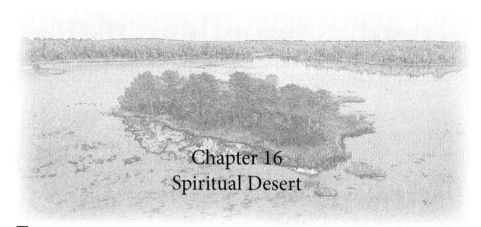

Chapter 16
Spiritual Desert

I T HAPPENED SO INCREMENTALLY THAT Hiawatha didn't notice for months, but after the War of Central Park, his awareness was sharpened, and he realized how his spiritual senses were dulling. He began taking Bonnie for more walks through Central Park. He communed with Mikiziw telepathically, and he searched the neighborhoods for any signs of spiritual resonance. New York City wasn't exactly a dead zone, just very, very weak, like a faint HF radio signal ebbing and flowing through the static of the atmosphere. He visited the churches. The Catholic ones had a barely perceptible signal during services, but they were dead otherwise. Many of the old churches and cathedrals in poorer neighborhoods were bereft, with chains across their doors, their steps littered with feces, vomit, and hypodermic needles. Their alcoves, reeking urine, were populated by derelicts and their vile debris.

The frenetic noise of machinery and vehicles, the warbling of sirens, the stench of garbage on the surface and sewage wafting from below were just physical aspects, but the whole of it seemed to overlap into the spiritual realm as a form of pollution. Just the pure concrete inertia seemed to be part of the problem. Nothing was coming from the heart here because nothing was going in. The spiritual resonance Hiawatha had grown up with was drowned out.

Instead, these unfortunates were filled with worthless blather, day and night. Hiawatha tuned in to TV to find out what was there. Jerry Springberg refereed his stupid, crass participants as they hurled insults, vulgarities, and sometimes fists and furniture at their family members or neighbors. There was Murry Pilvitch and his game of "Who's the Father?", pitting boyfriends and husbands against each other with DNA tests. Then there were the vapid soaps with their endless sexual conflicts.

And that was network TV, purportedly regulated for content.

Hiawatha turned to the cable channels and was deluged with vulgarity, violence, and crude, poorly written storylines with no artistic value. He perused the professional sports and news programs, the evangelicals and the financials. He found nothing to hold his interest and much to turn away from.

Then there was the porn.

Cat helped him out. She created a favorites list for him, with NASA, The Weather Channel, The History Channel, The Discovery Channel, and Animal Planet. He settled on CSPAN, to witness the workings of government, and found it unexpectedly amusing.

After a week, he quit.

Then the twins came home one day and wanted to know something.

"Daddy, what does 'girls eating each other' mean?"

They had been waiting at the magazine rack in the neighborhood convenience store.

To change the subject, he got their minds on school.

"Tell me about your day. How do you like your teacher?"

"Well, she's not as good as Mommy, or Keep America."

"Why not?"

"She doesn't answer questions. She just wants us to remember what she says."

"Like what?"

"Like all the wars America started, and how bad slavery was, and how our soldiers murder innocent people, and how all the rich people keep us down, and especially how we Indians were slaughtered."

"In first grade?"

"She says we have to start early."

Hiawatha made a mental note. Time for homeschooling again.

The next morning, Hiawatha went out for his Bonnie walk, searching for spirituality. He decided to turn right instead of left for some reason. Just to change it up, probably. So they headed for Brooklyn. Up past 112 St.

As they passed 125th, his spiritual Geiger counter went ballistic!

It was the Ebenezer Baptist Church, and it was rocking.

They went in, Bonnie and he, and took a seat in the back pew.

So, here is where the spiritual germ is planted and growing.

Reverend Cecil Maxwell delivered a heartfelt sermon about accountability and responsibility. About looking after your fellow man, your brothers and sisters. Especially your children.

About fidelity and steadfastness, perseverance, and determination.

About charity and philanthropy.

About tithing, and the love of God.

Hiawatha had no formal religious training, but he liked the values.

And then the choir started. They were beautiful and perfect. The hymns hit Hiawatha with significant impact.

His immediate thought was, *Do they have a school? Let's enroll the girls.*

They didn't have an accredited school, but there was children's choir rehearsal on Tuesday night, and singing and dancing lessons on Thursday night and Sunday afternoon after services.

The classes proved invaluable, and the twins took their singing to a new level, with a flavor and nuance they never would have developed elsewhere.

Since the War of Central Park, the band of paleface Ojibwa had started to cut back on street performances. Keep America Green Bookkeeping Service was picking up, and Cat suggested a website for the crafts. Hiawatha had taught everybody, and now even Chuck and Cat tried their hand at creating with deerskin, beads, and wampum. They started doing a brisk mail order business.

Hiawatha went back to the authentic and expensive things using Great Daddy's artifacts as models. One Saturday, he was alone at the site when an elegantly dressed gay man approached with a large, muscular black man in impenetrable sunshades.

Boyfriend or bodyguard?

"Oh, they're beautiful. Oh, it's perfect! Look at the breastplate. Sioux?"

"No, Ojibwa."

"Well, we'll need all you have, and I'll order more for the chorus. And loincloths. Do you make loincloths? I need thirty of them. Leggings too, or maybe high-topped moccasins."

Then, to the expressionless bodyguard/boyfriend, "Oh, Otis, can you believe the luck? Three weeks before opening night, and we finally find something good enough for the show."

Hiawatha would have given two weeks' allowance for Keep America right now. She could have calculated everything in her head instantly.

Hiawatha asked, "Do you mind if I ask what all this is for?"

The dainty man pointed flamboyantly across the street to a large electronic poster with a border of chasing neon lights.

THE LAST OF THE MOHICANS
The Musical
Starring: David Ladd
With: Sally Bowden & Suz Di'Caprio
OPENING AUGUST 19th
THE GASLIGHT THEATER

Hiawatha stood to introduce himself. As he extended his hand, Otis took a half-step forward.

"It's okay, honey. This is business."

The small man gave Hiawatha a quick glance up and down, stopping just below the belt buckle.

"Oh, my Gawd, what a stud! I think I'm going to faint!"

"I'm Hiawatha Heywood of the Paleface Band of Ojibwa."

"Well, I'm just *so* lucky to meet *you*. You have *no idea* how lucky. I am Ascot Saint, the producer, and this is my guardian, Otis Johnson. We were desperate, and you were sent from heaven!"

"Otis, hand me my purse. I need to write the deposit."

"Well, Mr. Saint, I don't know what to charge you."

"Ascot, please. Here, I'll take all you have now, and here is a permanent pass that will get you into the theater at any time. They'll do the photo ID later. Here is my personal check for ten thousand dollars. I'm sure it will be more. Is that enough for a deposit?"

"Well, Mr. Saint."

"Ascot."

"Ascot, these are museum quality. They're very expensive and take time to make."

"Don't you have elves? All artists need elves."

"I guess I could put the whole band on the job. When do you need them by, the nineteenth?"

"Sooner. Quick as you can. Chop, chop. Deliver the rest at the theater as you get them done and bring an invoice for the balance. I'll pay cash in advance."

As they turned to leave, Hiawatha heard him whisper, "Do you suppose he can act?"

Chapter 17
Stardom

KEEP AMERICA WAS GETTING USED to surprises—first the Packard, then KAGBS taking off like a rocket. Now Hiawatha comes home with a check for ten grand and a contract for, how much?

"That's $500 each for breastplates, then $300 for the moccasins, and $250 for the loincloths times thirty is $31,500 total, plus the tax. Not bad for three weeks work. We better get cranking."

Hiawatha corrected, "Three weeks is opening night. If we deliver it that late, poor Ascot will have a cow! The dress rehearsal is next weekend. We *really* need to crank."

With everybody working at a fever pace, including Cat and Chuck, the project moved along on schedule.

Hiawatha delivered the first load two days later and dropped off the invoice for $21,500 at the business office. The secretary cut the check right there on the spot. As Hiawatha headed for the side door, he was brought up short by Ascot's shrill tenor.

"Hiawatha, Ohmigod! I forgot the feathers! We don't have head-dresses!"

"Well, you're lucky they're Mohawks."

"What do you mean?"

"If it was Sioux war bonnets I couldn't finish in a month, but the Mohawks are simple. Porcupine and deer tail roaches. Three-feather chiefs. Shouldn't be a problem. I think I even have a few made up already."

Ascot clapped his hands and bounced on the balls of his feet.

"Oh, Hiawatha, thank you, thank you. You saved my show."

So there was another $7,500.

The next delivery brought another surprise. The check was already waiting at the business office. That was nice.

But as Hiawatha turned to go, here came Ascot with the director in tow.

"Hiawatha Heywood, this is our *gifted* director, Harold Prince. He would like you to read for him."

"Read what? Can't he read it himself? I've got stuff to make."

"No, silly; read for a part. Audition."

"You mean to act? In this show?"

"Maybe. Really, he just wants to see how you look on the stage, and how you project."

"Project?"

"How your voice sounds. To the audience. How it goes out through the building. Fills the room."

Well, Hiawatha's voice sounded good anywhere. It was one of his strongest physical attributes. He didn't say much, but when he did, it was in a mellifluous, resonating baritone.

Ascot grabbed him by the hand and pulled. "C'mon; it won't take five minutes." They placed him at center stage with a script and disappeared into the dark of the fourth row seats.

"Okay, Hiawatha, start where it says Chingachgook."

Hiawatha cleared his throat and began. The mellifluous baritone rang out.

"We are sorry to kill you, brother. Forgive us. I do honor to your courage and speed, your strength."[4]

"Thank you," said Ascot. "Now down to where it says Ongewasgone."

"John Cameron, thank you for your hospitality. Twin River Mohawk got no quarrel with Les Francais. Trade furs with Les Francais. Now Les Francais bring Huron into Mohawk hunting grounds."[5]

"Thank you," said Ascot. "Now could you please sing a few bars of something?"

"I don't sing very much," said Hiawatha.

---

4. Dialogue originally from *The Last of the Mohicans* 1992 film.
5. Ibid.

"That's okay. We just want to hear some tone and range."
Hiawatha called on his most strident patriotism:

> O beautiful for spacious skies,
> For amber waves of grain,
> For purple mountain majesties
> Above the fruited plain!
> America! America!
> God shed His grace on thee
> And crown thy good with brotherhood
> From sea to shining sea!

"Jesus Christ, he sounds like Paul Robeson!" said Harold.

Hiawatha squinted into the dark. "What did you say?"

"You have a wonderful voice, Hiawatha," Ascot replied. "Thank you. Now just one more minute while we shine some lights on you."

Hiawatha stood there a while more while they trained the spotlight on him. First green, then yellow, then red. Then another light from below.

From the dark. "Look at the features."

"And the poise."

"Okay, Hiawatha," said Ascot. "That's it. We'll see you next delivery."

"Good thing we're done," Hiawatha replied, "or you would be minus a few headdresses for the rehearsal. You know, if you want singers, you should be listening to my daughters. Now, they've got talent."

"Okay, why don't you bring them when you come day after tomorrow."

"I will; they'll be very excited. I won't tell them till the last minute, or they won't sleep for two nights."

When Hiawatha handed the check over to Keep America, her mouth dropped open and her brow wrinkled up in a questioning arc.

Hiawatha drew a chair up next to Kamali at her sewing machine. She was putting borders on the loincloths. He stroked her hair and kissed her cheek.

"Headdresses. Porcupine roach and three-feather chiefs. We need to make twenty-seven of the roaches and three chiefs, and then we're done, except for the acting."

"Acting!"

"I auditioned. They might use me. Bit part probably. You know, just stand there and look like an Indian. They liked the way the light shined on my face. Ojibwa genes. It's union scale, you know, and a steady gig."

"Gig?"

"Yeah, that's the way we talk in show business."

Kamali smiled her impish grin. "Can I have your autograph?"

"I only give autographs after a special interview. It has to be in private in my upstairs quarters."

"Kids, Daddy and I are going to take a little nap. We'll be back in half an hour."

Keep America looked up from her stitching. "Not going to be a lot of sleeping going on in that nap."

The last batch of leather costumes was done in forty-eight hours. Hiawatha made the delivery and brought the girls for their first exposure to a theater of any kind, including the movies. They came in through the side door, into the frenetic energy of a set under construction.

They were struck dumb. They stood arm in arm with eyes like dinner plates. Six years old, and they knew this was where they wanted to be for an entire lifetime. At that moment, destiny was revealed to them, and they just knew, instinctively, without a word spoken, that this was where they belonged.

Hiawatha sought out Ascot and the director, Mr. King.

Ascot slid the last five feet on his knees, and came to rest before the twins, right at their own height.

"Oh, look how pretty. Now who is Minnie and who is Danci? Let's see, hmm."

He did an eeny, meeny, miney, moe and came up right. Big points! Ascot was a magician with kids; he had them loosened up and laughing at his antics right away. They joined hands with him and went around the stage on a mini-tour, looking at all the interesting stuff.

In a couple of minutes, he propositioned them.

"Here, come stand in the spotlight. George, can you darken the theater and give me a spot at center stage?"

They stood.

"Okay, lights up and applause!"

George turned up the chandelier and piped recorded applause through the PA. It was as if the girls were being welcomed by a full house.

"Now, what would you like to sing for the imaginary people?" Ascot asked.

The mirror image twins responded in unison.

"'Ojibwa Love Song' and 'Shawl Dance.'"

They glanced and nodded to get in sync, and began one of their most practiced and familiar routines.

Ascot and Harold could not believe their ears. And the ringing, resonating note at the end was sensational! It was still reverberating when the twins turned and exited the spotlight.

Harold was adamant.

"I have to have these girls! We need to write them in! Call Steven and tell him he has to change the script."

Ascot winced. "He's going to *love* this."

"It doesn't matter. Once he hears them, he'll understand."

The men approached Hiawatha with hopeful smiles, and Ascot spoke up.

"Mr. Heywood, we think your daughters are the freshest, most prodigious talent we've seen in years, maybe ever. Please meet with us and bring your lawyer and agent. We need an exclusive contract with you. It will absolutely make the show. Also, we talked about your own audition, and we want you to understudy the character of Uncas. It's too late for you to learn the part, let alone acting in general, but you will be guaranteed union scale, seven days a week, whether you work or not. That way you can learn how theater is done, and actually play the part when we think you're ready, if needed. Once you reach a proficient level, we'll keep you on as standby."

Harold continued, "As far as the twins go, we'll just plug that act in. I know right where it goes. They're ready just the way they are. They will have to leave regular school because we perform six days a week, and twice a day on weekends. Are you comfortable with homeschooling and tutors?"

Hiawatha laughed. "A lot more comfortable than PS 59. Problem is, I don't have an agent, but I guess my landlord could set me up with one."

The twins skipped and bounced all the way home.

They burst into the brownstone and overwhelmed Bernard with enthusiasm. Finally, after thirty seconds of waiting for the elevator, they completely lost patience and bolted out the door to use the fire escape route. They peeked through the windows of each floor in search of Kamali. She was all the way up on the fourth, where a bedroom had been converted into the workshop. Kamali looked up from her eighth Mohawk porcupine roach to see the twins flying toward her in a blur.

"Mommy, we're stars!"

"We're hired! We start tomorrow. Rehearsal!"

Keep America figured. Two at union scale, that's fifteen hundred each a week! Times two is three thousand. Whoa!

"And Daddy's undersomething. He gets to study every day."

Keep America's mind was starting to reel. That's forty-five hundred. Times four weeks is …*eighteen thousand a month*! "I'm getting dizzy!" she exclaimed.

Hiawatha arrived in the elevator just as the girls needed it. "We need to go tell Cat." Minnie pushed "One" and then "Door Close" to speed it up.

Cat was subjected to the same onslaught, and had to keep slowing them down. Then Uncle Chuck came home from the firm, and he got the same treatment.

There. Everybody's notified. "No, wait. Bonnie!"

They dashed for the elevator to fill the little Border Collie in on all the details.

So, in a week's time, the whole family routine had changed exponentially.

The street theater period was finished for good. Keep America Green Bookkeeping Service was successfully launched. Sky Blue Waters Indian Crafts was now internet-based and would probably need its own facility soon. Forrest was teaching after school at the dojo. The twins were removed from PS 59, and Kamali started back in with homeschooling, which she had sorely missed and loved to do. Keep America was starting at Columbia in the Math Department, with hopes of working for Dr. Solomon as an assistant. Hayowenta was least affected, with Tae Kwon Do replacing the fighting show, and tenth grade at Eleanor Roosevelt being fine with him.

The twins said their tearful goodbyes at the Ebenezer Baptist Church, and promised to come for services every Sunday, once they were settled into their routine. This made Sundays intense. Get to bed before midnight Saturday night. Get up early and dress for church at Ebenezer. Out to lunch, and then to the theater for the matinee. Home for rest and light dinner, then back for the evening show.

Hiawatha's appointment with Ascot was scheduled for Wednesday, and he asked Chuck where to find an agent.

Chuck was protective. "Let's not go rushing out hastily. After all, agents are for finding work. You already have jobs. I'll write a contract for you and represent you. We're a pretty respected law firm" (understatement of the century) "and nobody's going to try anything cute with us in your corner."

They all settled into their routines, and the countdown started for opening night.

As predicted, playwright Steven Beckhoff did fuss a little about the changes. Actually, he fussed a lot, and broke some china dishes. But he did change his mind immediately when he saw the twins trying their new "Mohican Love Song with Shawl Dance." In the end, they were written into the play in four places, including the finale.

The entire band had good seats on opening night. Hiawatha sat in the audience for the first and last time. Henceforth, he would remain back stage with his script, learning his part. Aping it, really, reading or reciting from memory every line, night after night.

The band embellished their best deerskin garments, and wore them. Hiawatha yearned to bring Kamali in her wedding dress, but that was gone forever, and he didn't have a month of Sundays to make a new one.

Still, she was a sensation, as always. People pointed and whispered. They figured she was the leading lady. When she took her seat in the audience, they figured she was from Hollywood, but no one could place her.

Forrest got some attention, too, from the teenagers in the audience. Girls gathered in groups at intermission and gawked in disbelief. He was turning into quite a specimen in his eighteenth year, and the daily workouts at the dojo had him in terrific shape. He was very handsome and self-assured. It was the demeanor, the confidence, that slayed them.

So the curtain went up, and the play went forth. The audience was abuzz at intermission. In the end, when the curtain fell, there was a standing ovation and three curtain calls.

The paleface band went backstage with flowers for the twins. The girls were excited, but spent. Kamali could tell that the anticipation had taken its toll, and they were ready to spool down and get some rest. She prompted Hiawatha, and the band slipped out the side door early and went home. As they emerged, a scream rose up from the crowd of autograph seekers who waited for David Ladd, the star who played Hawkeye. This scream, though, from a small group of teens, was for Forrest, even though he wasn't in the play. Kamali and Keep America glanced at each other with arched eyebrows that said:

We're entering new territory with new dangers. Powerful ones.

Everybody waited for the first reviews. They were very good, not great: 8 out of 10, and the twins were mentioned favorably in most, and very favorably in two reviews. They gave the show momentum, and ticket sales, and the hope that life would continue for *The Last of the Mohicans*.

Life did go on for the Mohicans, and Hiawatha got his part down pretty well, to the point that he secretly wished Will Jones might take some time off. Not that he wished Will misfortune, but he was starting to wonder what it would be like out there, with the lights and the audience, the interaction with the cast, improvising when the timing faltered. Dealing with the unforeseen.

So every day, Hayowenta went off to school. So did Forrest. Then they did Tae Kwan Do until time to come home.

Keep America did the books early in the morning and left for Columbia at about ten. She carried a full load. Eighteen credit hours.

The twins got homeschooling until mid-afternoon, when they reported to the theater. They traveled together with Hiawatha, performed, and got home about midnight.

Cat was left with Kamali running Sky Blue Waters Bookeeping.

One Friday morning, Kamali woke Hiawatha at eight. It had become his habit to sleep in since his hours had become abnormally nocturnal for him.

"Hy, wake up. Ascot called; he wants you to call him back right away; says it's urgent."

As Hiawatha was at the toilet, the phone rang again. It was Ascot, and he was in an inconsolable tizzy.

"Hiawatha, we're *screwed*. The show is dead in the water. David Ladd *quit* last night, and he took the understudy with him!"

"What? Why?"

"Oh, he's such a *jerk*. He got a Hollywood offer, and he tried to extort me. When I resisted, he just got up and walked out the door."

"Well, call him up and tell him to come back, and you'll pay."

"I tried all night, and now his partner says he already left for LA on the early morning flight. We'll have to cancel the performance for tonight, and I don't know *how* long it will take to replace him. I hope he falls off the airplane and breaks his neck, the dirty little queer."

"Watch who you're calling names, Ascot. It's bad karma."

"Well, he just ordered up a double-helping of bad karma for himself then. The little shakedown artist should burn in hell."

"Calm yourself, Ascot. Everything is going to be fine."

"How can you say that? It's *not* fine; it's completely fucked."

"It's fine because I know the part."

"You *what*?"

"I know the part as well as I do Uncas. Ascot, I've been sitting backstage every night for two months. Once I memorized Uncas, I figured I might as well start on Hawkeye. I know it by heart. All of it. The songs, the spoken lines, all of it."

There was a long silence on the other end. Hiawatha realized Ascot was crying.

There was a snuffling sound and then, softly. "Hiawatha, I loved you the moment I set eyes on you. You are my hero."

"Well, I guess I better come down early today for costuming and makeup. Plus, we could run through it a couple of times."

The rumor spread like lightning. The trades splashed it on the front page: LADD QUITS MOHICANS.

That night, the entertainment press thronged in to chronicle the death knell of a Broadway show. There was no way Ascot Saint could pull this off, and the reporters would deliver the coup de grâce with withering reviews. A lot of them bore no love for Ascot, whom they dismissed as a gadfly and flibbertigibbet.

When the curtain went up, the audience was treated to a new and imposing Natty Bumppo, his makeup deemphasizing the Ojibwa features and highlighting Hiawatha's Anglo-Saxon traits. Still, the Ojibwa blood provided the perfect expression of the character's enigmatic identity. Hawkeye's European mind incarnate in Hiawatha's mixed-blood body.

From the first scene, they were held spellbound by the baritone, and the first solo sent a murmur of wonder through the audience.

When the finale arrived, the audience was already on its feet, cheering.

The twins lit up with pride and beamed up at their father with radiant admiration.

As the cast gathered for the first curtain call, the crowd roared its approval, cheering, whistling and yelling. When the entire cast gestured toward Hiawatha, the reaction was deafening.

On Saturday, the reviews were out of this world:

MOHICANS MADE MARVELOUS!
SHINING STAR ON SCENE!
HIAWATHA HEYWOOD HOT!

Every critic raved. By Monday evening, the show was sold-out for six months. Hiawatha was invited on the morning shows. A week later, he was on Oprah!

Now the side door crowd was spilling out onto the street. Pads and pens were offered from every angle, and Hiawatha graciously signed. Kamali developed the habit of picking up the twins and getting them home to bed as soon as possible. Hiawatha followed later and Kamali waited up. Sometimes, she had some home-cooked goodies in the fridge for him. Other times, they made love.

After the first month, Ascot called him in with Chuck Derry, and a new contract was signed.

This time, Keep America dropped the checkbook on the floor and wrung her hair in disbelief.

A month later, Hiawatha appeared in full Ojibwa regalia on the cover of *TIME*, taken from a perspective down near his feet, making him look very imposing.

Chuck and Cat were on everybody's short list now. They had a cast party and invited her socialite friends. All the rich and powerful wanted to meet the North Woods Curiosity. Kamali would never forget one ironic scene. Daniel Triumph, the billionaire, regaling friends with the story of his old friend Hiawatha, who sold him the Packard Dietrich convertible "for a song."

Chapter 18
9/11

So September arrived and Keep America started her commute. She rode her bike the six miles to campus, angling across Central Park. It was great exercise with interesting sights along the way. Dr. Solomon loved her and was grateful for her diligence and work ethic. She devoured the classroom material readily, and advanced ahead of schedule. After counseling, she was allowed to accelerate through to the advanced courses.

She was pedaling through the park at 8:46 on a brilliant Tuesday morning, the eleventh of September, 2001.

That same morning, Forrest took Hayowenta and his fifth grade class on a field trip. Forrest had convinced Hayowenta's teacher to visit a dojo to learn about Korean culture and martial arts. They rose at first light and put their gear together. At 8:00 a.m., they met the class and boarded the downtown subway, bound for Chambers Street in Lower Manhattan.

Back at the brownstone, Hiawatha and Kamali rose at eight. She was preparing breakfast for the twins when Minnie came in from the TV room.

"Mommy, I think something bad happened."

"Did you spill your OJ?"

"No, on the TV. A big tall building is on fire."

Kamali went in to see, drying her hands on a dishtowel.

"Hy, come in here and see this. I think it's the Twin Towers."

So they sat and watched the whole thing happen.

The shock and disbelief of the second plane.

The rumor of the third and fourth.

The conjecture.

The collapse.

"Oh my God, the boys!"

Hiawatha started for the door. "What's the name of that place they were going?"

"It's a dojo like theirs. It's big. That's why they picked it. I'll call Tae Kwan Do Masters, but everybody's probably gone. I think the whole team went."

Now Kamali kicked herself for not going along with the cell phone plan. The boys had appealed with all the practical reasons for everybody in the band to have one, and the parents had resisted.

Too much kid independence.

Foolish.

Hiawatha jumped on the first southbound train. It took him all the way to the World Trade Center.

All the way into bedlam.

All the way to Hell.

In the confusion, Hiawatha's sheriff's badge worked. Everybody accepted that he was law enforcement. They didn't inspect the credential in detail. By this time, the atmosphere was starting to clear, and he went to work systematically searching for a group of martial arts pupils somewhere among the thousands of refugees.

Forrest had been readying himself, focusing on his match. The tournament was to begin at nine. That would be the little ones, the bottom of the ladder. He stood where he could observe and supervise.

Hayowenta's female primary school teacher was quite taken by Mr. Kim Sae Park, the dojo master. He was the embodiment of Tae Kwan Do values.

Humility.

Responsibility.

Honesty.

Discipline.

Strength.

Hayowenta figured to fight at noon or so, but it never hurt to loosen up early.

Then: Whoosh. Boom.

The windows rattled and there was a general discomfiture.

The alarm spread from without. They were drawn to the sidewalks to join the pointing and gesticulating crowd. They stood and witnessed the incredible monstrosity that would be revealed in later days.

Forrest and the teacher gathered their charges and took shelter in the locker room. That's when the first tower collapsed, and the dust entered everywhere.

When they couldn't breathe anymore and the lights went out, they exited the back door and started marching for safety.

Forrest and Hayowenta linked them all together with their karate belts and led them, single file, in the general direction of the crowd, trusting the instinct of the masses.

The teacher had disappeared.

As Forrest looked back over his shoulder, he witnessed the sight that would define the remainder of his life here in our world of three dimensions.

Three desperate victims jumped one hundred stories to their deaths. A man first, slowly somersaulting.

Then two women, their dresses trailing out behind them.

After that, the second tower, Number One, collapsed.

At that point, Forrest could not reconcile the vile hatred that coursed through his veins. His Ojibwa sense of vendetta was kindled. He was at one with his tribal instinct.

On the warpath.

Meanwhile, Hiawatha crisscrossed the wave of refugees systematically.

On the seventh crossing, he found them all at City Hall, encamped in a half-circle. Forrest and Hayowenta stood before the group taking roll call. Nobody was hurt. When the boys turned to see him approaching, Hiawatha noticed a transformation. Their eyes were intense, and their mouths were drawn tight and thin. Their energy was heightened, and they were acutely tuned in to their surroundings.

Warriors.

During the American Revolution, they would have enlisted. Forrest, the soldier, and Hayowenta, the drummer boy.

In 2001, Forrest joined the Navy at eighteen to begin his distin-guished military career.

Hayowenta was left to seethe. He joined the Army in 2003.

BOOK TWO

Chapter 1
Forrest

I AM FORREST GREEN. I WAS an eyewitness to the 9/11 attack on the Twin Towers. I felt the earth tremor when they collapsed. I breathed in the dust and particulate matter for an hour after that. Probably will kill me if I live long enough.

As soon as things opened up again, I went into the US Navy Recruitment Center on Chambers Street, in the same part of town. Seemed like my revenge instinct was stronger in that neighborhood. It kept me in touch with my motive, and made me feel more like my decision was directly tied to getting even. Kind of like, "Okay, martyrs, here's the scene of the crime. This is where we start." That was when I wished I had pushed harder for a West Point assignment. Our congressman came by school my senior year screening for scholarship candidates. Since I'm a pretty good student and a first class jock, I probably would have got in. But that was then, and this was now. I could swim for miles, thanks to Gitche Gumi. Hayowenta and I had been into martial arts our whole lives. By this time, I was a first degree black belt in Brazilian jiu jitsu, and Hayowenta was just as good, just not certified yet. After all, that's what we were doing on 9/11. It all made perfect sense. Sometimes people ask me, "Didn't your parents gather around the kitchen table to talk about that kind of important stuff, helping with the decision?" Nope. They felt their obligation was simply to raise a decent human being; after that, leave your kids' personal decisions up to them.

I felt bad for Hayowenta, getting left behind and all, but he's so tough and his character is so strong, he wouldn't let it bother him for long. He'd just use the time to improve all his skills. They'd be amazed on enlistment day. "He's already ready to graduate Ranger School. Should we use him as an instructor?"

On my first day at RTC Great Lakes, I was sworn in. We stood in line for our government-issued uniforms and equipment. They showed us to our barracks and assigned beds. They briefed us and briefed us some more. We got one more (official) medical exam. At the end of it was a commissioning ceremony. Then the fun began.

I really felt for most of the other recruits. Week one after indoctrination starts with swimming, drill, and teaching the basic sins and punishments for infractions like fraternization and sexual harassment, basic PC rules we already knew, but delivered loudly and harshly by our RDC (Rank Division Commander). They taught us how to recognize superior ranks. (Everybody was in uniform, besides us and our class, at this point.) We learned the right way to address them. You don't call your RDC "Sir" or "Ma'am." That's reserved for officers, and RDCs are petty officers (halfway between officers and enlisted). You call them "petty officer" or "chief petty officer." Any other title you use will get you a day of extra PT. Running laps, endless calisthenics, and no sleep, which makes the following day hell on earth.

I couldn't believe how poor the average recruit was at swimming. That was the single biggest washout factor. Why didn't they test them before they ever showed up, like at the local YMCA or something? Anyway, about a third busted out right then and there. I never felt so comfortable in my life. I could see the instructors pointing at me and talking. I thought, *Okay, so now I have their attention. Next, they'll get to see me kill it in general conditioning and obstacle course, and they haven't even seen me fight yet.* I didn't want to look arrogant, but my next question was "How do I sign up for SEAL training?"

When I asked my RDC, he said, "Didn't you sign up at the recruitment center? That's the fast track. Now you've got more hoops to jump through."

Inside my brain, I was kicking myself for not knowing all the options, but outwardly, I stayed calm, and my RDC, Petty Officer Devonte Harris, put me through with his connections. I heard his end of the phone call. "Yes, he's a special case. Yes, the best I've seen in a long time. Can you call Olsonowsky? He could replace a washout. Yes, he's that far along." About ten minutes later, Jones' cell phone rang. "You did? He can? Okay, I'll send him over on Monday, the fourth."

So that's how I got my start toward SEAL training in San Diego. First, I had to change over to Special Naval Warfare School right there in Great Lakes. The Physical Training Test was more of what I'd already been doing. Next was the Modified Physical Training Test. To make it through and get qualified for SEALS training in San Diego, you had to pass a pretty stringent battery of tests. Seventy push-ups in two minutes, no problem. A four-mile run in thirty-one minutes, also, not that bad. A 1000-meter swim in twenty minutes with fins, which I could have done without the fins. There were more washouts. I didn't keep count because those of us who passed went on to Naval Amphibious Base Coronado and SQT. We never saw the washouts again. No time for a nose count. I would guess more than half of us made it through.

They announced the scores within a day or two. I forget. My orders were printed out that night. I was on the airliner ORD-SAN two days later, and I reported to Naval Special Warfare Center for BUD/S training. Everybody says it's the toughest military training in the world, and here I was coming into the program after two weeks of Basic (not eight) and they were already started, meaning I had to make up a week of work to catch up with the class, or pass a series of tests to prove I was up to speed. No way I could have made up the work I missed and kept up with the class on four hours of sleep per night. Luckily, I passed the tests.

Mustering out for my first BUD/S day (the class's seventh), I passed a ship's bell mounted in front of the Master Chief's office. On the ground all around it were helmets each with a name and class number.

When we formed up, I asked my new partner about them. "If you terminate," he said, "you have to ring the bell to get attention, then place your helmet on the ground. They accumulate until graduation day."

Psychological warfare!

I didn't count each one, but it seemed like a lot of helmets after just one week. We had twenty-three more weeks to go. If we made it, we would go on to Qualification Training. That's the advanced course, and it's twenty-six more weeks. So, a year. I didn't know what I was up against. I figured I would sail through and watch the others struggle out of morbid curiosity.

Most people interested in the SEALS know a little about the BUD/S program. The continual exposure to cold water. Never dry, never warm, sleep-deprived, stretched to the limit of your physical strength and endurance every day. Never a break for a year. So instead of leisurely observation of the weaker candidates, my every moment was devoted to survival, just like for everybody else. Going in, termination never occurred to me. Halfway through, I battled the temptation of it every day.

Once we made it out, we went on to Mississippi for medic training. That's another six months, plus there's extra training once you've finally joined your unit, in between deployments.

Coming out of medic school, I thought back to my original pledge back in Lower Manhattan. I never dreamed the commitment would involve all of this. On one hand, I felt "Just send me over the way I am, and I'll take out my share of the martyrs one by one." Kind of an immature view, based on an emotional response all that while ago. But look where that response got me. On the way to being a true warrior with a full complement of fighting skills, all this technical knowledge and tactical expertise, and the finest Navy in the world to put my unit on target.

So, now I've been through all these programs, plus parachute training. I'm on the way to the SEALS. Big question is East Coast or West Coast? I'm totally fixated on Virginia Beach where the Little Creek Base is located. It's home to SEALS teams 2, 4, 8, 10, and 18. More importantly for me, it's responsible for Atlantic operations, including the Middle East. Not that teams can't be deployed from Coronado, just less likely. Most importantly, SEAL Team Six is headquartered there, at NAS Oceana. That's what I want. SEAL Team Six aka DEVGRU (Development Group). No matter what happens, I will make it there sooner or later.

As it turned out, I didn't have to look for political connections or pull any strings, like using Chief Jones earlier. One day, a crowd of students huddled around the bulletin board. List of assignments. My eyes sought out "NAS Little Creek, Virginia Beach, VA," and there I was.

What a relief. I had made it straight through to my dream assignment by sheer luck (so I thought at the time). Time to get my orders, pack my stuff, and head east! I've got to call Hayowenta.

Chapter 2
Hayowenta

I AM HAYOWENTA HEYWOOD. WHEN I got the call from Forrest, I was bouncing around in circles on the balls of my feet. My friends couldn't figure me out. I wasn't expecting a baby, I didn't even have a girlfriend, and I didn't play the lottery as a matter of principle. But I was acting like it. Forrest's victories were my victories. We had started this military quest together. Even though we were in separate branches, and only talked by phone on big occasions, we were still in this together. A few times over the years, we got to see each other personally, and it was as if no time had passed at all. We were blood brothers in the Indian sense, and not just fingertips. (I will carry my scar to the grave.) We could read each other's mind from thousands of miles away. My blood brother was a SEAL! How great is that!

Now it was my turn to find a way to excel. For me, it was aviation. First thing was not to commit Forrest's mistake. Right away at the Recruitment Center, I applied for Warrant Officer Candidate School in order to attend and graduate Warrant Officer Flight School. I picked it because entry is much easier than USAF or US Navy Flight School, where you need a BA degree minimum. In the Army, you need a high school diploma, a passing grade in the Selection Instrument for Flight Training test, and a minimum of 110 on the US Armed Forces General Technical Battery. I had the diploma and I passed the tests. I entered Flight School to study visual and instrument flight, weather, night flying, and combat maneuvers. My idea was to fly the Apache, but the Blackhawk wouldn't be all that bad! It all depended on what assignments were open on your graduation day. Luck of the draw! First of all, before I chose an aircraft, or it was chosen for me, I had to report to Fort Rucker for aviation school. First, they set you up with housing. Then you go through the Basic Officer Leadership course. That's two months training. Then you have to go through Dunker Training and SERE (Survival, Evasion, Resistance and Escape). Then you have Aeromedical Training, too, before you get started earning your wings. For that to happen, you need to pass Basic Flight Training, Instrument Flight Training, and Combat Skills Training. It's an eighteen-month commitment. You fly the Bell Jet Ranger for the basic stuff, and the CH-58 for combat.

What I'll never figure out is how the brass comes up with other stuff for us to do while we're fighting every day just to keep our heads above water. Sometimes, I let myself think they're trying to make a name for themselves, but I try to remain charitable. They come up with something fun to do, just for the distraction value.

In this case, it was a week-long exchange program with the Navy or Air Force, just to experience how they ran their programs. Naturally, I picked Navy since Forrest was in it. Naturally, I got Air Force. Does the military have algorithms that make sure you get channeled into what you don't want? Sometimes it seems that way, if you let your internal conspiracy theorist rule the day.

We sat through an academic class (boring). We did a half day of PT (Why?). We got a ride in the T-38 twin jet supersonic trainer with afterburners (shit hot). Part of the prep for the jet ride was the ejection seat trainer. In those days, it wasn't a nice smooth rocket that launched you to safe altitude for parachute deployment. It was an artillery shell, right under your seat, and it had been fired and reloaded thousands of times. Once for every student, for years. The handles down by your thighs were worn down to the hair trigger stage. Big thing about the exercise was posture. Make sure legs are locked, your feet are flat on the floor, and your spine is perfectly straight all the way up to, and including, most importantly, your head.

I got in position, and they gave the signal.

Wait! Where's the trigger? I looked down to be sure, and Bam! When it fired, I was looking down for the handle. Everything went black. They got me out of the seat and off to the medic. Fractured vertebra. Just a hairline, but fractured just the same. I was lucky. They put me under observation. After a week, I showed them I had mobility. They released me and put me back in class. I graduated on schedule, but the neck's never been right since then. Small price to pay, I guess. Better than my four classmates who got killed.

I'll never forget getting my wings pinned onto my chest. Might as well have been the Medal of Honor. I know eighteen months doesn't seem that long to the average person, but the intensity of it is incredibly stressful. And the washout rate. Every week, the class is a little smaller. You wonder, *Will I make it?*

Well, I did make it, and I walked out of Fort Rucker with wings. Now how do I get into Apaches?

What a disappointment when assignments came down. My grades were pretty high, but only two Apaches were on the list. I got Blackhawks. In a way, it was better, since you have a wider range of missions. An Apache is essentially a fighter who shoots at stuff on the ground. Blackhawks haul soldiers and equipment into and out of combat, plus they're armed to the teeth with rockets and machine guns. I wonder what my first deployment will be?

Chapter 3
Kamali

I AM KAMALI HEYWOOD. KELLEY GREEN originally, before I became an Ojibwa princess by marrying Hiawatha. Technically, in the old days I probably couldn't have been a princess, since Hy is only mixed blood, but these days, your status in the tribe is as much what you can get done in Washington (think money), as it is the blood.

Politically, the whole blood thing is a touchy subject. Let's say you accepted nothing but those who were 100 percent Ojibwa into the tribe. Your tribe would be so tiny the politicians would ignore you, and Washington is where a lot of our money and special rights come from. It's about healthcare and education on the money side, and, let's say, subsistence fishing and minerals on the rights side. But if you grew your tribe to include everybody with any tribal blood at all, the shares would be tiny. For the healthcare, it probably wouldn't matter that much. Everybody would get it. But the fishing, or especially mineral rights, would divide down to almost nothing in some cases. In the case of Inuit in Alaska, it's really a factor. Tribe members want a bigger cut, and they don't want to share it with some Cheechako from Anchorage or Fairbanks who's never set foot on the reservation, let alone some supposed tribe member from the Lower 48 who's never even been to Alaska. So, they limit membership to a small number, but not too small. Tribes have different political positions because of rights, too. For example, the environmentalists love quoting the Gwitch'in tribe on the North Slope. No oil there, so they're against drilling.

The Inupiat tribe near the Arctic National Wilderness Refuge claim mineral rights on their reservation, and they get big bucks. They're all for drilling. They love Exxon. You never hear from them in the media, though.

Anyway, if you took a cross section of all the tribes in America, you'd come up with an average of somewhere around 1/32 Indian blood to make you legit. That seems to be about the right size for most tribes. A lot of them have other requirements. Were you born on the reservation? Do you come back home and spend time? Do you attend meetings? Do your relatives still live here? If you live far away, do you send money?

Our band of Ojibwa don't have money issues. A couple of hundred years ago, we had copper. White men took it, or bartered for it. These days, companies are drilling for nickel, chrome, and a little gold all around us, but so far, no deal on the reservation. That's okay with me. You should see some of the tribes who get big money. Rampant alcoholism, gambling addiction, domestic violence, super-high traffic deaths. Bad deal.

I'm originally a Green, from Enchanted Forest, Illinois. We were green in a lot of ways. My sister was named "Keep America" for a reason. My parents were environmental activists. Hippies. Trustafarians. Beneficiaries of the Gilded Age. The Green family made their money manufacturing prepared food. TV dinners and the like. So that made us green in money. We were also Greenhorns. Loved the forest and wild animals, but put us alone in the wilderness for two weeks and we'd be dead.

Hiawatha changed all that for me. I transformed into a self-sufficient being with aboriginal talents. I can make fire four different ways without conventional ignition. I can find a trail, read water, follow sign. I know trapping and I'm a dead shot. You could walk inside ten feet of me in the forest and never know I was there.

My first trip to the Chippewa Club was in the womb. Since then, I've never missed a summer. As soon as I could think for myself, I chose Hiawatha Heywood as the most important person in my life. All children of members are enrolled in Niijaanis, the children's program. Hiawatha was the head of it. His magnetism overwhelmed me. I followed him everywhere he would allow me to. Some of my woodsman's skills started in the Niijaanis program. Braiding hemlock bark into twine. Creating signs for the trail system with the wood burning set. Proper quenching of campfires. Following a blazed trail.

Once I was too old for the program, Hiawatha made me an intern. I started by laying out the materials for each day's lesson and cleaning everything up at the end of the day. Then I got my own art class and became a teacher/mentor for a few of the girls. Pretty soon, Hiawatha and I were equals. We're still equals, and not just in teaching.

After our magical betrothal on the beach of Gitche Gumi and our wedding on the Jack Pine River, we sequestered ourselves within the Chippewa Club as a band of two. Nine months later, we were three. Then five. Then, if you add Keep America and Forrest, that makes seven, plus Bonnie makes eight. I often wonder what our little band would have been like without the fire. Maybe we would have stayed semi-aboriginal. Maybe we never would have left the UP in our whole lives. A trip to Joliette once in a while.

Actually, Hayowenta would have left for the Army because of 9/11 no matter where we lived, because of Forrest.

I wonder if Keep America would ever have discovered her aptitude for higher mathematics without New York. She likely wouldn't have wound up at Columbia. And would another professor have been as prescient as Dr. Solomon in recognizing her potential? Others might have noted her proficiency, but would they have perceived the genius?

Chapter 4
Keep America

I AM KEEP AMERICA GREEN. AFTER our family escaped the nearly deadly fire, we moved to New York City, and I got a math scholarship to Columbia.

After three semesters of straight As in record time, my professors looked back at my SAT score, which was high, but it still didn't explain my unusual performance. They got curious, and had me sit the William Lowell Putnam math competition. When my result came back with a score of 100 (120 being perfect), they thought it was in error. One official suggested "something dishonest." The Putnam test is taken by the most promising math prodigies in America and Canada. The average score is between 0 and 1. That sounds like a joke, but I'm not kidding. It's the hardest test in the world. Fewer than 5 percent of contestants score higher than 41 percent. Those who score well have included Nobel laureates like Richard Feynman.

Over time, all the doubts faded, and Columbia thought I had a chance at preeminence. Dr. Solomon called me in for counseling.

"Keep America, we've learned a few things about you since you've been here, and I wonder how it is that you solve these complicated problems so much quicker than other students."

"I see them."

"How do you mean that?"

"I guess you could say I live within a mathematical landscape. A lot of my math doesn't involve computation. When you show me a numerical problem on paper, it appears to me as a picture, and I understand it perfectly, like you would a painting or a photograph, only I'm in it. I'm in the picture. I'm part of the scene I'm observing, kind of. It's as if I'm processing the math within the primary visual cortex of the brain. You know, in the occipital lobe, instead of the cerebral cortex like most people. A lot of my math doesn't involve computation. At least the foundational part of it. It's like starting the 1500 meter run at the 1000 meter point, in a way. I'm not doing a very good job of explaining, but then, words are not my strong point. Just the opposite. I have trouble expressing concepts verbally. You give a little to get a little, I suppose."

"Or in your case," said Dr. Solomon, "to get a lot more than ordinary people can even imagine, let alone strive for. So, what do you want to strive for, Keep America? Honestly, I would be comfortable conferring your degree right here in this room, right now, but I don't know what good that would do. What's next, then? Long term, where will you apply this gift of yours?"

"Well, being visual and all," I said, "geometry is what attracts me. Geography of the universe, maybe? My friend here at Columbia took some classes from Murad Toqqu, who studied under Benoit Mandelbrot before he left for Cal Tech. That's what I'd like to do. Study fractal geometry like Mandelbrot. Follow his tracks to Cal Tech, and continue refining fractals as they occur in nature. Maybe find some people who knew or studied under Mandelbrot."

"How did you become so interested in fractals?" asked Dr. Solomon.

I told Dr. Solomon about a day when I was waiting in line to register last semester. A freshman girl had placed her cell phone on the table next to me for a second. It had this continually evolving pattern recreating itself on the screen.

I couldn't help asking, "What's that thing on your cell phone?"

"That's my infinite eyedazzler," said the girl. "My friend calls it the Mandelbrot Set."

"You mean Benoit Mandelbrot, the mathematician?" I asked.

"Bennett who?" asked the girl. "I don't know anything about math. I'm a poet. I just find the pattern comforting."

"Well," I said, unable to resist sharing information, whether asked to or not, "he was a brilliant scientist who was also lucky. First, he got out of Poland when his parents escaped to the haven of Paris in 1936. He studied at the Ecole Polytechnique. He continued his emigration to the United States where he added US citizenship to go with his French, and earned a Master's Degree in aeronautics from California Institute of Technology. Then he returned to Paris and studied under the eminent Gaston Julia, earning his PhD in Mathematics in 1952. Oddly enough, Gaston Julia was on track toward fractal geometry around World War I. He just didn't possess the tools to carry out the calculations. They were too complex and took too long. Many years, if done by hand in those days. He knew the concept, but for the proof, he needed Mandelbrot and his computers to run the equations millions and billions of times over. To complete the set, one had to run the calculation from a known geographical spot, using $fc(z) = z2 + c$. Then you had to take your result, and plug it back into the equation again. Over and over and over. Luckily for all of us, he was hired by IBM in 1958. This placed the eminent mathematical genius in position to compute the solutions, and also to transform his calculations to visual form in the computer, creating the Mandelbrot Zoom, which the hippies love so much. I wonder if that was the first pictorial depiction of mathematical formulae? Anyway, besides being the physical representation of fractal geometry and self-similarity, it turns out to be a great tool to help non-mathematicians get the basic concept of the infinite depiction of abstract patterns in nature. You could say, the building blocks of nature, or at least of certain areas of nature. Mandelbrot was initially interested in whether there were formulae to define irregular natural forms like coastlines or clouds. It was like, if you can define a triangle with math, why not everything else? He called it the 'art of roughness.' It was about quantifying the uncontrolled and seemingly uncontrollable in life. Turns out, fractals are everywhere. Ferns and cauliflower exhibit the infinite repetition of self-similarity. You could say much of what occurs in our earthly reality actually adheres to a symmetrical rule of order, even when it's not apparently ordered."

The girl in line stared at me with her mouth open for a second, then said, "Interesting," and turned around.

I barely noticed. I had begun to wonder, *Where else do fractals exist?* Cardiologists say the human heart is fractal in the way the arteries branch off and divide themselves smaller and smaller. Tree branches are that way. So is lightning. At first glance, it seems pretty ordinary, but then it seems like there's a whole body of math that's always existed, but Mandelbrot brought to light. I've got to know more about this.

And so I told Dr. Solomon I wanted to study fractals more. He was so good to me. He made sure my paperwork for the transfer to Cal Tech went through smoothly. Now I've got to decide. Sell my car and fly, so I can start over in Pasadena, or do the drive?

Wait a minute! I'm twenty-four. How many chances do you have to see the USA from the ground floor? Actually, I can head north across the border and do my first trip to Canada too. Plus Sault Sainte Marie is the best spot to come back across, and then I'm in the UP. Half a day to the Chippewa Club. This is awesome! But I have to trust myself not to just go home to the Chippewa Club and never leave again. I'm making the vow right now, before I ever start the trip. Maximum time at the Chippewa Club: one week.

So, if I take the long way (the picturesque way), it's 4,249 statute miles, or seventy hours of actual road time at 60 mph. If I went the fast way, it's about 2,800 miles, or forty hours behind the wheel. Being young and supple, I'm good for ten hours per day.

Well, I've already been on Interstate 80. I hate it. The boring perspective. The packs of semis, all slipstreaming off each other and obstructing us little people with their turbulence and visual blockage. The fast food and motels and gas stations at the exits, which have replaced the Midwest villages of the past, where families raised their kids and educated them in towns with names like Kearney and Brady.

Take the time to venture the four miles into one of those towns some day. They're just short of ghost towns. The old greasy spoon replaced by Taco Bell and Motel 6 out by the interstate.

Some of the descendants of farming families that moved off their land live there in those deserted towns. The original farm families were the salt of the earth, and some still are, but a lot of the modern generations are lost. They survive on welfare, drug money, and part-time farming work when they're desperate. The towns that jumped into the casino business right away did well (money wise, at least.) It all depends on the state and county laws on gambling, or if there's a reservation nearby. Like, if you take the Rosebud Casino in western Nebraska, they're in the boondocks in Valentine, near the Sandhills. It's cattle. Beef cattle, and that would be it, except for the gambling, only there's nobody within 200 miles, so they just barely stay alive on the cowboys. Most pathetic casino I ever saw. Then you have mediocre ones, like in Winner, South Dakota. All the wholesome family businesses left town. Now, it's bars and strip clubs. The local restaurants caved in to Perkins and McDonald's out by the interstate. The whores do business in the Motel 6. Actually, there's only one real season in that part of South Dakota: pheasant season. The men who come from all over the country do some hunting at night too. I was checking in to the Motel 6, and there was a pretty young woman struggling with several suitcases at the front door. When she went to her room, I asked the clerk about her luggage.

"Looks like she's here for an extended stay."

"Till end of pheasant season. They all are."

"Oh, the strip joints, I guess."

"Well, they do that too!"

So, that was my first exposure to the Great Plains States on my way to grad school in California.

Well, I should say it was my most surprising and unexpected exposure. In those days, fracking hadn't really started yet, at least not in the Dakotas. There was an exodus of the human population leaving for work in the Midwestern cities, and that left a scarce human civilization and a growing population of wildlife. The herds of pronghorn were thriving, and beautiful to watch. Man, they're fast. Actually, the fastest animal in the New World.

I saw a black bear in the middle of the day, out in the open. Bison were being reintroduced, and every time I saw a herd, I imagined them in their millions back in aboriginal times.

Back when I started out from Brooklyn, I wasn't thinking about the Great Plains at all. I was wondering about power and fuel, and my effect on the climate. My friend Connie from the dorm was a social science type from the School of Humanities, and she bought into the whole global warming movement to the max. She lived it on a daily basis, as if the fate of Earth and humanity depended on Connie's own behavior. Right away, she had me trading my Corolla for an electric Prius, the only hybrid available in America in those days. Problem was, the plug-in electrics weren't even a thing, yet. I mean, Tesla was working on the roadster, but it wasn't really a mainstream product, and Joe Sixpack was definitely not in the equation at those prices, let alone me, and I was way below Jane Sixpack. At least she had a steady income, theoretically. Connie was an idealist with no connection to reality. What was I going to do, magically find more than $100,000 somewhere, and drive to California in a roadster with room for one small suitcase? Ridiculous. Problem was, she didn't understand the technology at the time. She thought all you did was plug it in and drive it.

Back in 2002, the technology was hybrid. It helped mileage, but still used gasoline to generate electricity. That, and the energy produced by slowing the car from cruise speed. Regenerative braking, it's called. They hook up a generator to the axle, essentially, which robs the energy of a cruising car as it slows to zero, and sends it to a battery, instead of just letting it go to waste. Not very efficient, and not independent of gasoline.

What Connie and her friends didn't get was electric cars aren't clean. Even if they were available to the general public at the time, which they weren't, the power they get from their plug has to come from somewhere. So, let's say for the sake of argument, I left for my trip to California in a plug-in electric car. A Tesla Model S magically produced ahead of time in 2002. First off, where am I going to plug it in, going across the country? The range of a Model S isn't that great. Not like a gas car, especially at high speed. I could get stranded. Then there's the pollution. The car itself runs clean, but what about the power plant that produces the energy it uses? My first leg from NYC to Montreal would be as clean as you could ever want. Environmentally perfect. Hydroelectric power from Niagara Falls. Trouble is, it doesn't stay that way. Down the road, it might be fossil fuel. Nuclear is a big part of Canadian power. Then there's gas, coal, and oil. Pennsylvania is coal, if you choose to go through there, you're burning coal. Not as simple as Connie thinks. Listening to her was a little like depending on Greta Tunberg for personal advice.

And so, my choice for a route was influenced by fuel efficiency, since Connie's plug-in car idea was a childish dream. The Corolla got 35-39 mpg. Closer to the 39 at highway speed. Much better vehicle for a cross country trip in 2002. I can't believe how gullible I was in my youth. It's easy to get a young person to go along with idealistic nonsense she might never have considered on her own.

The more I thought of Montreal and the traffic and expense of the place, the more I realized it was a bad choice, especially if I stayed overnight. The meals, the rooms, the cost of refueling all penciled out as prohibitive. I made a strategic decision and turned off of Highway 87 at Champlain. That way, I bypassed the whole Montreal Metroplex and entered into Canada at Cornwall, Ontario. So, I just cut off to the west on Highway 11 across New York State, and crossed the two Saint Lawrence Seaway bridges into Ontario. South Bridge was a nice, modern, open-style suspension span to Cornwall Island, then the North Bridge, a lumpy, rollercoaster of a thing designed to make your passengers barf all over your upholstery. You can smell the paper plant 100 miles before you get there, and that doesn't help.

Customs was no big deal in those days. They barely looked at my stuff.

So, now I was on my first international trip! Not very exotic, though. Everybody looked American. Dressed American. Talked American except for the "Eh?" The guys seemed to think everybody else was a "Fookin' Idgit," but they liked me okay. Maybe I was a Fookin' Idgit when I turned my back.

It was nice spending my time in the countryside, in the boreal forest and the clean air. This whole area suggested a wilderness-style trip. Good thing I brought my sleeping bag and yoga mat, plus my one-man tent. Maybe I should get a camping stove and make this a real outdoor adventure. There were rustic rest stops all along the highway, every fifty miles or so. Plus, being early enough in the fall, they weren't closed yet, but summer was over, so lots of vacancies. Perfect! I was planning on Motel 6 and the like, but camping would put me in Pasadena way under my budget. Nice way to start out my new life in a pricey town.

This whole trip was a transformation. I mean, the whole entire life change, including grad school, was transformative, but I hadn't planned on the driving part being this big a deal. I was really doing my own thing! I guess it kind of crept up on me. I wasn't just studying math anymore. I was out there!

By the third night, I had the rest stop routine down pat. Find my spot. Build a campfire for the ambiance and cooking. (I rejected the camp stove. Not rustic enough.) Play a little guitar. Put on my headlamp and read some stories. Then turn out the light and do my calculations from memory till sleep came. It was 11 p.m. to 7 a.m. pretty much every night. Then wake up, clean up, have a yogurt, do my workout, and hit the road. Some nights, I had company. My last rest stop, it was a nice old retired couple with their dog. They said the dog helped them meet people. Plus it was protection. They had the dog and the gun.

"The dog raises the alarm, and I blast 'em," said the husband.

"Do you really feel like you need to protect yourselves out here? It's peaceful," I replied.

"I guess you don't know about these rest stops," said the wife. "They have a reputation. Do you know about Blind River?'

"Yeah," I said, "I stayed there last night. Beautiful."

"Well," the husband said, "that's where the McAllisters got killed. Guy posing as law enforcement with a badge. Mutilated them. Can't be too careful."

"George, that was ten years ago," said his wife, "and they caught him. Life sentence. No parole. Don't scare the poor young thing."

"Just sayin'. Can't be too careful," he replied.

So, my routine changed. Headlamp strapped on, .410 by my side, knife in undies, phone open to keypad and dialed to 91-.

Maybe I'll stop at the pound in Sudbury and pick out my alarm dog. I could be like John Steinbeck in *Travels With Charley.*

That was my last Canadian rest stop anyway. Next leg was across the bridge at Sault Sainte Marie, and on to the Chippewa Club. Then after that, maybe stick to campgrounds with supervision.

Policy is, you call as far in advance as possible to let the Chippewa Club know you're coming and how long you can stay. I still had my family membership because of Hiawatha and Mom. Once I hit twenty-six, though, I'm supposed to apply for my own membership. Something big better happen between now and then, 'cause I can't afford it. Way too expensive.

I pulled up to the gate, and they had my name on the list. Marv was on duty. Forty years as an employee. I've known him my whole life.

"Keep America! Welcome to Chippewa! How long you here for?"

"Hi, Marv. Just a few days, for old times' sake. I'm on my way to California to start a new life. How's the fishing?"

"Stick with Scow Lake. Big rainbows in there, I'm told. You have a good time, and don't stay away so long next time. Oh, wait! Come on in and see the pups!"

"I didn't know you liked dogs."

"I like them okay, but my place is small. Management had me bring them out here to the gate and try to give them away. Do you remember Bonnie? Remember that litter she had the year before the big fire? Four—she had three bitches and a dog. These are her great grandpups. Four months old. Got their shots. Ready to go. Four left. Take one!"

"Now, what am I going to do with a dog on my way to LA?"

"She'll protect you, bark at strangers. She'll keep you happy. No fun on the highway all alone, anyway. You can talk to yourself and not look crazy. Take that nice girl that keeps watching you. That's Birdie. See? She loves you already."

I didn't even have to say, "Get in." Birdie worked her way into the half-cracked driver's door before I had even turned around. We headed for the cabin.

I opened the door to Magnificent Green and let Birdie in. That's my pet name for our family cabin. We entered into Green Cabin's spiritual space. She greeted us and invited me to enjoy her perspective across the pink sand beach and the mighty Gitche Gumi. I never felt alone in Green Cabin. She had a comforting personality, a presence, as if she were a living entity. I could never figure if she retained the souls of humans departed, or if she had her own spirit that never left. Maybe it was both. I felt lovingly welcomed by her as she embraced me. Can a cabin have a spirit?

I could have navigated blindfolded directly to my bed in room number eight, "Minoshin." That's where I fell forward into the down comforter and slept for sixteen hours straight. I threw a pillow on the floor for Birdie.

I awoke with the sun in my eyes. First, I thought it was dusk, but wait a minute! My bed faces due east. That meant I had slept all the rest of yesterday, all through the night, and now it was dawn. Every morning, the sun breaks above the horizon and shines right into my field of vision. Birdie was at the door waiting. Five miles of beach all for her and her morning toilet.

Sometimes I just lay there and pondered the continuity of it all. The Great Lakes are young. Remnants of the Laurentide Ice Sheet. I find myself considering the Glaciation of North America. It wasn't really all that long ago. When you consider the Egyptian Empire being about 5,000 years old, the last glacial period seems like yesterday. It was all ice 16,000 years ago. What's now New York was frozen two miles deep. Then, 10,000 years ago, it all melted, and the Great Lakes were left. Humans and mega fauna were here, spread widely about the earth. Certain cultures were very advanced, but not in this part of America. People here were aboriginal. Hunter-gatherers. Most likely, somebody woke up out on the sand with the sun in her face every day, almost like I did this morning. They stayed aboriginal all the way to the European Invasion, and every time I returned, I felt that way too. Is that devolution? I don't think so.

My plan was to stay isolated there at the Club, on my own, in the wilderness. After some yogurt I found in the fridge (not spoiled, but since when?), I grabbed my big fishing vest. It was an inspired invention. Somebody should make a modern version of it, made of lighter, stronger material. This one was from my grandfather's era. Canvas and leather. I always rubbed the leather with bear grease before putting it away, so it was still supple after all these years. It had twenty-eight pockets. I had them all organized for a week in the wilderness. Just add dried food and you're good. A little pocket of fire starters, waterproof matches in a Dayglo red waterproof case (never green, gets lost), a flint sparker, a magnifying glass, magnesium flakes. Another small pocket for cutting tools and a Lumberman. A big pocket for six feet of baling wire and micro-thin tarp. Micro fly rod rolled up in the yoga mat. A head lamp and batteries. Small pocket with a small envelope of flies, mostly streamers, but some dry. Soap. Deep Woods Off. You get the idea. Never fall short. My survival food was dried soup, jerky, oats, and pasta shells. Goal was never to touch it. Live off the land. My olive oil was a four-ounce vial. Luxury! On the way out the door, I grabbed the .410 and a half-full box of #6 shells. Two per day. The natural pantry out there was full. Trout, bass, pike, squirrel, rabbit, grouse. Leave the predators alone, though. I can't kill a canid, or a cat.

My idea was to relive my childhood Ojibwa lifestyle in all the old places. Our old camps. I waited till dark and left through the side door to avoid detection. My first destination was Rust Lake and the hidden cave. Nobody but us old-timers knew about it. As kids, we were pretty good about secrets. The cave wasn't that far away from the main camp and its cabins. Maybe four miles. First, you had to hike. Then you got to the island by canoe. My personal fourteen-foot birch bark was right there in the Rust Lake boathouse where I left it. Water was the first level of protection. Nobody's swimming that far. Members would row out to the closest shore for lunch on nice days, but they had no reason to go farther. Otherwise, a few fishermen visited it now and then when the weather was nice, but they weren't exploring. They were concentrating on the surface. The cave was all the way on the other end of the island. West facing. Hard to see. Most members didn't know it existed, and you could miss it easily floating by in a canoe.

Best to stay hunkered there, and let people get used to not seeing me. Out of sight, out of mind. Birdie explored the general area, then came back to the firepit. Good instinct.

Next destination would be the Magical Falls, on Magic Stream. We could camp at Odyssey Beach. Plenty of nice fresh water right there. Nice wide, flat sandy beach for sleeping. We used to spend weeks in that area, 'cause there's so much variety. Go to the Red Pine Grove for solitude and peace. Play music, write poetry, make love, sing. Walk over to Magic Falls. Bathe, sunbathe, search for artifacts. It was an Ojibwa site back to antiquity. Don't dig for stuff. That's sacrilege. Look around the gopher holes where they come up with the castings. Look in the downstream water pockets for obsidian points, beads, ceramics, wampum, and spearheads of flint. Then climb up Mt. Argon. Plan on climbing all day. Highest point in 300 miles. You can see where you've been, where you're going, and where you might go someday. You can see down Valley Lake, the biggest lake on Chippewa Club property. Four miles long and a mile and a half wide. Full of bass. Look farther, all the way to our next destination down at the south end. It's Norway Creek, full of brook trout. Big ones, and a nice camping site on a clean, smooth, rocky point. Birdie thinks she went to heaven. It breaks my heart she'll wind up in LA, but that's okay. It's just for grad school; we'll be out of there and back in the real world for the rest of our lives together.

When the week was over, I grabbed the last of the shotgun shells, and we signed out with Marv at the Gate House.

I figured there was plenty of hunting in the Plains and the Rockies, so we might as well be equipped to take advantage of whatever came up.

"Don't stay away so long this time," said Marv.

I tried Birdie in a wire kennel on the backseat. People say it's safer. After day two, I threw the kennel out and scolded her when she tried to squeeze her way forward. By day four, she was riding shotgun, and that's the way it stayed. Willful dog, but obedient when she thought it mattered. She's not sleeping on her pillow anymore either. Now she's under the covers with her head on my pillow.

So, our route took us through the Land of 10,000 Lakes. I bet there really are 10,000, at least. And they're so blue, with the forest so green. I was almost like, *Okay, this is it. I can get a job at Starbucks and go to Lake Superior College*, but that was a moment of weakness. We pressed on, and pretty soon everything changed. The Northern Plains. Now this was different. I've never been on land like this. It reminded me of my friend Chip, who brought his new bride from Montana to the UP. She got quieter every day for a month. Finally, he got worried.

"Honey, I know something's wrong. Let me help. What is it?"

"Chip, I can't see."

His heart froze. "Do we have a medical problem?"

"I can't see for these trees. Take me back to Montana."

Well, now I see her point. A person could get used to seeing her destination an hour before she gets there. People out here drive an hour and a half one way to dinner. Pretty soon, I'll be getting close to Rapid City. That's where Dean Bryan raises his organic wild buffalo.

My friend Onnie Lund was the boat maker at the Chippewa Club. He was a permanent employee who lived on the property, and he prided himself in living off the land (against Club rules). Come late fall and throughout the winter, he was pretty much unsupervised. Due to his stealth, he was able to trap, shoot, net, and gather all his food. One deer was enough for getting through the winter, with ruffed grouse and trout (salmon, too) making up the remainder. Plus, he harvested blueberries from the same barrens the Ojibwa had used since prehistory. His booze was elderberry wine.

He traded with his old Yooper friend Dean Bryan for the bison meat he raised in the South Dakota Plains. I thought it was the best organic, wild meat in America, and now, because of my trip, I had a chance to visit the herd in its natural habitat along the Dismal River. When I called Dean to let him know where I was, Dean invited me for a tour.

The Dismal River Ranch was the iconic image of Wild West countryside. Just where you would expect to see Sitting Bull and his warriors on the bluff overlooking the valley below, with its blue ribbon of water meandering through a sea of green and dotted with thousands of ruminating bison. We sat on our mounts above the scene, absorbing the splendor, before he led me down a narrow trail to the valley floor to ride among them.

The pastoral herd remained in repose, only acknowledging our presence by a glance. Not appearing to consider rising to their feet, they were content to go on with their digestive process unalarmed as we passed through their midst.

Dean explained his idea of ranching.

"Now, this is the way you raise bison. I've got these thousand or so here, in Dismal Valley, and then the rest on the Pine Ridge Reservation south of here. The Oglala and Lakota never took to ranching. Turning my herds out there is as organic and natural as you can get. They just run wild, and the strongest survive. Totally hands-off. Even when a cow has a breech birth, I just let nature take its course. Tough to watch, especially when you know you could help, and it kills my bottom line, but that's how we do it here. God's way.

"That applies to harvesting too. These are wild animals. You should see how the big operations slaughter. Round them up like cattle in a corral, and drive them into trucks, whipping their hides raw. Stacked in there cheek by jowl. Literally. Then the two-hour ride to the slaughterhouse, while their adrenaline maxes out. Then the pandemonium of the actual killing. What a mess. No wonder they're tough and stringy and shot through with hormones. That's why they age that meat. They *have* to. If you tried to eat it too early, you'd have diarrhea for a week.

"Here at Dismal, we work with the Oglala. They come up from Pine Ridge in a spiritual state of mind. They smudge the sacred rifle (sacred, because it's blessed, and only used for one thing.) They thank the beast spiritually, and then it's one shot to the forehead. Instant death. The rest of the herd doesn't even look up. It's normal life for them. The field unit is on a trailer. Butchery is quick, and the site is cleaned up perfect. The offal and trim goes to dog food and fertilizer. (You know the Oglala and their dogs.) We butcher and wrap the rest for shipment to our clients. They pay extra, but they're eating the best organic meat on the planet. The waiting list is a year, and we're not speeding up production. Nobody resigns their spot on the list, and we're not growing it."

"So, Dean," I asked, "do you mind if I camp here tonight, among the herd? Just Birdie and me under the stars. I want to seem Oglala, but in my own way. I'll buy a steak from you, up at the Ranch House."

"Well, it's not part of the tour. You can't tell anybody you did this, but you being a Yooper and all, that makes you like family. Especially with the Onnie connection, so go ahead and stay the night. The week, for that matter. Birdie can wake you up if the wolf pack shows up. They're not likely, it being fall and all. They really only care about the herd in springtime when there's babies. Fire off three shots with that .410 of yours if you need help."

"Three shots! That's a day and a half of ammo! Let's make it two, and that will mean Godzilla just showed up to burn me out with his breath! Otherwise, I'll take care of myself."

"Okay, but promise me one thing. Come by the Ranch House when you start out for the Coast. I don't want to sit up here wondering if you're still around."

"Deal!"

So that's how it went at the Dismal Ranch. The two of us up hunting at dawn. Snowshoe hare were developing a mottled look getting ready for their white winter coats. Easy to see. There were cottontails too, which were okay, and ground squirrels, which we didn't bother with. The best game was the grouse. I never figured out which it was. Prairie chicken? Sage grouse? Ruffed? Now that's good eating over a wood fire.

Birdie was too young to point, but she took to flushing like a champ. I actually only ever shot one on the ground one day when I was desperate. One bird every other day (or none at all, sometimes) had me building a surplus of shells. I figured we could probably hunt the rest of the Plains and the Rockies before I had to put the .410 in the trunk for my entry into "civilization."

I realize I could have bought more ammo along the way, but the rationing aspect appealed to me on different levels. First, I'm Scottish. Second, I'm a starving student with a big gas bill. Most importantly, rationing enforced a level of efficiency that I wanted to hone carefully throughout my life. I guess it's comes from my auntie Annette, when I showed her my prize-worthy photo of a loon and her chicks.

Her first question was. "How many shots did you take?"

It wasn't lost on me. Any dope could get a good photo with a hundred shots. Plus, in her day, she came up as a photographer with no money. She had to buy film. The number of exposures she used determined whether she would be shooting next week or next month.

When the calendar started to itch at the back of my brain, I determined to leave Dismal. What a crazy name for such a beautiful place. I wonder who named the river. Some crazy explorer in a bad mood? We shot two nice grouse (sage?) for Dean, and drove up to the Ranch House. I got out of the long emotional farewell, which I find awkward and embarrassing. Said I was behind schedule, and maybe standing somebody up. Basically true (Dean of Admissions?). It didn't feel like lying, and my sense of purpose was restored.

"Set a long-term goal, and don't rest till you achieve it," Hiawatha used to say.

That's the way I felt. I was back in touch with my commitment to applied geometry. Back on track, with my mission in mind.

It was exhilarating, being on the road again. I sang Willie Nelson's song and Birdie howled along. Where to? Montana or Wyoming? What an amazing choice for a young Yooper and her dog. I imagined myself in my Stetson and spurs.

We decided on Bozeman.

I wasn't ready for it. So trendy. So full of Beautiful People walking arm in arm down West Main Street. The espresso kiosks. The brew pubs. The wine shops.

Sushi!

Where were the dirty cowboys in their beat-up pickup trucks? I was the only one with a herding dog. I guess the small towns would be more what I'm looking for.

We filled up with regular gas and kept on going.

We got to Butte. What a difference. A working man's town, but not a cowboy town.

Up in the UP I had read a book on mining towns. *Boom, Bust, Boom* by Bill Carter. A lot of UP towns were mentioned in it. It's about copper and mining. Butte was in there. I read all about it, but I still wasn't prepared for the giant open pit mines right in the center of town. I had never even heard of the Berkeley Pit, but it's famous. It filled up with groundwater when operations shut down. Now it's a lake. The place stinks of sulfur. You're not going to get any beautiful tourists strolling around downtown Butte, or sipping espresso. People do come and look, though. It's a Superfund toxic waste site, and they come to the viewing site to look across at it. It's full of lead, sulfide rock, and arsenic. City/County Council figured they had a problem back in the '80s when migrating geese made a stopover. Come next morning, they were all dead.

Copper is the price we pay for modern life. It's everywhere. Everything electrical, including cars, appliances, phones, even toothpaste has copper in it. I keep copper stuff with me to stay connected to the UP. I have a big nugget and a copper key ring. A copper trinket hangs from my rearview mirror. My coffee mug is pure copper. It's still not green yet, but my fingers are.

Butte is on the Continental Divide, so now we're on the Pacific side, but it doesn't seem that high up. We're a mile high, almost, but no craggy snowcapped peaks. Time to turn south to Wyoming. This is High Plains. I want Rockies. Yellowstone! The road winds back east a little, but mostly south. This is my big, big deal about being up here. I heard the wildlife is all over the place, and I think there's something to it because they're spilling out over here into Montana. You really have to look out on the sides of the highway. Elk everywhere. What's that over there in the rest stop next to the Coke machine? A buffalo!

This is perfect timing because the Labor Day weekend crowds aren't here yet, the campgrounds are half-empty, and stores are well stocked. I've got my pick of campsites, the animals are emboldened.

Everybody says Yellowstone is a super-volcano, and you sense it as soon as you crest out over the caldera coming in from the north or west. The crater is scalloped, revealing the multi-cored nature of the original eruption, and it's humongous. Actually, it was the largest volcano eruption in all of history, and now look. Thirteen-hundred square miles of pastureland for dozens of species. Right away, I'm threading my way through grizzly bears along the roadside. I guess this is where they beg during summer season. You see video of idiots stopping to pet them. The rangers keep them under control (the idiots, not the bears) during summer, and these grizzlies today are probably just optimistic holdovers. The last to give up and go forage for berries, grass, and carrion before the hibernation. I'm scouting for my campsite near Lake Yellowstone with access to trails and food. The best one has no tents or people, but some cars and trucks parked near the trailhead. They must be the hard core who hike in for miles and set up completely isolated camps for weeks at a time. I'm jealous. Most visitors never see 2 percent of the park, and this time I'm one of them.

We've got a good campsite, though. I warmed up my chili. Birdie had her kibble, and we drifted off. The wolves woke us up howling between midnight and one-thirty. Birdie joined in, but I shut her up. No use raising attention.

So, next morning, I'm lying on my backseat with Birdie, poaching off the Lake Yellowstone Hotel Wi-Fi in the parking lot. A bunch of emails float in. One jumps off the page in 3D. "Founder of fractal geometry to speak at Cal Tech. Dr. Benoit Mandelbrot will address his audience at 4 p.m. on Wednesday, September 12. Lecture is free and open to the public."

What? September 12. That's four days. My world just changed from early bedtime and howling wolves, to all engines full power. No breakfast. Just juice for me, and a Greenie for the Girl. Top off the tank. Check all the fluids (not just oil). Check tires, 34 PSI all around. Hit it hard. Speed limit plus 8 mph and extra vigilance. Maybe I should switch over to Nevada, where there's no speed limit.

Wait.

Calm yourself.

We have plenty of wiggle room. Call it eighteen hours. That's nine per day for two days, plus extra time for a flat tire or engine trouble. So, one stop in Utah should put me in Pasadena Monday evening. What about rush hour? At least the campus is north of LA proper. Not like we have to drive through the whole LA basin bumper to bumper all day.

Then I've got a day to find lodging and get unpacked. That's a generous amount of time. There's a grad student dorm. Call and register next fuel stop. Why didn't I do this already?

I've never been so stoked in my life!

After our first driving day, we pulled into Beaver, Utah. Motel 6. Perfect! That leaves a nice seven-hour trip, with plenty of time to spare. I'm feeling calm enough to play some guitar and....

Wait! Call the dorm! Get registered.

I called, and after I'm told my dorm room is #114, I ask the registration person, "Is the Mandelbrot lecture still scheduled for Wednesday?"

"What lecture?" she replied. "Classes don't start for a week. What's a manda brat? Like a kosher brat?"

"Never mind."

Monday morning, Birdie and I chilled with a leisurely breakfast and a long walk for Birdie. Poor thing is out of her element, but it's a good life lesson for humans to see how animals accept what their dealt and just live with their situation as normal. I need to adapt that attitude.

Pulling into campus, I was so relieved. The car held up fine. I got to the dorm office in time to sign my paperwork and get my key. I could at least get some of my most important stuff unloaded, but first some food. There's a Perkins. I like their Classic Burger.

So, I'm waiting for my burger. It's a shame about Perkins' fries. I almost asked to leave them off. I reviewed my dorm contract. I put it down and rubbed my eyes, and when I looked across the room, an electric charge hit me right in the middle of my chest.

"It's *him!*"

There was the most eminent mathematician alive, studying his notes. Munching mediocre fries and sipping a chocolate milkshake! I felt like Gladys from Mississippi spotting Elvis at Kroger!

I felt my body rising to a standing position, involuntarily.

"No. Sit! You've got nothing to say to him. If you tried, it would be embarrassingly mundane. Leave him alone with his fries. He's probably rehearsing Wednesday's lecture, which you're going to hear anyway." It's a reality check, though. Here I am attending a university where the greatest physicists and mathematicians have studied for over a century, starting my new life!

Chapter 5
Forrest

WHEN I ARRIVED AT NAS Little Creek, I was of two minds, and one of them needed to be dead and buried. That was the mind that was mentally and physically fatigued. They say a combat tour has a way of oppressing the mind in a subtle, almost unconscious way. You can reconcile the gunfire and threat of artillery bombardment and the fatigue, but it's that continued, ever-present unidentified threat. I guess you could call it the general feeling of stress and vulnerability that gets to you over time.

Listen to me talking like a combat veteran! Well, eventually, I became one, but at NAS Little Creek, I thought I understood the feeling just through the pressure of all that training. Okay, I got through physical training and evaluation and medic school, but now what about parachute training, advanced combat class, final exam, graduation?

During all that time in training, I never felt secure. I never felt I had any breathing space. I might flunk out. I might fall on the obstacle course and break my neck, like my classmate did. The stress stays with you 24/7 until you're out of there with a certificate of graduation.

Anyway, now I was done. Ready to report to active duty, but drained. Drained of energy and drained of emotion.

The second of my two minds was the commitment to excel at all costs. I had been doing a pretty good job of that so far, but now my state of mind was recommitted to excellence. I'm here on duty and qualified. Everybody else in my unit is too. I really had found my fraternity, my family.

The pattern of life at Little Creek was a cycle. Learn. Practice. Deploy. Deploying was the only reason to be participating at all, in my opinion. I found myself sympathizing with peacetime military personnel. What an unfulfilling way to spend a career. Vietnam was bad enough, from the vets I've known and talked to. Fighting an unpopular war for a dubious purpose, a purpose practically inexplicable to the average citizen. But to spend twenty-plus years going through the motions. Learning the details of a specialty, but only on the theoretical level—that would weigh heavily on a soldier's self-esteem. At least my kind of soldier. Maybe it attracts the sort of employee who's satisfied by a mid-level bureaucratic career. I could definitely see a young person spending a few years learning mechanics or aviation, or EMT work. Totally worth it. But for specialized combat troops? No way, not for me.

With that in mind, I loved the learning. Let's say EOD, for example. Explosive Ordnance Disposal. Fascinating and exciting. A little scary at first, but with proficiency comes confidence, and pretty soon you're right at home doing a chore that would terrify most people.

My first learning task as a team was how to effectively attack a Middle Eastern village half-full of insurgents. They constructed a mock-up village with adobe structures. They dressed the subjects correctly and armed them with appropriate weapons, carried just as they would in theater. An AK-47 on a sling with a Chinese chest rack for ammo underneath baggy Arab clothes. They constructed the doors and windows authentically. When we did night-time raids, the gas or oil lighting was just like what they used. By the time we really pulled one off in theater, it was second nature minus a few surprises and some last second innovation, but we were almost like war veterans on our first mission.

Speaking of the first mission, I felt lucky. Some guys show up at NAS Little Creek and their unit is already deployed. They get put on the next airlift to Iraq or Afghanistan totally green. On the job training is never easy, but it's a bitch in a life-or-death situation. Not that it was the normal plan, but a few guys did have it happen that way.

Our team was well-prepared, and we got called in for a specific raid. It was a village in Kunar Province, Afghanistan. The provincial elders asked for us. It started with a few radicals moving in. Once they felt comfortable, they called in the experienced local insurgents. Slowly, they took control of the dirt floor shacks in the middle of town. When al-Qaeda got the word that the town was under control, they moved in too. Now it was a military camp disguised as a village, and as usual, shielded effectively by innocent civilians. We had seen all this before. Well, in the case of our specific team, we had seen the simulation of this, and had raided and conquered it.

   So, here's how my first real battle went. As SEALS, we have options on how to approach a target. We can fly right into the target in helicopters, like we did in Abbottabad on Operation Neptune Spear when we killed Bin Laden. We're there quick, but they know it. They're surprised, but they can grab stuff and retaliate. We count on outnumbering them and crushing the whole target indiscriminately, or nearly so. This method is good for when we're overloaded with explosives and heavy weapons, like mortars and heavy machine guns. Then, we have the HAHO (High Altitude High Opening) method, where we parachute out of our aircraft miles away, sometimes even across an international border, and fly our chutes stealthily to the target. This is good for quick surprise when we're lightly armed. That way, you can catch them asleep in bed. For our Kunar raid, we used a third method; we got discharged out of our helicopters onto the ground miles away, out of earshot, and hiked in. It's the hardest way, physically. We used it because the terrain was too extreme to parachute in at night. Intelligence is paramount. We had to worry about scouts and sentinels. There's a much bigger chance of stumbling into an ambush, which endangers your team and ruins the mission. Plus, how do you get back out from some unknown enemy camp? It's much easier to extract us out of the target area after we're done than have the helicopter pilots navigate to an unknown location at night. They can do it. They're awesome, but why burden them when you don't have to?

   So, on the night of the raid, we deployed within a larger platoon as a distraction, with ourselves and another team embedded. The big group, all of us together, deployed up the main road in a frontal assault like they would have expected. Once we were inside the last sentinel outpost, and just behind a ridgeline for camouflage, we split off left, while our brother team Bravo went right. Eight guys each, with our Heckler and Koch assault rifles, hand grenades, and side arms, and our all-important night vision goggles. A couple of specialists had grenade launchers. Hopefully, the enemy wouldn't notice the main body of our assault team, still advancing directly in front of them, was now smaller. We had good light conditions, but not great. We wanted pitch black in a perfect world. That gave us a big advantage with our goggles. That particular night, it was a waning half moon. Not bright, like a full moon, but not perfectly black. We knew there was a goat trail along the ridgeline behind the village. They used it every day for ingress and egress. It made sense that when we opened fire, the first class insurgents would break uphill to the ridge, to gain the high ground. From there, they could survey the entire battleground and choose their targets easily. Raining down a defilading barrage on the combatants below. They had a problem, though. Our squad was already there, under protective cover and fully loaded, with our night vision goggles in operation. Shooting gallery! Once we started picking them off, and they realized their mistake, they peeled off to their left and scrambled downhill toward a little copse of bushes and some good-sized boulders for cover. Problem was Bravo Squad was already there, and the slaughter intensified.

The whole thing was over in a half hour, and that included rounding up the wounded. The bad guys were pretty much wiped out, and most of our casualties were accidental. Broken bones and the like. One petty officer took a grazing shot to the quad, femur intact. By the time we were done, it was first light. By dawn, the citizens and elders came out to see. They were delighted! We had to hold some of them back, or they might have hung a few.

After that deployment, it was back to Little Creek for more learning and practice. Actually less learning by this time, and more simulated combat operations. I could hardly wait to get ahold of Hayowenta and tell him the whole story. Poor guy hadn't been called up yet. Before I could find out where he was, we had a new deployment.

Everybody on earth already knew about the piracy of the *Maersk Alabama*. It was on FOX News every day. The four pirates captured Captain Richard Phillips and held him for two million US dollars ransom. It was like reliving the Barbary War of the 1800s. These small-time outlaws were encouraged by a series of similar hijackings and kidnappings over the previous week, which had, unfortunately, been rewarded with millions in ransom money. The final decision was to fly us, including the three snipers, all the way from Virginia in a C-17, and parachute us into the water directly next to our base of operation, the USS *Boxer*. The USS *Haliburton* had two Blackhawks aboard, but the operation never needed them. Eventually, with the wind gusting up over thirty, and their lifeboat losing power, Bainbridge Commander Frank Castillo offered to tow them to safety. The dummies accepted! In fairness, they were desperate by this time. Castillo sent them food and water. They probably thought they could drift to shore and negotiate from there. Who knows with characters like that? They never displayed any sign of judgment during the whole ordeal. They were teenagers. Seventeen to nineteen.

The snipers we jumped with from the C-17 set up a command station on the fantail and fired from there. Castillo roped the lifeboat in closer and closer till each sniper had a clean headshot and they all fired at once, killing the pirates instantly. That cleared us to go in by boat and rescue Phillips. We got him off the lifeboat and safely aboard the *Bainbridge* right away. He was quickly transferred to the *Boxer* by air. That was my second deployment.

Chapter 6
Hayowenta

I AM HAYOWENTA. ONCE I GOT my wings, I applied for the Night Stalkers. It was in keeping with my excellence idea. I got C Company of the 1st Battalion, 212th Aviation Regiment for advanced training. We added night vision to our list of qualifications. We got checked out in both models of the UH-60, the A model and the M.

From there, I got my first permanent assignment. The 160th Special Operations Aviation Regiment (SOAR). Our Company Commander was Captain Flitch. In our activation ceremony, he mostly talked about our being dual rated, creating a "hybrid mission," which I guess was a thing at the time. His last words stuck with me, though.

"We will do more than succeed; we will excel."

I knew I was in my element now. And the talk was flying around about a special deployment in the works. It was all about piracy off the coast of Somalia. Turned out it was a SEAL mission Forrest got involved in. For me, it was all rumor.

They already had a couple of Blackhawks aboard one of the ships over there in Somalia, so we didn't get called up. We were pretty close to being on the same mission together, though. Maybe someday.

Blackhawk pilots know every detail of the Battle of Mogadishu. They made it into a movie *Blackhawk Down*. It was before my time, back in 1993, but we've all lived it in our minds as if we were there. It's part of the lore. It's our nightmare. The commanders should have planned strong defensive presence on the ground where the Blackhawks crashed. We could have saved the nineteen soldiers we lost, but the Washington politicians (read, Clinton Administration) thought the "image" was too aggressive. Two airborne snipers, Gary Gordon and Randy Shugart, were the heroes who insisted on deplaning to defend the two downed Blackhawks and crews on the ground. They were both awarded the Medal of Honor posthumously. I guess you could call it a pyrrhic victory. They achieved the original goal, but what a cost.

The idea that we were defeated, plus the desecration of American bodies, which was shown around the world, was humiliating. It led to our nonintervention policy. It destroyed our reputation. It encouraged Osama bin Laden to ridicule America. It strengthened the courage of al-Qaeda. A lot of people who know about this International Relations stuff figure the whole thing kept us out of Rwanda too, so you can add a half-million more victims to the pile. I'm not a politician, I'm a helicopter pilot, but I'm entitled to an opinion, and that's it.

We collaborated with DEVGRU on a few raids on al-Qaeda camps. The assaults didn't get much recognition, but they were important to us for self-esteem and proficiency. Usually, we would fly in a couple of teams of eight or twelve SEALS. They would fast line in and wipe them out. It was a decapitation mission. Idea being, take out the leaders, and a little while later, come back and get their replacements. Let the snake grow a new head; then come in and cut that one off too. Destabilize them. Keep them off balance and insecure. Like we were after 9/11. Payback's a bitch.

There was a lot of operational practice stateside too. We would try combat scenarios in challenging situations, and sometimes they got too ambitious. For an example, the head sheds decided to include proficiency at high altitude, since so many of our missions were likely to be chasing bad guys in the mountains of Afghanistan and Pakistan, like Tora Bora. The elevation at Leadville, Colorado, is about the same, over 14,000 feet. At that altitude, lift is really compromised, especially if you're heavy. You have to plan ahead and revise your techniques, be light-handed, and slow with the stick. Drive like a little old lady. Keep airspeed up a little higher. Plus, you have to consider gusting wind, too. And the terrain.

Anyway, everybody on the Leadville Blackhawk was super-qualified. The pilots had 10-12 combat deployments, and the enlisted crewmembers were career aircrew. The flight data recorder showed low airspeed, rapid descent, and a high-power setting. Otherwise, the aircraft was in normal operating condition with no mechanical issues. It just shows you how intense a mission can get when you least expect it. This crash was in broad daylight in good weather, and Leadville would have seemed almost too ordinary to them. Normally, we Night Hawks fly dangerous missions. Low, fast, and mostly at night. Sometimes we're under fire. When you think you're on Easy Street, you can't let up and stop concentrating, especially in the mountains. I took some professional lessons from Leadville.

Chapter 7
Hiawatha

I AM HIAWATHA HEYWOOD. I'VE BEEN watching these kids develop in their separate ways their whole lives. I tried to give guidance when I thought they might benefit from it, but only when they had an open mind or asked for help. I guess we adults all learn to observe and make note of tendencies and practices we see in the young people we're responsible for. Then we keep quiet until the right moment.

These kids are basically good. They don't try to get away with stuff. There's not a liar among them. I mean a congenital liar. All kids tell the white lie. We all do, but I never caught one trying to get away with enhancing their wellbeing by lying. They're hardworking kids who were lucky enough to find their individual passions. And they all had the strength of character to carry themselves through to success, in some cases, excellence. Let me say a bit about each one of them here.

Forrest

My relationship with Forrest was a little different than with the others. Even though we're twenty-one years apart. He was like a kid brother. A kid brother-in-law, really. My wife's kid brother. But he fit in more with Hayowenta and Keep America. Then later, he fit in with the twins, Minihaha and Dancing Rain. Forrest was different in another way too. No Ojibwa blood. He comes from the Green family. Anglo-Saxon, like his sister Keep America. If you met my wife, Kamali, you would say, "Wait a minute. Anglo-Saxon? No way! She looks Native American, or Latina or something." To understand this situation, you need to suspend reality and embrace Ojibwa magic. Kamali was transformed. I say magically because that's what it was. You can explain it to yourself however you like, but I know the truth.

So, why is Forrest white? He came before the transformation, that's why. Kamali was whiter than him at one time. I know it sounds crazy, but I'm an elder in the Good River Band of Ojibwa. I'm on the council, and some day I'll be chief. I know about this stuff.

If we go back through the whole thing, I'm mixed blood through my mother, who was white, from a Chippewa Club family. My father was Ojibwa. Nobody knew his name. He ran off somewhere. My wife is Kelley Green, and her sister is Keep America. Their kid brother is Forrest Green. They were all white, Anglo-Saxon (English) until Kelley transformed to Kamali and magically became 100 percent Ojibwa. Then there were two white Greens and Kamali, the princess. She transformed just before we got married. Kelley/Kamali and I had three kids: Hayowenta, Minihaha, and Dancing Rain (Minnie and Danci). Minnie and Danci are mirror image twins, and they sing in perfect harmony together.

So, if I'm mixed blood and Kamali is a 100 percent Ojibwa princess, that makes our kids three-quarter Ojibwa. But if you go the legal route and use Kelley's birth certificate from the Northwestern Hospital, she's 100 percent white, and the kids are a quarter Ojibwa. It makes for a big legal mess, but the kids are still okay for scholarships and tribal rights since they meet the 25 percent Ojibwa cutoff for "blood quantum." I hope they never ask for my father's birth certificate! For official government business, we use the Kelley Green heritage. For the family, and for tribal affairs, it's Princess Kamali.

For me, the first one to come along was Forrest, and he was my kind of guy. Self-confident, charming, star of the wrestling team, running back. What a sense of humor. That's why the girls loved him. I taught him all the skills of the Ojibwa woodsman. What a deal the SEALS got when he enlisted. We lived the idyllic life in the wilderness. We would pack in for two weeks at a time, living off the land. One summer we decided to pan for gold in Magic Stream. The idea was that the whole UP was awash in minerals, which it was. Copper had been mined by the Algonquin people since prehistoric times. Gold and silver mines were going in all over the area, plus nickel and trace minerals. To us teenagers, it made perfect sense. All the big mining concerns were overlooking the most obvious deposit right there in knee-deep water. Being kids, we believed what we wanted to be true. Fact was, all the easy ore had been gathered by the aboriginal peoples centuries before. The operations now were deep rock mining, thousands of feet down.

I'll never forget our first fool's gold nugget!

"Look at this! We were right! We're rich!"

It was our finest day. Our worst was the visit to the assayer's office. The next sluicing session was sheer drudgery. The water seemed colder and not so clear. Our shriveled fingers fumbled less enthusiastically. Our workdays got shorter and then less frequent, until it was all over a month later. I still have the nugget. I bought it from Forrest for a buck. It sits on my desk in the cabin to this day. In the end, we got a little dust, and I mean little, and a few scattered flakes.

The thing about Forrest was his intensity. He burned with an inner strength, even in the most mundane situations. In the deer blind, when I was prone to daydream or observe casual wildlife, he was tuned in with all his senses. You could be whispering to him about plans for tomorrow, and *click*, the sound of a twig would snap him into rapt attention. Safety off. Muzzle up. Fifty-meter stare locked in.

Every time I thought of something to prepare in advance—gather firewood, fix a leak in the tent, replenish the water supply, dump rainwater from canoe, cache the food—he already had it done.

I think of myself as a pretty good woodsman. I can build a fire on a rain-soaked day with ten knots of wind and nothing but a flint stone. I can find water in the desert. I know what plants to eat without poisoning myself. I can read the stars and navigate by dead reckoning. I am a stealthy hunter. I catch fish when nobody else does, with nothing but a fly rod. All that gives me confidence, but put me in a dangerous situation, a survival situation (bear attack, rattlesnake bite), I want one partner and one only to help me through the crisis. Forrest is my man. I got whacked by porcupine quills once, when we were deep in the forest. Two days brisk walk from civilization. He worked those things out, twisting just so, and cutting in the right places, till I was fit to go about an hour later. Hurt for days, though. He used to spot me five hundred yards in my little birchbark, the forerunner to *Exalted*, and beat me across Red Pine Lake every time. I think he had over a mile to catch me. No problem. Once he said I could use the canoe and he would swim. That prospect was tempting, but I turned him down. The potential for humiliation was too great.

I look forward to Forrest's reports from the SEALS. What a team to work with. Best in the world. He told me once as a young man that he wanted to excel. I guess this is it. In a way, he reminds me of the boxers and UFC fighters when they interview them after their championship victory in the ring. The announcer asks what the champ's plans are, and it's always "Work hard and learn new things to make myself even better." That's Forrest. Never satisfied.

I know he's already been on missions. Not search and destroy; they already know where the camps are. It's just destroy. The agencies use satellite images and refine them with high-altitude drones. It's the CIA and their contractors that do that stuff. Then they hand it over to the SEALS, and they take the training camps and outposts out. Take no prisoners. You didn't hear it from me, though, and it sure didn't come from Forrest. I'll deny that in the torture chamber with half my fingernails pulled out.

Hayowenta

Next came Hayowenta. Cut from the same cloth, but not quite so wilderness-oriented. He's more of a mechanical type. Speed demon. Snowmobiles, dirt bikes, ATVs. He started downhill skiing, but when he heard about snowboarding, he changed over and charged farther and farther into the extreme elements of it. The first crazy idea was take the snowboard down the ski jump ramp. It was a dare he took when he was twelve. Forrest opened his mouth about doing it himself, but he was on the wrestling team, and there were specific rules about self-endangerment. He worshiped the coach and they had a shot at winning State that year in their division (A), so if he hurt himself in an unauthorized activity, he could be DQ'd. Actually, so could the whole team. So, it was like, "I would pull that off, no problem, but I can't, 'cause of the team," and Hayowenta was like, "Okay, pussy; let me show you how this is done."

Word got around. There was a crowd. Bets got placed: Injury? Death? He chickens out and comes up with an excuse? (No takers for that last bet.) On the day of the event, it was still just the local snow freaks and school kids. TV news had caught wind of it, but nobody wanted them, so the kids gave out the wrong date and time. The jump is huge. The skiers start from the very top, twenty-five stories up, and reach more than 60 mph. Since Hayowenta was so young, they lowered him halfway with a rope, and he launched from there. It was still spectacular. More than ten stories up. He thought about a back flip, but Forrest talked him out of it. He flew more than fifty meters, and landed on his feet. You would expect this to start a "me too" craze, but it never caught on. Maybe there were no teens that year willing to risk coming in second to a twelve year old. Those things have a way of losing energy with the passage of time. Especially back then with no YouTube. The Rangers got more aggressive about patrolling too, so that made Hayowenta the one and only snowboard ski jumper in those days. Maybe some of them do it now. I don't know.

Later on, as a teen, he got into competition. Half Pipe and Giant Slalom to start with. Then the Alpine and Extreme. By the time he was in high school, he became the most influential boarder in Backcountry. You've probably seen it, where they go off cliffs, over trees and boulders. Backflips, cork 1080s. All the spectacular stuff.

Summers, he was a dirt bike and ATV enthusiast. They had an event they called the Mudhole Races in Little Bay, and Hayowenta always won his class. All about keeping your speed up in the deep parts. Once you get slow and bog down, you might as well sit and wait for somebody to come by and winch you out. The dirt bike scene was in its infancy in the UP. There were no real sanctioned races, so Hayowenta and his buddies raced cross-country among themselves along the trail systems set up for vehicles. The biggest challenge was staying away from the ATVs, so they would notify the area they were going to take over a segment, usually a loop, and ride hell-bent through the Red Dog Plains, finishing at the General Store for beer and BBQ.

When 9/11 happened and Forrest joined the SEALS, it just about killed Hayowenta. He was motivated by revenge, like a lot of us were. Forrest got right in the Navy, but Hayowenta was seventeen. He had to wait. He was livid. "Somebody lie for me. Get my birth certificate and doctor it up. I will. Where is it? What's wrong with this country these days. People lied and got in underage all the time back in the day. Famous people."

His family had to let him know things had changed. Records were kept more accurately these days. When he wouldn't leave it alone and kept ranting, I finally lost patience. "Shut up! I'm sick of your complaining. Look at you. You're seventeen, and a skinny seventeen at that. Do you want to hold your platoon members back waiting for you to catch up? Use this time to get ready. Get fit. Go to the gym. Put on muscle. Go look out in the garage for gun and ammo. I took your 22 apart. Put it back together. In fact, put it back together blindfolded. And when you've got that done, shoot that target in the backyard till you hit a full box without missing. That's fifty straight. There's a case of 22LR in the basement. You can start with those, and when they're gone, break into your paper route money and get more.

"OK, fifty shells per box, ten boxes per brick, ten bricks per case. Five thousand rounds to start with. Two boxes a day means almost two months of practice. You don't want to shoot too much. You lose focus, plus the gun gets dirty and starts jamming. Clean it thoroughly after every use. Never shoot more than three boxes without cleaning. Leave important time for conditioning. Start with simple calisthenics and move to the weights. Run sensibly until you're up to four miles a day, four days per week. That leaves plenty of time for the paper route, and you can wash cars in the neighborhood and mow lawns too."

Realistically, the initial plan was too much. He cut here and there. Customized the gym routine as his fitness changed. Cut way back on the shooting as he became more accurate. Just like everything, the tough part was getting started, then getting up to proficiency. Once you're up to expert level, maintaining is less intense. Just never skip sessions. Your biggest enemy is inconsistency and laziness. Always do at least something on workout days.

Hayowenta started to see this waiting period more as his preparation time. I asked, "What is your specific military goal? What service? What specialty?"

"It has to be machines, Dad," he told me. "It's just natural for me. I love them, and I'm good at using them and fixing them. The military is full of them. I just need to start narrowing it down."

Hayowenta's lifting buddy at the gym was Sylvester Coffey. "Sly." They played on the football team together. Sly was from a family of athletes. He was football, wrestling, baseball. Hayowenta was football, wrestling, track. One day they were finishing up their workout when Sly mentioned he was running late.

"What for?"

"Got to get my flying time in."

"What? You have a plane?"

"No. You know my background. We don't have extra money for big stuff like that. I take lessons. Come on out and see. My instructor might give you a demo flight. You could be a potential candidate. I get credit for bringing him new students."

It was a Cessna 150. All the basic student planes are. Cheap to fly. Aerodynamically honest. Enough power to get out of stupid mistakes. Ninety percent of private pilots' first flights were in a 150. Air Force pilots started in the 172. A little more power, I guess. Or they got to spend more of the taxpayers' money on a nicer plane.

The instructor was Pedro. He was smart and insightful. He had cultivated the art of recognizing potential flying addicts over the years. He detected a spark in Hayowenta, who had to wait on the ground for Sly to be done. They flew off somewhere to do air work. Stalls, turns over a point. VFR navigation. Then they came back to the traffic pattern for touch-and-go landings. They were smooth, for the most part. A couple of skips and one definite bounce. Hayowenta counted twelve landings total. When they taxied in, Sly jumped out, but Pedro kept the motor running.

"Pedro says go out for a ride with him."

Sly walked him out to make sure he didn't do something dumb, like walk into the prop. He opened the door. Wait a minute! This is the pilot's seat. Pedro ran him through the controls. Rudder pedals, control wheel, throttle.

Pedro gave instruction. "Go ahead and release the parking brake. It's on your side down by your left knee. Now, push the throttle forward a little and steer with the rudder. There you go. Taxi out to the end of Runway 29. No, left, there."

"Pedro, I wasn't planning for this. I thought you were going to show me some stuff."

"I am. No better way to learn than by doing."

So, an hour later, Hayowenta taxied in, set the brakes, killed the engine, acknowledged the chocks were installed by the ramp worker (two thumbs pointed inward toward each other), and stepped out on the macadam. Stall series. Turns over a point. Five touch-and-gos. He was hooked.

"Dad, I think my planning process is starting to take shape. I'm going to be a helicopter pilot in the Army."

"The Army has pilots? Why don't you join the Navy and fly jets off the carriers?"

"The Navy wants a college degree. Air Force too. Not want, they require. You can't even get started without it. That's four years. It would drive me crazy."

So, that's how Hayowenta wound up where he did. All the time with al-Qaeda on his mind.

Keep America

So, next is Keep America. She never let her name determine her direction in life. You probably know her parents were serious environmental activists. Very intelligent people with strong beliefs. You could say zealous beliefs. They were unappreciative products of the "Establishment" with an anti-establishment version of *noblesse oblige*. If you're around my age, you know the type. Their attitude toward their prosperous ancestors was dismissive. They talked as though the railroad tycoons and industrialists in their families had prosperity just dropped in their laps out of nowhere and used it to oppress the less fortunate out of meanness and greed. "Robber Barons." They renounced their family's country club society as shallow and irresponsible, while retaining their own trust income for vagrant drug-fueled wanderings through Europe and North Africa. None of them I knew were aware of their families' philanthropic orientation, of the trusts and estates that funded vast areas of education and medical research. The Vietnam generation had a wide variety of reasons to be anti-war. They flocked to any cause that would afford them a waiver or deferment from duty. The number of adamant atheists who applied to Yale Divinity School was comical. I loved to listen to the righteous arguments proffered by newly converted socialists at the Student Union. They never acknowledged their trust funds, which probably included large holdings of Boeing, Rockwell, and other defense contractors.

Keep America liked her name. She never considered a nickname or a change. She worshiped nature in general, and the wilderness in particular. She didn't share her parents' political philosophy. She liked capitalism. She did love nature like they did, but more as a conservationist than an environmentalist She thought America should help the less fortunate in the world, and that didn't rule out military action. She was religious. Her parents were not. She kept her beliefs completely private.

When I met her, Keep America was in the children's program at the Chippewa Club. She's my sister-in-law, so when I fell in love with Kelley, she was always right there with us. We did everything together. Well, almost everything. When I married Kelley/Kamali, Keep America became family. Everything changed for her when the academicians discovered she was a mathematical genius. That happened when she was at Columbia after we all moved to New York as a family. Now she's at Cal Tech in Pasadena studying fractal geometry. It has something to do with nature, and how if you look deep enough, you can see the basic design of the universe. Remember Stephen Hawking, the physicist who got famous? He said when we understood the Theory of Everything, we would "see the face of God," or we would "know God," or something like that. It didn't happen because there still isn't a Theory of Everything, a theory that unifies the world of the very small, as in subatomic particles, with the theory of the incomprehensibly large, relativity. I think Hawking was string theory, or maybe chaos theory. I think they're similar to fractal geometry. When you look down inside, it seems to get more and more basic. So, I think Keep America has this idea that there's something more fundamental to fractal geometry than just infinite replication.

All this fractal stuff is beyond me, really. She tries to explain, but when she gets frustrated with me, out come the formulae.

$D = \log(3)/\log(2) = 1585$ is supposed to calculate the dimension of a Sierpinski triangle, which is an iterated function system fractal that's supposed to be easy for me to understand.

Now you can see there's no point in me trying to explain what Keep America is doing at Cal Tech.

The Twins

The last two are the twins. Since they're mixed blood, they got an Ojibwa name and an English one. Minihaha and Dancing Rain. They go by Minnie and Danci. Since they're younger, I feel like I've had more of an influence over them. I don't have to encourage their singing, though. Neither does their mother. They do that all on their own. They became local celebrities among the tribe as small kids. First, it was birthday parties and baby showers. Then they started in the children's choir at church, and they were stars right away. Their voices have a way of vibrating off each other, creating a harmonic effect that is almost like an echo, or a third voice. There's a name for it—I forget. Soprano, though. Both definitely soprano, even though Danci is a little lower.

Once they got a little older, I got them into the casino on a technicality. I'm pretty influential in the tribe, so we can do stuff on the reservation that isn't possible in the rest of the country. Look at tobacco and cherry bombs, for example. The only casinos with smoking allowed are Indian. Fireworks are legal to buy and use on the reservation, no matter what the state law happens to be. We're in our own country when we're on the reservation, with our own legal system. Nobody ever complained about kids singing in the cocktail lounge. We had pretty good entertainment in the main showroom for a country casino. With no large population center nearby, we had a small transient clientele from around the UP. Tourists gambling as a major change from their lives at home. Loggers and miners looking to improve the size of their paychecks. We had the usual acts that came through. Dance acts, comedians, and a few traveling singers like Buddy Red Bow and Buffy Sainte-Marie.

The best act we ever had was a mysterious magician who entered the back of the room in Sioux chief's regalia, looking individual audience members in the eye as he made his way to the stage. He projected his personality as he passed by. During his act, the stage lights gradually darkened until it was just the chief and a classic Indian campfire with the smoke curling up and out of sight. He made his final bow, stepped into the fire, melded into the smoke, and disappeared. Then the fire did too, and the smoke. He was a hologram. They were all holograms, but since when? Was he always one from the time he entered, or did he transform from human form somehow during the act? When he passed me in the audience, he looked me straight in the eye and acknowledged me with a knowing smile. He was human. He recognized me, or I thought so. The mysterious thing was I never saw him outside the theater. His agent did everything for him until he appeared in the room, and they collected the pay in advance. His last performance, I snuck out to the parking lot and spied on the agent's car. He came out of the stage door, got in the car, and left alone. I searched the whole backstage and asked all the cast and staff.

"Where's the chief? I need to pay him." (Lie, he was already paid.)

"Beats me, Boss. I only see him during the act."

One week, he never showed up and that was the end of it. I called up the other casino managers.

"Red who?'

"Red Otter. Kiowa Medicine Man."

"Never heard of him. Ask the Kiowa."

I started using the girls for openers. It was their graduation from children's birthday songs and hymns. They had some pretty standards for the first opening act. Just one per show. Then, as they got a little older, I moved them to an occasional featured act on weekdays. Their standard was "A Million Dreams." Later, they brought in "Tennessee Waltz."

One day, Chief Buffalo, from one of the Potawatomi bands, came through for a visit. It happened the girls were practicing for an afternoon show they were going to do on the weekend. He was obsessed.

"We need these girls for our place too. You need to put them on tour. They could hit all the Upper Midwest. We've got ten casinos just here in the UP. We don't have that many Native singers. We need to get away from Elvis impersonators and Wayne Newton lookalikes. We need to get an identity of our own going."

"Buff, these are my daughters. They're young girls. They need their family, their friends, and their own tribe. There is no way I would do that to them. When they're twenty-one, it's their choice, but now it's mine and Kamali's. Even when they're twenty-one, I'll still vote against it."

"Well, do me a favor and just have Kamali bring them over to our place for a daytime weekend show. Just one time a week. Make it Saturday afternoon. It's not that far, and it won't screw up their homework."

That's how it started, and they loved it. It was definitely the high point of their week. They even wrote their own song. "Indian Summer."

They came to me with it.

"Dad!" (They always called me Dad when they wanted something.) "Can you get somebody to write this in proper fashion, with notes and stanzas and stuff? We could sing it on tape so they can write it down. Who's a good musician around here?"

"Well," I said, "Keep America took piano. She plays from sheet music. I guess she could do it, or her piano teacher, Ms. Winona."

"Winona? Yes! We know her. She likes us. Can you take the tape to Joliette? She has her studio there."

"I'm going in Saturday for bait and ammunition. I'll take it then. You could come too and sing it in person, but it's your day for Potawatomi."

"Call the chief. Tell him we'll make it up Sunday, or we could sing two shows next weekend. Please. Please. Please!"

So, they came into town that Saturday, and it turned out to be a bigger deal than they thought, like it always does. Winona wanted them to sing each part of the song bit by bit so she could make notes on the vibrato and do a better job. It was fine with me. I got the stuff I needed right away, so I sat around and drank tea and watched the process. I was clear they were truly driven. They came at it with true passion. I began to question my resistance to their commitment. They were teens. Their schoolwork hadn't suffered, at least so far. Maybe we could add more performances.

So, little by little, Kamali branched out, taking the girls to Native American casinos all over the UP until she found the right combination of convenient location and size. The ones in big cities had more business and paid more money, so it came down to a couple of Ojibwa ones, which was nice, being our own tribe, and the Potawatomi one the chief had, plus a couple in Wisconsin. One day, the girls were singing at Potawatomi and Kamali watched with the chief.

"Kamali," said the chief, "did you know I'm part Mohegan?"

"Really?"

"Yeah. There's only a few thousand of us left. My cousin came through last month from Connecticut. He's in the Uncasville tribe. Same as mine. They might open a new place in Las Vegas. I might invest some Potawatomi money in it. Then you could bring the girls and turn them into real stars!"

"Yeah, right. Just where we always wanted to put down roots. A cute little family town with plenty of natural beauty. Ugh. I can't think of a worse place in the world. Well, maybe New York City, and we already tried that once. Got bombed out by the Muslim terrorists. Don't call me any time soon."

"Kamali, think about it. Maybe a few short visits per year. It could be big bucks for just a little bit of time. Do you know what Siegfried & Roy make? Take a guess."

"I don't know. Really big bucks, I guess. Ten grand a week?"

"You're off a little. Actually, you're off a lot. An exponential lot."

"Okay, fifty grand a week! Haha."

"You're getting closer. Take a look at a ticket some day. They're not cheap, and they sell out every day, two shows a day, seven days a week. I'll save you some time. I know the number from being in the business. We managers keep close track of this stuff. Last time I checked, they were averaging $140,000 per night. That's average. That's about fifty million every year for decades. I'll take that back. They made much less in the beginning, so that would bring the average down a little. Still, the 140 Gs, that's today's money. You could decide to stay in the woods and continue like you are, or change your family's life in a big way."

"Chief, they're Siegfried & Roy. We're not. You can't make a comparison like that."

"I'm just showing you a difference in degrees. Of course the girls wouldn't make anywhere near that money. They probably never would in their whole lives, but the potential is there for a big improvement and anything is possible. Sky's the limit."

"Oh, why did God give them these voices, and why do they love it so much?" asked Kamali. "I just want my babies happy together in the North Woods with me."

"Think about it, Kamali. That's all I ask. It might not even happen. Maybe my cousin won't get the casino deal done at all. I just wanted you to know what's happening and what could happen so you don't have a surprise offer pop up in your face some day unexpectedly."

"Okay, you told me. You told me something that could happen maybe some day. Now you listen to what I'm telling you. I'm not mentioning anything about this to the girls, and I don't want you even to insinuate in the mildest way to them that anything like this is even remotely possible. They're innocent and joyful, and their lives are perfect at the moment. If you so much as hint to them, I will tell Hiawatha. You don't want that. In fact, I'm going home and telling him every detail of our talk right away. We share everything, and I know exactly what he'll think about it. Chief, I'm sorry I got so churned up about this, but I'm a mother, and I sense danger to my daughters. Thank you for thinking of us, but we're nowhere near considering a life like that and probably never will be. The only way we're even going off our own reservation right now is I'm with them every minute we're on the road."

"I understand, and I pledge to you."

Chief's pledge lasted five years, from when the girls were thirteen until they were eighteen. Now it was 2008. High school was done. They had gotten grades and graduated in the top quarter of their class, with music at the very top. They came to Kamali and me for a kitchen table talk.

"Hy," Kamali asked me beforehand, "did the girls talk to you about a family meeting?"

"Yeah. Three guesses about the subject."

"I know. It's been boiling under the surface for a while now. What do you think about the Vegas thing? Before you answer, I can commit to being there with them for their trial period."

"Trial period? Do you know more than I think you do?"

"Well, the only way I see it can work is a few short trips like Chief was talking about when he brought it up back then. A few engagements over a short period, and then a reevaluation to see if it's workable over time."

"Okay, let's hear what they have to say."

Minnie and Danci had been working on their proposal for a long time, and they agreed the timing was really important. Catch them in a good mood. Be on our good behavior for a while. Be polite and respectful. Agree on a date in advance, so they don't feel bushwhacked.

Then it happened. Kitchen table. The place where everything important was discussed.

Kamali opened the meeting. "Okay, girls, just so we know we're all on the same page and we don't waste time, is this about singing in Las Vegas?"

Danci turned out to be the spokesperson.

"Yes. We found out Chief's Uncle Dakota got the casino and it's starting up. Mohegan Sun. Chief's an investor. He invited us to sing there. We could be one of the first acts in the main showroom. Buffy's opening, since she's the most famous Native American singer, even if she is Cree. Actually, I'm kidding about the Cree stuff. We know her from singing together. She likes us. You could even say we're a "thing." So, Mom (they always call her "Mom" when they want something), could you be our chaperone? And maybe Dad too, when it's practical?"

You can tell they see Kamali as the easy mark on big decisions. I actually think I'm the easy one. Funny the girls haven't figured that out yet. Fathers are always the softies in the end, at least for daughters. So, I gave the approval, which was really Kamali's approval, and we called the chief to arrange the opening day at Mohegan Sun. February 4 with Buffy.

OPENING NIGHT
FEBRUARY 4th
BUFFY SAINTE MARIE
THE CHIPPEWA GIRLS

Chapter 8
Keep America

The Fractalist

S O, THERE I AM IN a Perkins Restaurant sitting in my booth, fixated on Benoit Mandelbrot in the flesh for the first time in my life, after committing my entire intellectual identity to his life's work. I sat frozen there.

I listened to the little robot in my ear. I have a robot that advises me on matters of judgment, especially survival. He lives within my consciousness somewhere, mostly hanging out in my brain stem, the primordial part, casually observing my life go by, like a football fan might watch a game from across the room. One he's only mildly interested in. Then when the big play comes up; it's like if I'm about to punt on fourth down with ten seconds left in the game, he pops up in my frontal cortex and yells, "No!" Like Hayowenta jumping up from the sofa and spilling his beer.

This time I was about to introduce myself to the most important mathematician of the twentieth century (besides Einstein, maybe) when I had nothing meaningful to say to him. My robot saved me. He put me in my place so securely that not only did I not introduce myself, I never even raised my hand in class that whole first semester. I introduced myself to the whole class on Day One, like everybody else did. That was it. So Mandelbrot never knew I was devoted to him and his work. He probably thought he was just another teacher to me, like he was to the rest of the students.

I was fascinated with the self-similarity of fractal design. The code-pendence of mathematics and art. The mind and the eye. The impact of the Mandelbrot set, and its influence on seemingly non-mathematical aspects of reality. Most people see the Mandelbrot Zoom as their first exposure to the phenomenon. Your everyday curious student leaves it there. Pretty picture, leading who knows where? With me, it was about the ubiquitous nature of fractal geometry in the natural world. It was inside me, in my vascular system, my nervous system, my brain. Plus, it was everywhere in nature. Ferns, cauliflower, trees, river systems, coastlines.

Wait a minute. Are you saying that a coastline, which is totally nat-ural and constantly modified and reconfigured by water, has its basis in mathematics? To me, that would mean nothing exists outside of math. It's the foundation of everything. It gave me a sense of importance that I was becoming highly proficient at fractal geometry. It was becoming my youthful identity. Maybe my job was to become masterful at it.

So, looking back, I began to see Mandelbrot as founding the notion that the geometry we always applied to manmade things, like triangles and cubes, buildings and bridges, applied to everything, including us as individuals.

Mandelbrot calls it the math of roughness, as opposed to the smooth nature of triangles and spheres in regular geometry. I think of it as the math of the apparently disorganized. The purely random, like a forest full of trees. Then he comes along and says: "You see the con-tinuous branching of a tree trunk to the branches, to the twigs, to the leaves and their veins? Well, the whole forest is laid out the same way. It's predictably mathematical."

Our high school valedictorian got straight As in math, physics, German and Russian, and he was a concert pianist. He had a perfect SAT score that he took as fast as he could write. He became like a vale-dictorian at Stanford too, if they even had such a thing. He didn't even bother with the lesser degrees. Straight to PhD in Theoretical Physics. I asked him what he studied, expecting a practical answer.

"The behavior of fluid in a vacuum," was the answer.

I objected. "How can there be anything in a vacuum? If there's fluid in there, then it's not a vacuum."

He was like, "I could spend the rest of the afternoon trying to explain the formulation of certain principles of theoretical physics, and how we modify them to perfect their application to practical matters useful to the science of engineering, like rocket fuel and flight paths in space travel, but you probably wouldn't get it anyway."

And I was supposed to be a genius.

Well, now I was in the same situation, of being in over my head, but I had to figure out a way to learn it. First, I had to read his books:

- *The Fractal Geometry of Nature*
- *The Misbehavior of Markets*
- *The Fractalist: A Memoir*

Maybe after the first semester, I could be conversational enough to engage him.

"Okay, Robot?"

Later, I learned it was a bad plan. He decided to limit his tenure to one semester only, and return to his full-time job at Yale.

Dimensions

Some of my electives offered the temptation to diversify my field of study within physics. Fractal geometry led to chaos theory and string theory, which then led toward the idea of multiple, and then parallel, dimensions. Every time I got to the dead end of one theory, another would pop up.

So, you get into these equations, and they all seem to indicate there have to be seven to ten dimensions. Mathematically, they all prove out that way. That's what Stephen Hawking and Brian Greene were calculating. All of them were then, really—Nigel Calder, Kip Thorne, Max Tegmark. The more they pursued the possibility of Grand Unified Theory (the Theory of Everything), the more persistently the ten-dimensional universe appeared. Actually, Brian Greene later calculated eleven dimensions. But where are these dimensions, and what form do they take? One version was curled up dimensions too tiny to be seen, or even detected. Others include membranes floating in the cosmos, or universes and their dimensions stacked together like panes of glass. When the calculations of quantum mechanics are used to examine the tiniest subatomic particles, they cease being matter and become energy instead. More precisely, they become likely (probable) to be one or the other. It's wave-particle theory. They don't exist. They only have a probability to exist. No matter whether you're dealing with the infinitely large realm of relativity or the impossibly small realm of quantum mechanics, they lead to indefinite conclusions, or, you could say, they become too fuzzy to identify.

As you're travelling (zooming) through the Mandelbrot set, interesting features appear. It isn't just a continuously repeating pattern of images. It's more of a landscape of unique creations. In the fourteenth level of zoom, past the seahorses, there's one called Julia Island, named for Gaston Julia, the originator of the equations. I got to thinking about certain features, Julia Island for example, as possibly being portals, jumping off points. Gateways from our three (four) dimensional universe to the other parallel universes. Now I'm beginning to imagine the Mandelbrot set as the super-highway through the parallel universes of the multiverse.

Chapter 9
Forrest

I AM FORREST GREEN, NAVY SEAL. As my experience level became more seasoned, I got more responsibility and promotions. In the SEALS, you make E-4 (petty officer third class) pretty quick, and by the time I got to Afghanistan, I was an E-5. Between that mission and the *Maersk Alabama* rescue, they gave me the Bronze Star and the Navy Commendation Medal.

In 2010, we started hearing about a top-secret mission we were supposed to train for. They were just rumors at that time, but they really intensified when we got scheduled for a last-minute briefing in Washington, DC. I was in Virginia Beach doing routine training, but when I got to DC and walked into the special secure briefing room, a model of a building and its surroundings was in the middle of the room, obviously the objective at hand. I walked around it and inspected. It was a large three-story, domestic-looking house on a large triangular lot surrounded by a concrete wall between twelve and eighteen feet high. It appeared to be on about an acre of land. The closer I looked at the detail, the more familiar it looked. Wait a minute; it's that facility out in Nevada we've been using for proficiency training! This mission has been on the drawing board for a while now. I sat down and waited for the facilitator to break the news.

The rumor mill had been working overtime, and this meeting was a way for us to forage some hard facts and some educated guesses about what we were getting into. Question time was our best opportunity for harvesting information.

"Sir, what equipment are we taking?"

"Will we be near a base?"

"Do we cook in the field, or are we surviving on rations?"

"Is there air support?"

Afterwards, we got together and assembled the pieces of the puzzle. It's amazing what detail can develop using the process of elimination. We figured out it was an international operation, starting in one country and finishing in another. We were deploying from a US military base. It was a helicopter mission. We were a platoon of two squads of twelve. Our target was the compound depicted by the model in the briefing room. My friend Jack said he looked at the model from different directions. "It's that place we've been practicing on out in Nevada. It's like we've already been there." More informal intelligence revealed the initial destination was Jalalabad, specifically Bagram AFB. There was no active military conflict in the area. Our group was too high level to fly halfway around the world for a routine operation. Our two squads comprised the most-experienced, most-proficient, and highest-ranking members of SEAL Team Six. As the facts came together and the situation clarified, there was only one explanation for that sort of mission: We were going to assassinate Osama bin Laden.

I remember when the realization hit me, and it really physically hit me with a burst of adrenaline, like the first time you come under attack in a firefight, or when the toughest bully in the schoolyard picks a fight with you. Ten years of anticipation and preparation finally paid off in that moment. I thanked God under my breath. What were the chances that the young man from the Upper Peninsula of Michigan, who vowed revenge on September 11, 2001, would wind up on SEAL Team Six, made up of two dozen of the world's most dangerous fighters exacting the ultimate vengeance? I mean, I had set the long-term goal and worked ten years to achieve it, but to have it all fall into place perfectly was a miracle. I can't wait to tell Hayowenta. No, wait a minute—this is top secret. I'll have that pleasure over a couple of beers when it's all over and we're back in the UP.

The mission came together from that point pretty quickly. Everybody was thoroughly trained, proficient, and current. The defense policy really came to fruition during the term of Donald Rumsfeld. The idea was that after 9/11, our adversaries changed from being world powers with large armies to a scattered group of independent Islamist underground organizations, and we needed to revolutionize in the US military. We were faced with lightly armed, highly agile adversaries, which required movement toward a high-speed, information-driven, readily deployable strike force. Quick Reaction Forces. Units like Delta Force and us, the SEALs. The days of large permanent bases around the world were not over, but the business end of our elite forces was to be nimble, efficient, and intensely effective. Our SEAL teams and the Army's Delta Force were the ultimate version of the Rumsfeld plan. It was supposed to limit occupational bases to use as launching facilities and, hopefully, end or greatly reduce decades-long occupations like Iraq or Afghanistan, with their exposure to random IED attacks against uniformed personnel. We keep the bare minimum of troops on the ground, mostly support personnel and combat advisors. When a brush-fire war breaks out or a terrorist leader pops up, we respond with lightning-fast teams, destroy the enemy, and withdraw. Decapitate the serpent, go home, and wait for the new head to grow. Immediate response to aggressive attacks on our allies or acts of terrorism was swift punishment. I figured it was modeled on Israel's strategy in the Middle East.

So, that was us, and we were about to execute the decapitation scheme. We had a little over a week to get ready. I was in an electrified state, and I had to do a few five-mile runs during the week just to take the edge off.

We each have a closet for our assault gear at Virginia Beach. We call it our cage. It's got every piece of the personal equipment you might need for a deployment anywhere in the world. Some of it is automatic and always included for any mission. Some of it is very specific, like my HAHO chute for long-distance parachute assaults. Among the automatically included were one of my pistols, either a Sig Sauer P226 or an H&K 45C. My rifles, which were H&K 416 with a ten-inch barrel and a suppressor and an MP7 submachine gun, deadly and silent. They all have laser sights, a must for this mission. I had a grenade launcher too, not needed this time, plus a longer version (14" barrel) H&K 416. Making my choices was a tough decision. I was going to have to learn a little more before deciding on it. I was right on the cut line due to weight. My body armor was made of boron carbide ceramic plates in a vest, which weighed sixty pounds. It had an all-purpose Gerber tool, like a Leatherman, which was always in the same pocket. You can't believe how essential that little thing can be. Just a normal household item. I had a fixed blade knife on my belt, just like they had in World War II. All my stuff was always in the same place, and I had it memorized. I could find anything on my body in a microsecond, blindfolded. Then I would constantly drill. I would "lose" them and retrieve them with my eyes closed.

I selected my kit thoughtfully and carefully, considering its importance to this specific mission and factoring in weight. I erred on the heavy side. You can always ditch stuff.

Going through my mental checklist, I felt ready to rumble. Best physical shape of my life. Astute. Courageous. Purposeful. Perfectly equipped for this specific deployment. Let's get it on!

Then the orders came down, and we moved on out to NAS Oceana. Back into the trusty C-17 for another deployment. I was getting used to the facilities by now, but they weren't always the same. The aircraft can be quickly reconfigured many different ways. For pure cargo payloads, it's just a big empty fuselage, able to accept palletized cargo. I don't mean wooden pallets like warehouses use. These are steel and aluminum wheeled pallets that slide in on rollers built to fit perfectly into sunken tracks. There's eighteen of them, and they can carry almost any piece of equipment required for logistics or warfare. I've seen thousands of pounds of ammunition of any caliber, up to and including artillery shells. I've seen palletized artillery pieces, hospital operating rooms, often airline style passenger seats for long trips or VIPs. That's in addition to fifty-four canvas seats on each side of the fuselage (not comfortable). It carries wheeled or tracked vehicles, including the Abrams M1 tank, which weighs sixty-nine tons. I guess you could put a Greyhound bus in it. The larger C-5 Galaxy could carry six of them. The maximum number of paratroopers is 102 men with their equipment. That's six platoons plus. Being a smaller, lighter strike force, we SEALs don't take up much room. We had lots of extra space on the *Maersk Alabama* rescue. They slid in a pallet of airline seats that reclined for sleeping. Pretty luxurious combat quarters.

I triple-checked my equipment bags for the last time before I drove my pickup to HQ at Virginia Beach. Ten extra magazines for the HK416 seemed like a lot. The way I had it in mind, we better not have an extended gunfight entering the compound. Ideally, the element of surprise eliminates that. This is a stealthy, fast-paced raid. In and out in a hurry, and CIA said the property is lightly defended to keep their profile low. Who knows what might happen inside the house, though? Ten magazines seems like a lot, especially with my Sig Sauer P226 too. Weight's not all that much of a deal this time since we're not covering much distance. Nimbleness is more of a factor.

So, we all made our way to SEAL Headquarters at Virginia Beach. Busses took us out to our C-17 at an airport I won't mention.

The loadmaster was doing his exterior preflight inspection. Sometimes the aft cargo ramp is open, and we have an easy way into the airplane with our gear. This time we had to struggle up the passenger ladder.

Dang! No airline seats. Some guys were smart and brought their hammocks. Plenty of room to spread out on the floor, though. I was happy to have my inflatable camping mattress. Time to get comfortable for the long flight. The Middle East, Africa, and South Asia all required a stop at Ramstein AFB, Germany, so that was the plan. Funny how people think of Afghanistan as Middle East. It's not. It's South Asia.

Right before takeoff, the loadmaster made us get up and strap into our canvas-side-facing passenger seats attached to the side bulkheads. No big deal. We had to be there for landing too, but the rest of the time, we were camped out on the floor. About halfway through the flight, we hit some massive turbulence and I got up and strapped in again. That's a big space for a human to be bouncing around in like a ping-pong ball.

So, at Ramstein, we got fuel. A guy in the terminal was selling small sausages in a crusty bun. Delicious. They sold beautiful-looking German beer too. We declined. Now we're on to Jalalabad, in combat uniforms with duffels full of deadly equipment. I'm stoked!

Jalalabad. Now everything is different. There's a feel to Islamic culture that definitely sets it apart from Americans or Europeans. I don't need to get into it. If you've been there, you know what I'm talking about. They emphasize that we are different. We didn't really enter into their society on this trip. We stayed on base, but even the local citizens who work there don't relate to us on a personal level. As long as I live, I will never forget the toothless old local who handled my bags, set them down on the helicopter pad, and caught my eye. He looked at me directly with an aggressive stare, and with his index finger, he slit his (my) throat.

I get to catch up on some legitimate sleep in the officers quarters. Holy shit! I'm in the officers quarters as an E-5? I felt weird, guilty, like I was a trespasser of some kind, but here I was, chosen for an historic mission, which meant I got to sleep on fresh sheets, laundered by a housemaid. Then, when I woke up in the morning, the boots I left outside my door as ordered were freshly polished. I don't believe this!

First thing in the morning is the briefing that we get on all the details of how we're supposed to pull this off. I'm even included in the top secret session because we all have to be on the same page.

Here's how it's supposed to go. We stay up late and sleep as long as we can. We get up and start our personal preparation for the assault. By about 2 p.m., we have all our equipment in order, and every detail of the timeline. We need to know if all the pre-existing conditions are satisfactory, everyone is prepared, and all systems are operational. There's plenty of time left for a catnap, a card game, or communications with family at home. We don't rendezvous with the choppers till after ten at night. That's when the bus shows up for the short trip to the flight line.

We go down to the airport and enter the Blackhawks (special, top secret stealth technology Blackhawks) en route to Abbottabad. I enter through the forward passenger ladder and instinctively glance to my left, into the cockpit, like most of us do when we enter an airplane.

Hayowenta!

I'm supposed to be finding my place to sit so I can be in the correct order for fast-lining to the ground when we hit the target, but I can't. I'm frozen. When I come to my senses, I sneak forward and grab his shoulder.

"Bro!" I exclaim. "We're together on a mission! Love you, man!"

My team members are completely freaked out. What is going on here? We are about to risk our lives, and you have a man love thing going on with the pilot?

I can't help myself. I drop my stuff and go up there, into the cockpit. We have a man hug and we cry. Now the teams are even more freaked out.

After I break it off and make my way back to assume my place in line (second), my team members look weirded out. "You know the pilot? No way."

"He's my best friend from the UP," I explain. "Hayowenta Heywood. He's the one I always talk about. Wrestler, running back, woodsman. I haven't seen him since I enlisted. We've got the best possible guy to fly this thing. Nobody better at what he does. He says we're going in first. Our call sign is Chalk One. He says flying time is ninety minutes, most of it in Pakistan. Weather is like we thought. Dark, no moon, perfect for night vision goggles. We're flying in low, under the radar, and fast."

Ten minutes later, we lifted off. The air was smooth. It was pitch black. Back on the job! They had me just inside the door. Noisiest place on the chopper, but at least it wasn't open. The next thing I remember was a call over the intercom. Hayowenta's voice said, "Six minutes out." Six minutes? We just lifted off! Was I sleeping for the whole flight? I guess so. That's a good sign. A nice, refreshing nap before work. Fresh and ready to go. We came in low over the city. Nice neighborhood with lighted backyards and swimming pools. Most houses were dark inside, being after midnight. We started to slow down. The loadmaster opened the door, and we deployed the fast rope. Just about the time we cleared the privacy fence, which was 12-15 feet high in that spot, the turbulence increased exponentially. I'd never felt anything like it. In hindsight, I guess we created a maelstrom of agitated air with our rotors turning it into a whirlpool inside the abnormally small, closed-in environment. This was not like a normal helipad. More like landing in a giant blender. The deck started pitching violently. We were getting tossed around like a beach ball in class-five rapids. I could see Hayowenta's control stick moving around in a giant circular pattern. Later, he told me he tried to add power and get us out of there, but that just added to the disruption of the airmass. We would have flipped upside down, and we all would have been killed. He chose to rotate the tail over the fence, and drop the nose to the ground, so we were upright and hanging with the tail rotor on the fence, and the nose embedded in

the ground. It wasn't pretty, but we were upright with a six-foot jump
to safety. The news reported it as a crash, but it was a masterful job of
high-level airmanship in an unexpected situation. Get the commandos
on the ground, no matter how. That was Admiral McRaven's last order,
and that's what he did.

Everybody bailed out and we went charging toward the target, the
guest house. There was resistance. We could tell our fire from the enemy's since we all had suppressors and they didn't. They liked AK-47s,
and those have a unique sound. Somebody was in the house really unloading with an AK. I stopped and surveyed my troops. I yelled that
we were up against serious firepower, and right next to me, charging
the target unarmed was Hayowenta. "Hay, for Christ's sake, what are
you doing? You should stay with the chopper." He says, "The chopper
is dead. I might as well help you guys."

I'm like, "Here, at least take my pistol. You stay out here and pick
off escapees."

My kill was right inside the front door. It was Ahmed al-Kuwaiti.
He fell on his back, luckily, because it exposed the four magazines of
ammo in his vest. I picked them up and threw them out the front door,
along with the AK for Hayowenta. "Come on, bro; let's get them all!

"Get them all" was a terrible thing to say because a large population
of women and children were in there. In the big house, and in the guest
house, where al-Kuwaiti and his family lived. Luckily, nobody took me
at my word. In the heat of battle, they probably never even heard me.
Thank God. You can see how some "atrocities" originate. Fog of war.
Misinterpretation.

We cleared out the guesthouse women and children and removed
them to safety. There were probably wives and children of Bin Laden
up there with him. Our goal was now the surgical removal of the target, but we were now the second team.

After we gained control of the guesthouse and the first story of
the big house, our focus intensified. All the relevant obstacles were
removed. We have one objective remaining, the primary objective, the
purpose of the mission. Time to get upstairs and finish the job. But at
this point, we're the backup team. Chalk 2, who were supposed to land
on the roof of the main house, had to land outside the wall when they

saw us "crash." They breached a door in the twelve-foot wall to gain entry.

So we're going up the stairs behind Chalk 2 and somebody yells, "Khalid!" And there's a shot. Hayowenta says, "Well, if they missed the helicopter crash and the gunfight outside, they're ready for us now." Always the joker. We keep moving up the stairs. Our progress is slowing because everybody has to step over the dead body of Osama's son Khalid on the landing and continue on with slippery blood on their feet. We can hear them breach the door, and then it's bang, and then, bang, bang, bang! Women are screaming, and in moments of relative silence, a child is crying. Chalk 2 has gained entry, and between them and the women and children, and Bin Laden's dead body, there's no room for us.

"Well, that's it for the fighting. What do we do now?"

"Collection time. We need to get all the paperwork. Empty the file cabinets. Gather the discs and laptops." There was more than that, though—recorders, thumb drives, memory cards, DVD recorders. They were mostly all here on the second floor, which seemed to be the office.

Everybody had a collapsible net bag with them for carrying this stuff away with us. The problem was we had got twenty-four guys and all these bags now filled with confiscated data and equipment, but only one Black Hawk left. Somebody better radio for one of the Chinooks to come in and get us out of here.

In the middle of our data acquisition job, Chalk 2 comes downstairs. The first group had the wives and children. They're all in shock. They wound up in the guesthouse where the first group had been. Next thing coming through is going to be the corpse. I squeezed Hayowenta's shoulder and nodded toward the staircase. We ran up the stairs to get a look at the scene. It was our only chance to admire the team's work and get a firsthand look at the layout of the room and the space involved. A snapshot to remember. He really was tall, just like they said. You could tell that, even with him lying there dead. His beard was shorter than in the pictures, with streaks of gray in it. Later, the guys said there was a bottle of Just For Men in the bathroom. Probably for when he did DVDs. The side of his head was pretty much exploded with brains leaking out onto the floor. Somebody had finished him with shots to the heart or thereabouts, as if he needed finishing after that head shot. I guess that was the bang-bang-bang-bang we heard after the first shot. Classic case of overkill. It was definitely him, though. The nose and mouth were unmistakable. The Chalk 2 guys were taking DNA samples. At least that's what it looked like to me. What else was there to do with a body at that point?

I'm really glad we went up there and looked. It gave me a sense of accomplishment in a vivid way I would never forget. I didn't get to pull the trigger, but this was the next best thing. I was there. I was on the team. I got my man on the first floor, and the special bonus was it was my first and maybe my only operation with Hayowenta, through a series of coincidences. The craziest one being that our helicopter had to crash to put us together, on the ground in battle. A pilot and a SEAL. What are the chances of that?

So, we helicoptered back to Bagram with our intelligence booty and Bin Laden's corpse in the body bag. Later, he was buried somewhere in the Arabian Sea within twenty-four hours, according to Muslim custom.

After a debriefing session and sixteen hours of dreamless sleep, I was back on the C-17 en route to NAS Oceana, and back to my apartment in Virginia Beach in time for the Orioles game on TV.

Chapter 10
Hayowenta

I AM HAYOWENTA HEYWOOD, WARRANT OFFICER, US Army. I serve
in the 160th Special Operations Aviation Regiment, the Night Hawks.
Our job often involves joint operations with Quick Reaction Forces,
like the SEALs and Delta Force troops. I enlisted after 9/11. It was eight
years after the Battle of Mogadishu, which was the milestone event
for us Black Hawk pilots. It was our "never again" moment, which
cost us two UH 60 Black Hawk helicopters and dozens of casualties,
including nineteen killed in action. I think every American alive at
the time remembers the footage of American bodies mutilated and
hung in public view. In the long term, even though it was a Pyrrhic
victory, it strengthened us as a unit. I know I am personally committed
to never allowing myself a lax moment, to retain the highest standard
of airmanship in all situations, especially in battle, because I know
what can happen. It's easy to fall into complacency or overconfidence,
especially when you're a twenty-something-year-old military pilot.

I thought I would be included in the *Maersk Alabama* rescue mission, but the Navy supplied its own helicopter. I did get included in
Operation Neptune Spear, though, and it came out successful in the
end, even though nothing seemed to go right at thc time. The worst
part was I had to crash land the only time in my career. In my defense,
we were more than 4,200 feet in elevation. Not as high as Leadville, but
still, it's thin air, and that means less lift. The compound was only an
acre, including the houses, and the high walls held all our rotor wash
within. I've never been in anywhere near as much turbulence that close
to the ground. As soon as I realized we were in a deadly situation, I

tried to go around and set down outside the compound, but as soon as I added power, the turbulence went exponential and the aircraft went out of control. We were in a roll axis of almost sixty degrees side to side. There was no way to land normally. I made a split-second decision to hook the tail rotor on the wall and drop the nose in the dirt. That way, we could all jump about six feet to the ground and get on with the mission. Well, they could. I was unarmed and unarmored. I finally decided I might as well go in with the team anyway. Maybe a weapon would fall into my hands somehow, or I could at least be an extra set of eyes. No sense just standing around with a crashed chopper. After the attack, on our way out, the aircraft had to be destroyed to protect against revealing top secret technology to the enemy. They blew it up with several plastic charges. It takes a lot of explosive power to destroy a Black Hawk. It was going to be a glass-breaking concussion within that walled compound. I felt for the kids in the guesthouse going through that with no warning, especially after what they'd been through already. We were either making peaceniks out of them, or America haters for life. Probably the latter, considering the culture they were going to be brought up in.

Here's how it went down. We were prepositioned with two Blackhawks on the ramp at Bagram AFB, in Jalalabad, Afghanistan, with orders to transport two twelve-man teams of US Navy SEALs to Osama bin Laden's secret compound in Abbottabad, Pakistan, with the goal of assassinating him. Officially, it was termed a "capture or kill" mission, but I know those SEALs, and I don't believe they had any intention of capturing him. It doesn't suit our purposes to try him in a court of law and provide him with the witness stand as his podium for Islamist propaganda. I'm not saying a trial was one of the options for the Obama Administration, but it was a strong rumor. Even imprisoning him at Guantanamo provides the terrorists motivation for kidnapping as a means to get him released. We have paid them off with important Gitmo prisoners in the past.

So, we're waiting there on the ramp, ready to start engines once the SEAL team loads up. No way we were going to wait, burning Jet-A at idle power with fuel such a critical issue. As it was, even with full tanks, we were going to need refueling for the trip back to Bagram. We had one Chinook outfitted as a tanker for that. He would wait for us in the desert outside Abbottabad.

Right on schedule, a bus pulls up with the SEALs. We had them load up through the forward passenger door. I called tower for clearance and we started engines. The copilot is reading the After Engine Start Checklist, and we're halfway through the overhead panel, when somebody squeezes my shoulder. That's how SEALs communicate in the dark when they are in silent mode. It distracted me, and I turned around to tell him to go aft and find a place to sit.

Forrest!

There are about 2,500 SEALs stationed around the world. What are the chances Forrest would be on this mission, let alone in my aircraft? We both yelled and hugged. I think it freaked out his teammates. I briefed him on the flight time and weather conditions en route and at destination.

I flew at 200 feet and 160 knots. There was just starlight, no moonlight. I knew all the obstacles and military outposts. I was mostly concerned with the Pakistani Air Force. What if they think we're invading from, like India, and they scramble F-16s? We're toast! It went off fine, though, and we got there right on schedule, and found the compound right away. It was the biggest place in the Bilal neighborhood. Chalk 2 was right with us, in close trail formation. We were to land in the compound. Chalk 2 was going to land on the roof of Building A. Osama lived on the third floor. We needed to take the guest house and kill Ahmed al-Kuwaiti and his guards. Al-Kuwaiti was the courier the CIA followed to the compound when they finally achieved their goal of locating bin Laden. Since UBL didn't communicate electronically from the house, al-Kuwaiti was his link to the outside world. He would send and receive messages elsewhere, then come back to his guesthouse home and wait for more. The CIA followed him home. Once they knew the house, they set up surveillance from above. Drones, aircraft, and satellite. They got high definition images of an unusually tall individual who made a daily habit of walking the grounds. They named him "The Pacer." When the CIA gave us our briefing in Washington, I asked the question: "How sure are you that this is UBL?" The female agent who spent ten years of sixteen-hour days searching for him replied, "One hundred percent."

We came in hot, slowed over the compound yard, deployed the fast rope, and attempted to hover. I've already told you what a disaster that turned out to be. It didn't take long to realize this was a hopeless situation. That was when I felt like I was being telepathically coached by Admiral McRaven. "Get them on the ground any way you can." I love my Black Hawks. I've never put a scratch on one in my whole career with the exception of that night. Funny, though, it didn't bother me a bit to munch that thing. You know the rest of the story. Our attack on the two buildings. Forrest flinging me an AK-47 and ammo. Kind of a spooky situation with me potentially firing an enemy weapon. Could have got me killed by friendly fire.

Actually, considering all the stuff that went wrong, Neptune Spear was a spectacular success. We took no casualties. There was no human collateral damage, unless you think that Bushra al-Kuwaiti, Abrar's wife, was an innocent civilian, which she wasn't. The other wives and all the kids were uninjured, except one of Osama's wives, who was shot in the calf. On the other hand, we killed the most dangerous Islamist terrorist in the world, and his henchman, for a murderous act of ideological hatred. They killed 2,977 innocent civilians going about their daily business. We killed five al-Qaeda terrorists, including the founder and leader, for committing that crime.

Chapter 11
Minnie and Danci

STARTING OUT, WE STAYED IN the casino on the employee discount. Back in those days, they didn't charge much for rooms because of all the money they made on gambling, and we got a discount on top of that cheap rate. The room charge was an incentive to get gamblers to Vegas. Once they got the tourists in town, the money came pouring out of their pockets. It was perfect for us since we didn't believe in gambling. One time we stayed at the Nugget for $17 per night. As long as we were coming out from the UP for short gigs, it was the perfect situation. If we ever got our own show, or a steady gig, it would be cheaper to get an apartment. As time went on, we made more and more trips, and Uncle Dakota started putting on the pressure to get us to Vegas for good.

Our first night in Las Vegas was when we opened for Buffy Sainte Marie. This was pretty intimidating. There was a big difference between the St. Kateri Tekakwitha Catholic Church, where we got our start, and the Mohegan Sun Casino. Now, instead of a country church with a normal congregation at ten in the morning, it was the main showroom at a Las Vegas Casino at nine-thirty at night. A real Green Room dressing area. Our own toilet. All the noise and excitement of the main gambling area, with the slot machines chiming away, and the scantily clad waitresses. I could tell right away what Mom was talking about back home. This is an unhealthy place for kids. Not nutritionally unhealthy, but spiritually. But now, for us at eighteen, our biggest problem was guys coming on to us inappropriately. In a way, we would have been better off with an apartment, a place we could call home, instead of living our entire Las Vegas life within a casino. We had fun, though. There was a large luxurious swimming pool with no limitations on time of day. The restaurants and snack bars were open all the time. There was tennis down the street, which was okay except summer afternoons when it was 115 °F. That was the biggest change for me. No more dinner at six and bedtime at nine-thirty. Except for singing, our schedule was wide open. No telling what might have happened without Kamali or Hiawatha there to keep an eye on things. Before, it was a daytime show once or twice a week in the UP. Now, it was a show at 7:30 p.m. and another at 9:30 p.m. every night. When Buffy left to go on the road, other acts came through wondering about us, and whether we could be their opening act. We were starting to get generic, in a way. Not just concentrating on our Native American heritage so much. We kept the Chippewa Girls name and some of the Native American songs, but we branched out into pop ballads (not too pop), and stuff like "A Million Dreams" and "Tennessee Waltz" that featured our unique style of harmony.

Bonnie Raitt came through Vegas and went to Uncle Dakota about us singing with her. She heard us singing "Tennessee Waltz" from backstage, and it moved her. She loves the song. Later, she would make a viral video of her and Nora Jones doing it. We were first, though, and it brought down the house. One night, Bonnie finished up her show and looked out in the audience, where the two of us were taking it in from the orchestra seats. Sometimes we grabbed empty seats to get the audience perspective on how a really good show pulled it off, and how we should try to look to the audience. We found two seats, stage left, fifth row, and she saw us.

"Ladies and Gentlemen, I see two talented young women out there named Minnie and Danci. Let's get them up here to join me in one of my favorite songs. Come on! Let them hear you! Minnie and Danci, get up here!" The house broke into long and persistent applause. We really had no choice, at that point. The applause got louder when we got to our feet and made our way to the stage.

Bonnie gave us the key, which was the one we always sing "Tennessee Waltz" in anyway, and started it off with her guitar. Now, you have to understand that we never sang with anybody but each other, so my stomach was full of butterflies. She sang the first verse solo, and then we joined in. It was the biggest and most surprising event of my life because the three of us blended perfectly, and our harmonics really complemented her voice. It was like our little duo got supercharged. There's no recording of it, but if you use your imagination, and try to add in a third voice, a high soprano, you can watch the Bonnie and Nora video and get an idea of the sound. It was a sold-out night, and the nine-thirty show, so the audience probably had a few drinks in their system, which didn't hurt. When the last note died out, there was an explosion of applause and cheers. It so startled me that I actually jumped. I looked out through the glare of the stage lights, and they were all on their feet, whistling and yelling for "MORE! MORE! MORE!" Nobody knew they had just heard the only thing the three of us could do together. After a couple of curtain calls, Bonnie announced, "The Chippewa Girls! Minnie and Danci!" and we exited stage left.

There was no way we were getting our seats back, so we just went out the stage door and made our way around to the main entrance and up the elevator to our room. Neither of us slept that night. Speaking for myself, the electricity coursing through my veins made my breathing irregular and my heart rate went through the roof.

First thing in the morning, I dialed Mom's room and said we had to come up and see her. When we walked into the room, she noticed our states of mind immediately, and unbelievably, she confessed. "I know! I was there last night in the last row." She came to all our shows with a backstage pass, but who would have thought she would buy a ticket to a Bonnie Raitt show. Turns out, she's a big fan. Up till then, I never paid any attention to what she listened to or who she liked besides us. That night she came backstage, but we were already gone, so she checked the room and saw the "Do Not Disturb" sign.

"I really thought hard about knocking," she said, "but that whole scene was so stupendous, I just figured you should have that time to yourselves, and we could talk when you were ready."

"Thanks, Mom. That experience had a huge effect on both of us. We're changed for life. We know who we are and what God put us on this earth to do. To say we are energized would be the understatement of all time. We stayed up all night and talked about it. There's no way we're going back to the UP. We're sorry, but we are eighteen now, and we're staying here and devoting ourselves to our career. We hope you and Dad can stay too, or come for long visits. Uncle Dakota had already offered us full-time pay at union scale, and he says all kinds of acts want us to open for them. He might want to try us for our own show, but we don't know that yet. Then we have to go on a full-time search to see if we should have our own band, and maybe a third singer. Maybe an agent. We've got enough income for a small apartment close by and everything else we need for this life. Even enough for a savings account."

"Okay, kids, after last night, I can't argue for the UP anymore. We were already thinking about spending more time here because your dad has been getting offers to sing backup baritone for some groups. Well, one group in particular. It's a recreation of The Four Freshmen, and they like his baritone. The regular guy has health problems."

"The four who?"

"The Four Freshmen. It's a quartet that started in the 1940s. They sang with all the old Big Bands like Woody Herman and Dizzy Gillespie. Then they had a career on their own. They're still performing with new singers added through the years as the old ones retire. Just the four of them. Google them, or watch them on YouTube."

Dad was going to try it for a while. If it turned out to be permanent, he would give up being Chief of the Ojibwa, which he always thought would be his life's work. The tribe depends on him for lobbying in Washington. He's got to find a replacement with political skill, one who knows how to raise money, preferably a young man. It's all up in the air right now. He can't leave the tribe hanging. That would be immoral. A sin, even.

"Holy moly! Dad is singing in Las Vegas like us? This is unbelievable!"

"Well," said Mom, "he did have his time on Broadway, and he is very comfortable on stage. He liked it, and he liked being part of the cast. This is the same kind of thing."

So we stayed, and we found our apartment. It was a one bedroom, which was fine, since we've been sleeping together in the same bed since birth. We registered to vote and got our driver's licenses. We were

officially Las Vegans! The Mohegan Sun staff knew us from our resi-
dency there. They liked us. To the older ones, we were like their kids.
There was the Native American thing too. Uncle Dakota had brought
in Potawatomis from Connecticut, and there were Navajos who mi-
grated up from the big reservation down by Four Corners. So we had
a brotherhood. People, Mom included, take Las Vegas for a superficial
place, and it probably is for the visitors. It wasn't for us, though. Sure,
we missed the rugged, glacially eroded wilderness of the UP, studded
with its myriad blue lakes. It will always be in our blood, but this was
here and this was now for us. The gurus say, "Live in the present." It's
especially important when you're performing an intense and complex
job. So we lived in the present, and tried to keep getting better. We
added songs, and built a large repertoire we could draw from and sing
from memory any time an occasion would come up. We added Bonnie Raitt's hits just in case she ever came through again. "Something
to Talk About," "Nick of Time." They were hard-hitting songs with a
heavy beat. Not like "A Million Dreams."

For you twins like us out there, tell me something. Do you think of
yourselves sometimes as part of one person instead of two? That's got
to sound really strange to you single sperm, single egg people, but my
natural answer when people ask me my name is "We are Minnie and
Danci." We each have to consciously stop ourselves when the other's
around. Now, we're fraternal, so we're single sperm people too, in a
way. Single sperm, each in our own egg, but birthed at the same time,
or almost at the same time. It must be even more of a feeling of unity among identical twins. It really helps our singing that we think so
much alike. We anticipate each other's thoughts all the time. We can ad
lib together right in the middle of a song. When we were starting out
as kids, if one of us hit the wrong note, or a pitchy note, we both did.
I'm grateful that we're fraternal because our voices are a little different.
Minnie's a high soprano, and I'm a regular one. That's what gives us our
harmonic ring that's so unique. If you asked me my dominant philosophy in life, it would be gratitude. Every time I walk out on that stage,
I thank God. How many eighteen year olds have a full-time career that
they're actually making a living at, and that they know will be their
life's work?

Chapter 12
Keep America

Visiting the Little Bighorn

AT COLUMBIA, SOME OF MY friends nicknamed me "Kiki" to keep it short. When people get introduced to me, they acknowledge Keep America in various ways. Some are straight-faced, like the social science majors, who are taught to be painstakingly sensitive to people's feelings. I could just watch their insecurity over something unexpected like a crazy-sounding name. Their minds are going "Is it a joke?" "Is it political?" "Could it be racist?" English majors wanted to know why my parents chose it and searched for symbolism. Psych majors thought it was cruel and an example of bad parenting. I was probably damaged, even if I didn't think so. The jocks were guaranteed to make it a joke, no matter what. "At least it's not Keep America Red, or Kreepy America." I thought of some of my own, like Krie instead of Brie, or Kerry or Kagey, but they didn't seem right. I accepted Kiki at Columbia, but now I was at Cal Tech and a graduate student. I needed dignity. I decided on Kamara, Kam for short. That didn't stop me from being Keep America, but it gave me a way to present myself professionally in a more conventional but exotic way.

I met some of the most impressive students, listened to the best lectures from the finest science professors on earth, took part in stimulating seminars on subjects like wave functions, probabilities, and quantum tunneling. I took my books to the beach at Santa Monica on the days when LA traffic wasn't as awful as usual. Pasadena is right at the foot of the San Gabriel Mountains, and you can be in nature quickly, using the Santa Anita Trail road to the Angeles National Forest. Big Bear and Lake Arrowhead aren't far, and then there's Desert Hot Springs and Palm Springs out in the Coachella Valley. It's just the crush of people, in Los Angeles Basin itself, that got to me, though. The frenetic pace of life. The eight lanes of traffic everywhere you go filled with what seems like bumper-to-bumper traffic at eighty miles per hour. Nobody drives the speed limit. They're good drivers, and they're used to the conditions, but for a country girl from the boreal wilderness, it's an alien world. I met some nice guys and I went on some dates, but nothing magnetic happened. By the fifth date, it was usually over.

I thought I was following Mandelbrot to Cal Tech so I could figure out how to be his protégé, maybe by being his grad assistant, doing his grunt work, if advanced mathematics and theoretical computations can be considered grunt work. The problem was, he accepted the position of Sterling Professor of Mathematical Sciences at Yale, and was here to deliver a one-time lecture, open to the public, and teach one more semester on fractal geometry to the post-graduate students. Then he was to return to Yale. Later on, I attended his TED Talk in 2010, just before his death.

I talked myself out of introducing myself to him at Perkins and again several times in the dining room at the Student Union because I didn't have anything substantive to say. During my semester as his student, I never had a personal relationship with him. He didn't have a grad assistant and didn't want one. He delivered his lectures and left the room. He didn't take questions, and didn't engage personally with anyone. Totally aloof. After his last lecture, he said "Goodbye" and left. That was my relationship with Benoit Mandelbrot.

That night, sitting in my dorm room, I reflected on my goals. If the relationship with my idol was no longer a factor, what was I doing on this campus, spending all this money in expensive California and paying money to live in a dorm room and eat cafeteria food? I could do everything online, including all the coursework and seminars. I could go back to the Chippewa Club, live in Green Cabin for free, and go all the way through to PhD, if I wanted, or almost all the way. The atmosphere here on this beautiful campus was inspirational, and personal contact with some of the smartest people on earth is invaluable, but what about doing the bulk of the work at home, and then coming back to complete the degree in the last semester? I was already a registered student at the school. My GPA was 4.0. I could be like my friend Francesca. She did 90 percent of her coursework at California State University Chico, an ordinary school meant for average students. She transferred her straight As to Cal Tech, and got her Cal Tech BA in one semester. Think of the money she saved, and the courses she took were probably easier at Chico. After graduation, nobody knows the difference. She's got her sheepskin, and it's an impressive one: 4.0 GPA from California Institute of Technology. Well, I guess the academic world would know if she chose to get other advanced degrees; they evaluate the transcripts, but the prospective employers don't always ask for them, and after graduation, associates and clients don't know. I'm just saying, especially if I come back and do the last part in person, and do the commencement ceremony, it's the best of both worlds.

So, I finished the semester, maintained my 4.0, and put my stuff together for the trip back to the UP. Same basic style of travel as on the way out, except this time I pulled a U-Haul, the smallest one they had, for the personal stuff I accumulated. My plan was different this time. I really thought hard about speed versus substance, and the Little Bighorn battleground finally convinced me to go back the north route. Highway 80 was really tempting. Much faster through the southern Plains States to Chicago. It would probably save two full days, but it's the main east-west route for trucking. My friends all use it, but it's not scenic. Hundreds of miles of wheat waving in the wind like an ocean is beautiful, but monotonous. In the end, it was the semi-trailers that convinced me. They travel together in herds, like horses, and slipstream off of each other so you have to deal with the combined slipstream when you pass a herd, and it yanks you sideways. They tend to drive aggressively, and they like to tailgate on the downslopes. Also, you don't go through any interesting towns. There's the gas stations, truck stops, and chain motels just off the interstate at the exits, sometimes big box stores too (small versions of them), and if there's a town, it's a mile or two off the road. They're almost like ghost towns. The motel and restaurant employees from out by the interstate might still live there, but the towns are depleted down to skeletons with boarded-up hardware stores and gas stations, maybe a small grocery with no produce section. My butt gets tired like everybody's does, so saving two days would help that, but the Little Bighorn seduced me.

I bought a book that my nephew Hayowenta recommended. *A Terrible Glory* by James Donovan. It's a detailed account of the Battle of the Little Bighorn from both perspectives, including maps. Perfect preparation for the visit. I learned that the Crow were allied with the Union Army, being traditional enemies of the Sioux. How many people know that Indian scouts fought with Custer? Well, the Crow scouts let him know that the Sioux were coming, and they fought with him when they arrived. The Arikara scouts were Custer allies too, and they fought. They were recruited and they enlisted in the Union Army. They were issued uniforms and weapons.

The Lakota Sioux came for Custer with their Arapaho and Northern Cheyenne allies, and thanks to his scouts, he was ready for them, not that it did him any good in the end. I'm devoting a full day to touring the battlefield. I have a visual impression of the valley in my imagination, with its rolling grassland and river valleys. I guess we all have that image in our minds, what with all the Western movies and their silhouettes of mounted Sioux braves along the tops of the cliffs, controlling the high country, looking down on the enemy.

As long as I'm committed to the northern route, I'll be able to transit Yellowstone again too. There's some of the best fly fishing in the world up there, and farther north on the Gallatin and Madison rivers. Now that's the way to save my aching butt. Not the fast route. The long route with plenty of stops. No more ten-hour days. Four driving hours a day max, and some days with no driving at all.

The accessible stuff I have with me in the car includes the new Apple iPhone with camera and my regular Nikon with telephoto zoom. I also have my sheath knife, which I depend upon to brandish in case of road rage attacks or robbery attempts. I keep the guitar on the backseat on top of the extra blanket, for easy access on rest stops and motel layovers. In the trunk are the .410 and ammo, the hatchet, the tent, and my air mattress. I keep a tote on the right front floor in front of Birdie. It's got what I need in the motel room, and what I want to access when underway. My toiletries and a set of clean clothes, a week's worth of undies and socks (on days when I wear socks), and the book I'm reading. Granola bars stay in the tote too, so Birdie doesn't pilfer them. There are scratches all over the glove box door from when I left jerky in there.

I planned to be on Interstate 10 eastbound before 5 a.m. to avoid the toxic LA traffic. Probably not necessary, since I was in the reverse commute direction, but I love an early start anyway. I was out of the LA basin and approaching Ontario when the sun broke the horizon. That gave me a blinding headache for the first hour, till the sun got high enough in the sky. Overall, my trip unfolded about the reverse of the original cross-country from New York to Pasadena. I stopped in the same places in Nevada and Utah, Motel 6. Same routine, same campouts, same Birdie, who didn't know yet that her life was about to change exponentially for the better. Even the trip through Yellowstone with its bison, elk, grizzlies, and wolf packs was similar but different. I got some great photos with the Nikon. One of a wolf pack relaxing around their elk kill, cleaning the blood off their faces, and one big black one (alpha male?) with his snout pointed to the sky, howling. I fished the Yellowstone River in the shadow of the Grand Tetons. Caught a nice rainbow and roasted it on a stick over the campfire. Nothing better.

The Little Bighorn was unique, though. I stayed in Sheridan the night before, and I arrived in Crow Agency right when the Battlefield Monument opened. The book really prepared me to make the most of my visit. They have a little grandstand—bleachers, really—which is covered to protect us from sun and rain. We sat there together, we tourists from different places in the world. There were about twenty of us. Then the ranger on duty started his presentation. It was a very cool lecture, because there he was, talking about what happened in 1876, and he could point out to the hill where the Crow encampment was, and where the scouts stole the Sioux horses, and stand there and point out Last Stand Hill, right in front of us. When the lecture was over, we got to walk the mile-and-a-half loop and see the gravestones where the soldiers and Sioux warriors fell and were buried, including Custer. There's a nice monument to the Sioux warriors with all their names in a steel sculpture, and even a monument to the horses buried in a mass grave. I wonder if any other country in history has erected a monument honoring their individual enemy soldiers.

The basic story is George Armstrong Custer, who graduated last in his class at West Point, thought 750 Union Soldiers would have no problem annihilating 2,500 Sioux and their allies. He was so overconfident that he left his artillery behind for being too unwieldy. He was a mediocre commander who lost control of his supporting battalion commanders, Major Reno and Captain Benteen, allowing them to abandon their effort and fail to come to his aid.

I'm not a big battlefield tourist. My dentist is. Other people go to art museums and cafés in Paris. All her vacations are to battlefields. I don't know how many it might be. Some that I know she's visited are Shiloh and Gettysburg, Utah Beach, Anzio, Iwo Jima, and Khe Sahn. I'll probably never visit another one, but Little Bighorn moved me. You can look at it from so many different perspectives. Manifest Destiny. The injustice of the Indian Wars of the 1870s. The conquest, subjugation, and relocation of the tribes, the unique revenge of the Native Americans. The glorious battle against all odds, the Pyrrhic victory. It makes for a revealing exposure of human nature during a period of conflict. More than anything, it discloses the stark comparison of the European conquering culture, and the comparative simplicity of the various Native American cultures as a whole. Essentially, to the tribes, these new Blue Coats were just another tribe from a faraway unknown place, behaving as the Native American tribes always had. Conquering the more vulnerable culture and using their assets for their own purposes. They brought with them revolutionary weaponry, including rifles and horses, which the tribes quickly learned about and used with great effectiveness.

Before I go any further with this subject, I am going on the record with my personal history and personal attitude toward the Native American culture. I am from Ojibwa country. This statement is not one of those often ridiculed justifications for criticizing certain cultures, like "I have black friends." I have legitimately grown up within the Ojibwa culture. My brother-in-law is half-Ojibwa. I attended my sister's Ojibwa wedding. I have a useful and practical knowledge of the language. I can sing the songs and chants from memory. I respect many traits and values of the culture, including, first and foremost, courage and stoicism. All that said, the Native cultures were not noble savages, slaughtered and enslaved by the cruel xenophobic European invaders. Their cultures were based primarily on war. Their treatment of women and animals was disgusting. They, meaning all the tribes across the North American continent, were continuously at war with each other. They killed all the elders and unattractive women; they conscripted the military-age men and boys and took the young women as sex slaves. The universal act of scalping was ingrained as common practice, and one of the milder forms of cruelty. Kidnapping, rape, and slavery were fundamental parts of society. A large body of work was created by Christian missionaries about the nature of these cultures. Before you start rejecting their journals as inspired by their ingrained Christian bias and xenophobic prejudice, you have to consider the large number of them who acculturated into the tribes, learned their languages, took wives from these cultures, and raised children within them. An obscure book was written by one of those missionaries who joined the Ojibwa, was formally initiated by them, accepted as a tribal member, bestowed with an Ojibwa name, and established himself with an Ojibwa family. He lived and died within their culture. He describes the most-respected aspect of character as being stoicism within the most grueling circumstances. Torture was a common practice against prisoners of war, and it wasn't just a military tactic. It was a form of entertainment and recreation. Like most Indian cultures, the Ojibwa enjoyed smoking tobacco. The missionary author uses the following example. When they obtained a suitable subject, preferably an enemy warrior, they cut off his fingers one by one and smoked them in their pipes before enjoying them as food in front of him. The victim was expected to endure the process without any sign of distress, as a sign of his stoic character. If he remained strong and indifferent, he was rewarded with death. Any sign of weakness resulted in more perverse forms of cruelty.

The Ojibwa were not unique; the Sioux, Arapaho, and Cheyenne had their own forms of torture. A Union Army soldier's worst night-mare was capture. Among the Sioux, the likely forms were live burial, burning at the stake, and quartering. It's not hard to imagine the motivation of Custer's troops in their fight to the death. They were right. Since some of the elaborate methods were impractical on the battlefield, due to the confusion and turmoil of war, the Indian warriors satisfied themselves with simple mutilation. Later on, soldiers who submitted to capture found themselves the subject of entertainment in the various Indian camps. In this more leisurely environment, torture reverted to the time-honored methods of beheading, slow hanging, and all of the aforementioned cruelties.

People think every Union soldier in the battle died. That is not so, but it was not only Custer and his immediate party who fought to the death. The other battalions, led by Captain Benteen and Major Reno, survived, but not without casualties. Four Crow and two Arikara scouts died fighting with Custer's troops. Thanks to two Union Army columns commanded by General Alfred Terry and Colonel John Gibbon, acting as reinforcements, only five of the Seventh Cavalry's twelve companies were annihilated. A large number of survivors died of alcoholism after the battle, including Benteen and Reno.

Lt. Colonel George Armstrong Custer was a high-profile, vainglorious showboat, and his boastfulness and cockiness worked in his favor. Due to his frequent appearance in the press and among the general public, his self-promotion made him the 1876 version of a celebrity. He was held in higher esteem than he deserved, so his loss at Little Bighorn was perceived by his following in the civilian world as heroism. Benteen and Reno received harsh criticism for their failure to come rapidly to Custer's aid, and some accused them of pure cowardice. There is strong evidence that this treatment might have hastened their decision to drink themselves to death.

I allotted a day to the Little Bighorn Monument, but four hours was enough. I spent more time than the average visitor, studying the battle sites and reading the plaques, asking some detailed questions of the ranger who lectured us. I spent a lot of time at the Native American Memorial, studying images of the warriors, and reading their stories. I moved on in the early afternoon and spent the next few layovers reading *A Terrible Glory* for the second time.

Frackin' on the Bakken

The big political cause at Cal Tech was global warming. On campus, there weren't factions for and against fossil fuels. Students were united in their disrespect for the industry, and the struggle against it. The most evil of the perpetrators were the frackers. They ruined the groundwater; they collapsed the terrain by removing the support of oil and gas. People who had enjoyed the purity of a rural life now had gas-fueled fire erupting from their kitchen faucets. People were dying in record numbers of cancer. The cattle were dying. Their pastures were collapsing.

I did a little research and found that the epicenter of fracking in our part of the world was Williston, North Dakota, up by the Canadian border. It's in the center of the Bakken Formation. Right on my way to the Chippewa Club.

I thought, *Let's go see what's going on up there.*

So I looked around for a place to stay, and found a Motel Six, naturally. My and Birdie's routine was wake up at daybreak, go for a long walk together after Birdie's breakfast of kibbles, so she could evacuate her bowels and be comfortable for the long car ride, then I would have breakfast in a diner, the most greasy-spoon-looking, and the most likely to have habitual local patrons. Usually, I could identify lifelong residents willing (eager) to engage with a traveler from out of town, and I would ask to join them in their booth to learn about them and their culture. Williston was no different. I was obviously not a journalist with preconceived notions, or an activist with an agenda.

In Williston, the first citizen I met was Dave Earl. He was born and raised on a ranch (he called it a farm) just outside of town. Mother, father, six kids on sixty acres of land handed down through the generations. Idyllic upbringing from his perspective, but no way for the farm to support them in any semblance of prosperity. They ran some beef cattle for sale, and had the usual ranch animals and a garden for food. Chickens and their eggs, pigs for meat, garden for vegetables in a hostile environment with a short growing season. A lot of canning and pickling. He went to school in hand-me-downs, and he wasn't the second generation to wear them. He lived in third and fourth generation, handed-down clothes, and it was a source of excruciating humiliation.

"There's Dave in his aunt's T-shirt. Do you wear her undies too? Ha-haha!"

Dave told me the story of his family, and their experience with fracking. Here's how it went. About the time he realized his grades weren't good enough to go to college, and he wasn't a good-enough athlete for a scholarship, his dad made an announcement.

"You're probably wondering why I called you here today." It was the humorous lead-in he used for routine family meetings. Everybody knew it was just another announcement about who had what duty for the next week, but it wasn't.

"I got an offer from the Independent Dakota Petroleum Company last week. It seems our little property has a reserve of oil underneath it. Not only that, but because of certain regulations, we can be used as a site from which to angle drill into large deposits of crude oil under surrounding properties. They made me an offer to sell them the ranch for three million dollars. I consulted some experts, and they say to hold on to the farm and take a percentage off what oil they get. Anybody have an objection to looking into this further?" (Silence.)

Dave's plans for another monotonous day of farming exploded in his face. This was the single most impactful experience of his life, besides being born in the first place.

"No objections? Okay, let's look into the situation we've been presented. Since there are eight of us, the sale price of the farm would give each of us $375,000 before taxes, or a little over $280,000 after tax. That yields an income of about $14,000 a year, or $1,200 a month, each. For a family like us, that sounds like a lot of money for doing nothing, but we would give up the farm and each of us would have to find a place to live. You can't live on $1,200 a month, even in North Dakota. If we go our separate ways, we will all have to get jobs. Working on the rigs pays big time, but this boom will be over at some point."

The girls kicked in first. "No, Dad! We love this place. Keep us together. Tell them to shove their oil well where the sun don't shine. We were raised here, and we want to raise our kids here too. If you sell this place, we're raising our kids in an apartment in Williston. We already work extra jobs anyway. We can make it work."

"Wait, kids. What about letting them do the work, and we get the royalties?" Dad continued, "The second plan is to keep living here and let Independent Dakota run the drilling operation. We get 12.4 percent in royalties. It costs $7,000,000 to $10,000,000 to drill a well around here. Independent Dakota pays for that. Then, the average Bakken well pumps somewhere over a half-million barrels in its lifetime of forty years or so. He said the average is 600,000. The yield doesn't stay constant over time. It comes in big in the beginning, and then slowly decreases over time. There's no way to forecast the income it might produce—too many variables, the most obvious being the market price per barrel, which changes continuously. Right now, we're at $50 a barrel, and a well like ours would probably produce a hundred barrels a day. That's $5,000 a day, and we get 12.5 percent, which is $625 a day, or $18,750 a month, or $225,000 a year. Since there's eight of us, that's $28,125 a year, or $2,343.75 per month for each of us, before taxes. Plus, they say the boom is coming, and jobs will pay big time for the boys on the rigs."

The old man almost never left the farm, and he never watched the news. Dave had to fill him in on current events.

"Dad the boom is here! Shorty Davis decided to drop out of college and drive a truck in the oil field. He said he couldn't turn down forty."

"Well, I agree, $40,000 a year is serious money for a nineteen year old."

"No, Dad, not forty grand—forty dollars an hour, guaranteed forty-hour work week. That's over eighty grand before overtime, and there's all the overtime he could possibly want. He's making over two grand a week so far. That's over a hundred grand a year if he keeps it up! I've got my application in, and I'm hoping for an interview next week. Rig hand, roustabout, pumper, or drive a truck like Shorty—whatever they've got."

Dave's sister Sara was the most adamant holdout. "What will they turn our ranch into? Heavy equipment stirring up dust all day long? The smell of diesel exhaust every day? The equipment grinding away 24-7? It's like raising your kids on a battlefield."

Dave explained, "Sara, that's just the construction phase. They try to get it done as soon as possible. It's expensive work that's not producing income until the well is pumping. After that, it's just a steel dinosaur bobbing his head up and down. You've seen them all over the state. Not that bad. After a while, you won't even notice it."

"Well, I hope they don't put it right next to the house."

"We have to agree on where they put it."

So, that was a positive effect fracking had on Williston. Next, I went looking for environmental damage. Most of the people in Williston were happy with the booming economy. Middle class people had good-paying jobs. The immigration of oil field workers led to prosperity in the local business environment, and a whopping influx of tax money into the city's coffers. Parks were improved. A municipal swimming pool was built. The city and county agencies got newer and better offices. One night, I called in an order to the Chinese restaurant and went to pick it up. About twenty strapping young roustabouts were waiting in line for their orders. Two young Asian girls were handing out what looked like supermarket bags of food. When I got to the head of the line, they handed me a bag that had to weigh three pounds. It was sweet and sour pork with rice, and some won tons. That's all. It took me a day and a half to finish it. Roustabouts have big appetites.

I found the greasy spoon the farmers seemed to like on the outskirts of town. That's where I got personal reports of environmental issues. One fifth-generation farmer reported brine spills on his property. Brine is the term for wastewater that's a byproduct of drilling. It's supposed to be pumped into chambers deep underground where it leaches harmlessly into the surrounding strata, deep below the aquifers. The farmer found streaks of dead grass, which turned out to be leakage from tankers trucking small amounts en route to above ground storage. The most toxic ingredient of brine is radium, which can affect groundwater and streams for years after exposure. There were reports of leaching into creeks and streams. Over a period of three years, there were fifty disciplinary actions against producers, mostly fines. Representatives of the Health Department and the Department of Mineral Resources went on record saying the number of spills was acceptable, and both said they saw little risk of long-term damage. The spills were small, relatively benign, and cleaned up quickly. I found some young people at the youth center, and at a high school baseball game, and I stopped as many twenty-somethings as I could around town. Most of them shrugged it off as a non-issue. It didn't affect them personally, and they hadn't been indoctrinated on the college campus yet. Overall, the relationship between the frackers and the population was benign. The townspeople, on average, were willing to accept mild and short-term environmental damage in return for a vigorous economy. I guess if it was an open pit copper mine, or uranium mining, people would have been up in arms.

Jocko, the greasy spoon owner, let me know about the activists who came to town to educate the farmers and citizens about the dangers of fracking. The flaming kitchen water faucets, the collapsing country-side, the poisonous undrinkable water, the dying cattle producing con-taminated milk, the creeks and streams running orange with chemical pollutants. A few years earlier, they might have bought into the dysto-pian predictions, but at this point, they were veteran fracking "victims." First of all, the townspeople didn't cotton to the face tattoos and nose rings. They were mildly insulted by their self-assured pretension. "Not our kind of people." Secondly, fracking had been going on at one level or another for years, and everything was pretty close to normal. The activists' rants fell on deaf ears, and they left town after one afternoon.

Next time I run into a fellow college student with strident opinions on the evils of fracking, I will fill them in on my personal, on-site ex-perience on the Bakken Formation.

Entering the Boreal

The next day, Birdie and I departed for the Land of 10,000 Lakes, on our penultimate leg of the return journey. Wow, two days to go, and I'll be ensconced in the rustic magnificence of the magnificent Green Cabin. I imagine I can smell the pines and hemlocks of my beloved Chippewa Club as I gaze out across the final few miles of the North-ern Great Plains. From the vast expanses of rolling grassland to the embrace of the great Northern Boreal Forest, with its fragrant conifers and brilliant hardwoods. Little Car has held up in fine style. Five thou-sand miles at highway speed, plus all the city driving in Los Angeles hasn't affected her at all. She hardly burns any oil. I didn't keep track of mileage in LA, but cross-country, if you count both directions, it turned out to be 38.4 mpg, plus no maintenance, except tires and tune-ups. Not bad for a two-thousand-dollar car.

The Land of 10,000 Lakes, Minnesota, made me feel like I was home already. I couldn't wait till I got to the Chippewa Club to cast my first fly line in a year. When we passed through Bemidji, the biggest city in Northern Minnesota, I got my fishing license and asked where the best smallmouth spot was. The young man waiting on me said, "Go to Leech Lake and the Hiawatha Beach Resort. They'll rent you a boat. If you get up at first light before the wind comes up, you can cast poppers onto water smooth as glass. They'll hit like the beasts they are, come up two feet out of the water, and fight you for five minutes, minimum."

"Great!" I replied. "I've been in Los Angeles for almost a year, and that's too long between hookups. When I was back in the UP, one week of no fishing was too long. By the way, I have a personal question for you. You look like you're nineteen or twenty. Why aren't you working in the oil fields?"

"You're close," he said. "I'm still eighteen. My parents say I have to finish college. I can work after my bachelor's."

"In LA, where I just came from, a lot of kids would tell their parents to butt out and go do what they want."

"This is the Midwest. Kids obey their parents, even twenty year olds. Plus, they're paying full tuition for me to go to St. Olaf's so I can get into Harvard Law."

The robot on my shoulder said, "Tell them to butt out and make your own money in the oil fields," but I didn't say anything.

So, I found the Hiawatha Beach Resort and got a tiny rustic cabin. Now I was home in the Upper Midwest. The place was classic. Acres of mown lawn leading down to a coarse, yellow sand beach and its shimmering blue water. After unloading, it was time for a game of catch and retrieve with Birdie, then a swim together with the sunset in the background. Once I got her dried off, we retired to the dog-friendly lodge for drinks with our fellow guests. I told my story, and the others told theirs. A couple accompanying their daughter to Bemidji State University showed me photos they had taken of the beautiful campus along the lakeshore. An older couple from Massachusetts on a cross-country trip showed me their itinerary. They were going west along the northern route like I had. I told them to stop and see the Little Bighorn on their way to Yellowstone. They were returning through the Southwest. They were keen on the Grand Canyon and Santa Fe, then a trip through Texas and the Deep South.

In the morning, I took a canoe instead of the runabout. The primitive vessel seemed more appropriate to me since I was working my way into a Chippewa Club state of mind. Powered boats are not allowed there. I felt stealthy, too, in the gray light of pre-dawn, searching for underwater structure along the shore. Waterlogged, hollow tree trunks were a good hiding spot. Rock outcroppings and whole fallen trees were the best. I reverted to my time-tested method of tossing a small frog imitation as close to shore as I dared, then swimming it at an irregular tempo. Actually, my first cast produced an instant reaction as it hit the water. The bass exploded on the surface and headed for deep water. The fight lasted a full five minutes, just like my teenage friend told me. Five minutes and twelve spectacular jumps later, I landed a twenty-three-inch monster, probably four pounds, give or take. Not having a net, I picked him up by the lower lip, like Hiawatha taught me, removed the barbless hook, and tossed him back in, none the worse for wear. At the end of the outing, just after sunrise, I totaled six smallmouth bass, two largemouth (slower and less aggressive, almost languid by comparison), and a nice brook trout. I kept the largemouth and cooked him on the barbeque with lemon and butter. Then it was time for some guitar practice, some physics equations from my textbook on alternative universes, and bed. I fell asleep to my favorite soporific sound, a cricket symphony.

Morning brought our usual routine, with an even more leisurely breakfast than usual. I was determined to take in the sights and sounds of the forest I had sorely missed. The Los Angeles experience served to underscore my devotion to the boreal forest. It was my Holy Land, and the Chippewa Club was my cathedral. One last grind through the "civilized" streets of Duluth, Minnesota, and Superior, Wisconsin, and we were back in the homeland.

We cruised along at a comfortable pace, catching glimpses of Lake Superior through the trees. We were back in the land of small lum-

bering and mining towns with names like Gogebic, Ishpeming, and
Ontonagon. Here's where you hold out hopes for a moose or black bear
sighting along the road—so far no luck. Just the occasional road-killed
deer beset by the usual scavengers—crows, vultures, and eagles.

Somebody told me once that a dog's memory lasts about three minutes. National Geographic verifies it. I don't know how they're defining
memory, but as we drove up to the guard shack at the Chippewa Club,
Birdie's demeanor transformed from the casual indifference of the past
week to wild enthusiasm, bouncing back and forth between the seats
and scratching at the windows. It's got to be the scent.

It was Marv's shift again, just like the day I left. "Well, I'll be switched!
Gol darn if it ain't the Green girl. Welcome home! And there's the pup
too. Glad you kept her. I heard you was an actress in Hollywood. How
long you stayin' this time?'

"I'm here to stay, Marv. By the way, it was college, not Hollywood.
How do these rumors get started?"

The four miles from the entrance gate to the cabin is along a
well-maintained dirt and gravel road, graded regularly to a crowned
surface to accommodate the membership, employees, utility companies, and contractors who handled remodels and maintenance. Then
there were the food and fuel suppliers. One thing that wasn't supplied
from the outside world was firewood. There were fifty thousand acres
of it on the property.

Look at this place; what a transformation! This used to be the deep,
dark primeval forest with fragrant red and white pines, hemlocks, and
hardwoods. This was the last known bit of boreal forest that had never been logged. Theoretically, if the Europeans hadn't immigrated, the
whole Northern Midwest would still have been just like this. Nothing
grew beneath its canopy. You could walk miles through the soft carpet
of pine needles and moss in the darkness. It was truly deepest, darkest
forest, just like in the nursery rhymes. Now, the fire had created a beautiful, young, bright population of young trees. It was green everywhere,
with grass and wildflowers among the stands of aspen and birch. And
deer! With no forage available in the old growth, they had moved on to
agricultural land and managed forest. Now, herds of them were back.
Hopefully, the fire had spared a few pockets of the old, mature, un-

touched forest left, just for the members to experience, as a trip back in time.

I pulled up to the magnificent Green Cabin at 8:00 p.m. I unloaded my Motel 6 tote and personals, including reading materials, and left the rest for tomorrow.

"Okay," I said to myself, "now that I'm here, let's make contact with the rest of the original group. I wonder if Hayowenta and Forrest could take leave from the military and relive old times, before everybody takes off and gets married and starts a new life. Speaking of that, I hear the twins have a new life and a career in Las Vegas. Maybe they can visit too. Do Vegas musicians get time off? I don't know. I'm emailing everybody about joining me here. They have their current contacts in the office."

Chapter 13
Hayowenta

E VER SINCE OPERATION NEPTUNE SPEAR, I've been struggling with a career decision. When am I ever going to operate in a situation as challenging, dangerous, and fulfilling as that mission was? I don't see a lot of combat aviation in our future. Since I got back stateside, I've been upgraded to instructor pilot, and flown training missions with student pilots in an observational and teaching role, not even flying the aircraft, really, except the occasional demonstration for a guy who doesn't get it. I'm not really set up for a command position. Commander at any level is a desk job; it requires a promotion to commissioned officer grade, which is not easy, and it's political. You find the most upwardly mobile officer and ingratiate yourself with him, hoping to ride his coattails to success. I became a warrant officer to avoid the bachelor's degree; now I would have to get one to meet the basic qualifications of commissioned officer status. I could stay a warrant and try to make CW5, the highest warrant officer grade, but you have to accrue a wealth of technical knowledge and understand the military strategy at the brigade level and higher. It's a special skill set that not many people have. CW5 is the rarest of Army ranks There are 199 CW5s and 231 generals. I'm coming up on my second six-year service obligation. Do I get out with no retirement benefit and chase a civilian career, or put in my twenty years of service and retire? I've got a much better civilian equivalent than Forrest. I can fly medevac, law enforcement, and corporate aviation to name a few. Forrest, as a Navy SEAL, could transfer over to law enforcement too, and just by virtue of the elite status of the SEALS, a lot of corporate recruiters would give him extra scrutiny, but I still think my chance of finding a good quality job is better than his.

Just about the time I'm mulling all this over, I get an email from Keep America Green. How did she find me? She's up at the old Chippewa Club, and she's coordinating a reunion of all us kids who hung out together up there. I wonder if Forrest knows anything about this. Of course he does; she's his sister. I think he's at NAS Oceana near Virginia Beach. I'm emailing him.

A week later, I get a telephone call.

"Hayowenta, it's Forrest. Whatup, Blood?"

"Forrest, you got my email. What do you think? Are you going up to your sister's reunion? It would be great. We could swap war stories over some beers and relive our adventures hunting and trapping."

"Yeah, and gold mining. We can bring the fool's gold nugget and roll dice to see who gets it for the next ten years. Yeah, I'm going up. I put in for two weeks' leave. I decided to stay in the Navy and go for twenty years and retirement. I've been getting early promotions every time so far. I could get out as E6 and have a nice monthly income. I'd only be forty-two years old. How about you?"

"I'm getting out. I can make at least twice the money in the civilian world, and there are plenty of jobs. When you see me at the Chippewa Club, I'll be a civilian. Has anybody seen the twins?"

"They're still singing in Vegas, and so is my dad. He went out there to chaperone them, and he got hired to sing as one of The Four Freshmen."

"The four who?"

"The Four Freshmen. They were a group from the 1940s. In Vegas, they keep hiring new people to sing old songs by groups that are dead. The Four Tops, The Beatles, The Coasters. That's what Dad is doing."

"I'll be damned. Okay, find out when they can get off, and we'll all go up there together. I've already got some ideas of what to do."

"Well, you can have all the ideas you want, but your big sister is the boss. I'm doing as I'm told."

Chapter 14
Minnie and Danci's Travel Plans

Hiawatha and Kamali got the news of the reunion first. Right away, they put the pressure on Uncle Dakota. "Okay, Chief, we've gone along with your whole Las Vegas plan, and it's been great for us. We will always be grateful for your persistently coaxing us from our comfortable nest in the UP and setting our daughters up in the career of their dreams. Now we need to ask you a favor. Find a way to give us two weeks off this next month. You can make it first two, middle two, or last two, but we're taking them off for a family reunion at the Chippewa Club."

"Last two."

"Okay, we're starting our plans right now."

So, that was the final decision, and that is how the seven Chippewa Club friends wound up on the most mysterious excursion in the history of the Upper Peninsula.

Chapter 15
Reunion

H AYOWENTA AND FORREST COORDINATED THEIR arrival in Chicago so they could ride to Joliette Airport together on the regional carrier and share the Chippewa Club van once they arrived in the UP. When they got to the guard shack, Herb was on duty.

"Well, I'll be damned. Here's two young studs I ain't seen in years. Back from your tours of duty. Nice to see that Army and Navy still talk to each other. Maybe that's my new nicknames for you two, Army and Navy. Here, put your John Hancocks on the sign-in sheet and your date of departure. It doesn't have to be exact. Just your best guess. It's a formality, plus it gives the kitchen a rough idea of how much food to order. Forrest, or should I say Navy, your big sister is here in Green Cabin. So, what's the plan? Fishing? Camping? You two ought to set up a skeet tournament. You'd dominate all the civilian hot shots!"

"We're here for gold mining," said Forrest.

"Well, good luck with that, the only gold ore around here is more than a thousand feet down. The Algonquins got all the surface ore five hundred years ago."

"Navy was just telling an inside joke, Herb," said Hayowenta. "We panned Magic Stream for gold when we were kids together. All we got was one fool's gold nugget. I've got it on my dresser in the cabin, in a jewel box. Maybe we should cut it in half with a hacksaw, but that means you owe me fifty cents of the buck I gave you, Forrest."

"No way."

"I guess my answer was right about what we're here for," Hayowenta continued. "Let's go back to Magic Stream and get another nugget to go with the one we already have. Then we'll both have one. It would be reliving the past, like a reunion should be."

"Okay, we're signed in," said Forrest, returning the paperwork to him. "Thanks, Herb. We're staying at Green Cabin if anybody asks."

Next to arrive were Hiawatha and Kamali with the twins. Herb was ready for them.

"Mr. Hiawatha, your new cabin is opened and cleaned, ready for occupancy. I think you're going to like it. Ed Bullis is the best log home builder in the country. Can you sign in please? But more importantly, I need autographs from the two celebrities in the backseat. I hear they're the stars of their own show in Las Vegas."

The twins autographed for Herb a first draft of an arrangement they were writing for Ms. Winona to score.

"Thank you, girls. I can't wait to come to Las Vegas and see your show."

So now, the reunion participants were all on the property. It consisted of Keep America, Hiawatha, Kamali, Hayowenta, Forrest, Minnie, and Danci. Let's see what Keep America has in mind.

In the morning, they all wandered into the Club dining room one or two at a time. Not enough people for steamer trays, so the waitress took individual breakfast orders.

Fine dining!

When everyone was done eating, Keep America announced her plan.

"I'm going for recreating our childhood experiences here, so here's what we're going to do:

"Remember the Red Pine Lake swim test? We all had to swim from the middle of the lake, clothed, to shore, in order to qualify for the sailing club. Theory being, any sail boater should be able to reach shore from a capsized boat, or more critically, from falling overboard off a boat that sails away. We'll reenact that swim test, but this time it will be timed, and there is a prize.

"Remember the five-mountain climb? We climbed the five highest and most difficult peaks on the property, including Mt. Argon, all in one day. We'll do it again, but this time, those who finish get a prize.

Oh, and the two military guys each get to wear a forty-pound pack. Sorry, boys!

"Remember the Club Road Run? We'll start at the Club House and run to the gate and back. Four miles each way. Sound like fun? There's a prize.

"Then there's the fishing derby. A hundred bucks for the biggest northern pike out of any lake you choose.

"This next one pains me, and I'm trying to figure out a way to handicap it. It's the skeet shoot."

"Wait, Keep America," Danci said, "we have a trap house now. You can shoot trap from different distances. We normal people shoot from sixteen feet, and the military experts from farther back, like twenty or twenty-five."

Forrest piped up. "Wait a minute. Just because we're qualified with the M-16 doesn't mean we can shoot trap any better than the rest of you."

He was overruled. "Sixteen for us, twenty-seven for you."

"Then, once the competition is over, it will be time for brotherhood and sisterhood. We camp out on the little island that saved us in the big forest fire, where the Heywood family felt protected, as if by a sentient being. Where we felt as if we were being drawn into the arms of a protective mother. We can have songs and drums and Ojibwa chants. I'm not being a phony spiritual materialist here; we're not hippies. I just want us to finish up as a spiritually connected group and take home a feeling of unity, connectedness, and universal love."

Hiawatha decided to assume the senior role of the athletic competitions, something like being a coach. "When I was your age," he said, "I would have dominated all of you, but now I'm the elder of the group, so I'll supervise. Keep America, what event comes first?"

"Well, I figure the fishing derby comes last; we can sit in a boat all day when we're all worn out from the physically demanding stuff. Plus, we'll have fresh fish for the campsite to go with whatever we order from the kitchen, like steaks and hot dogs. Forrest even knows how to fillet a northern pike and avoid the bones, a special talent. We can probably do the trap shoot the same day, it being a short event—maybe an hour or two. That way, we can listen to the war heroes brag about their prowess with firearms."

Hayowenta got to his feet. "Just a minute, Keeper. (That's what you are, by the way, a real keeper.) You guys are playing this military stuff up too much. I haven't touched a firearm since basic training. I'm a pilot. Forrest is the one who gets all the requalification training at the firing range every month. I'm going to accept the challenge and shoot back there from twenty-seven yards with him, but don't expect to see me bragging and kissing the trophy, up on the podium. There is a trophy, right, Keeper, and a podium?"

"You'll see what the prize is when you win it," Keep America replied. "Meanwhile, we have to come up with the other events. We could use the Club Road Run for the kickoff. Eight miles is no big thing for any of you guys. Kind of a warm-up jog. But there's a prize for the winner. Then, I suggest the Red Pine swim. It doesn't take all that long, and it's kind of refreshing. I can't think of a way to handicap that one, unless we make Forrest start from the opposite shore, instead of the middle of the lake. It's kind of ridiculous to enter a swimming contest against a Navy SEAL."

They all chimed in. "Yeah, that's a great idea! Does he have to wear his forty-pound pack too?"

Forrest was game. "Okay, I accept, but no pack. What's next?"

"Then," said Keep America, "it's the ball-buster that we all hated. The five-mountain climb. We have to start at daybreak and come dragging into the compound well after dark. I thought about handicapping the twins, since I think of them as kids, but they're actually at peak athletic age, and I found out they have a gym membership in Vegas. In reality, they could be favorites.

"So, just to review: Day one is the run. Day two is the swim. Day three is the five-mountain climb. Day four is the fishing derby and the trap shoot. Then we go camp out and tell stories. If anyone asks, I'll play guitar and the twins will sing."

Danci piped up. "We're singing whether anybody asks or not. And Daddy's got a harmonica. He says it's the Steinway of the campfire!"

Chapter 16
Competition

WHEN THE DAY OF THE Club Road run came around, everybody in their twenties joined in. It started at the Club House, and went out and back, ending in the parking lot with a small crowd in attendance. Members lined the road for the last hundred yards. The runner coming around the final curve first was no surprise. It was Forrest with no second place finisher in sight. When the second place runner showed up, everybody was shocked. It was Danci. All those one-hour sessions on the treadmill had paid off, plus being twenty years old was a big positive. Next to finish was Minnie, then Hayowenta and Keep America. So, the first contest kind of cemented the notion that a Navy SEAL is always going to beat everybody. Keep America kicked herself. "Should have handicapped it."

A big party was held in the main dining room that night, and two dozen or so of the regular members were treated to the award ceremony, which consisted of a funny speech by Hiawatha and a tiny loving cup filled with Club Road dirt for Forrest.

Next morning, everybody gathered for breakfast in the same dining room for the briefing on the Red Pine Lake swim. The big issue was the definition of "clothes." Forrest wanted to know if shorts and a T-shirt were clothes. Minnie wanted to know if she had to keep them on at all, whatever they were. "If I dump out of a Sunfish in the middle of the lake, first thing I do is strip down naked." The final judgment was any reasonable person would strip to some level. So stripping was legal, and the whole clothing thing was a minor inconvenience at the start of the race. Fall in, strip down, carry on. They decided starting Forrest on the far shore was unfair. The lake was a mile wide, and he needed to be treated better. In the end, he got about a two-hundred-yard penalty that everyone was comfortable with. They used the ten-gauge starting cannon from the Sunfish "Yacht Club." It was super-loud, and actually shook you to the core if you were close to it. People jumped when it went off even when they knew it was coming. The membership came out to see something completely different. Life at the Chippewa Club didn't change over the decades, or over the generations, for that matter. Sunfish racing, barbless fly fishing, grouse hunting, skeet, and bridge. That was it. So, a swimming contest was unique and exciting. Remarkably, Keep America won! She started out strong and held her lead. If there was wagering in the crowd, the odds were heavily against her, but she finished way ahead and waited to wrap the twins in towels for modesty, since they had both stripped completely in their desperation to pull off a victory. Hayowenta was second, and Forrest finished last. Too much of a penalty.

That night, another awards ceremony was held, this time with a ceramic trout vase as a trophy, and a rousing chorus of millennial victory chants, which nobody understood.

Day three dawned with a mugginess in the air. "Damn hot and humid on the toughest contest of the week."

Hiawatha stood at the end of the breakfast table with a map and some notes. "Sorry about the weather, troops. I wish I could have ordered up seventy-five degrees with a light wind. You've got a dilemma. Long sleeves and trousers and roast to death, or shorts and a T-shirt and let the bugs eat you alive. I was going to let you all go in different directions and climb different mountains at different times. It doesn't work. First, it would have to be the honor system. Not that I don't trust you, but I don't trust you. We're all getting into the club van, and we're starting at the base of Mt. Argon. It's the highest point in the state at 1,980 feet. Then it's Bass Mountain, Quartz Mountain, Red Pine Mountain, and Crane Peak. They're all together in kind of a semi-circle, and the longest distance between them is a mile, so almost all of the terrain you cover is uphill or downhill. It's not quite four miles from the foot of Crane Peak to the Club House. First one back gets a prize. I'm leaving the van and driver out there at the foot of the mountains in case somebody gets injured, or wants to quit. Good luck!"

There was no question about who would get the prize. It was a foregone conclusion unless Forrest fell off a cliff and broke his neck. They started up Mt. Argon single file for the first couple of hundred feet, then Army and Navy broke to the right, abandoned the trail, and went bushwhacking through the undergrowth. Hayowenta broke first, and Forrest followed a few yards farther up. That left Keep America and the twins with the easy route, up the blazed trail switchbacks to the summit.

"Hey, Keeper," the twins asked, "do Army and Navy know something we don't?"

"No. I told them they had to bushwhack to the top. The trail is too easy for them."

"No wonder. We couldn't figure out what the machetes were for."

When the girls made the summit, they each found their green-and-blue Chippewa Club flag, which was proof that they made it all the way. The flags went into their backpacks for the descent, mission accomplished. The best part of the summit wasn't the view or the energy bar and fruit juice. It was the two flags that were still there when they started back down.

"Keep bushwhacking, boys."

The twins were in great cardiovascular shape, with legs like sculpted steel. It wasn't the endurance that was the problem; it was balance. They didn't have a lot of hiking or climbing experience, and they didn't realize that a descent had its own set of challenges. In a way, it is harder. Any time they got to a steep spot, Minnie wanted to turn around and go down backwards. As always, they tried to work as a team. Danci was the eyes of the operation, and Minnie followed her lead.

"Min, do you remember if they have to bushwhack back down the mountain too?"

"They better have to," said Danci, "or they'll be on top of us in no time."

"Hey, Keeper, do you hear us?" asked Minnie. "Do Army and Navy have to bushwhack both ways?"

"They better," said Keep America. "Those were Hiawatha's orders."

Three quarters of the way down, a rock about the size of a baseball came sailing over their heads.

Minnie ducked. "Yikes! That thing could have knocked us out or killed us. I'm starting to wish they were ahead of us. We could be buried in a landslide if this keeps up. I wonder, since it came so close, does that mean they're on the trail too?"

Danci gave the order. "Just keep trucking. We're almost down. We should tell Keep America to make them go up the opposite side of the mountain from us on the next climb. Which one is it, Bass Mountain? By the way, where is she?"

"Down at the bottom already. I saw her through the trees. Easy does it; just a few more feet."

When they set foot on solid, level ground, there were the three of them: Army, Navy, and Keep America.

"Dang, we thought you were above us. How did we get passed up?" asked Danci.

Hayowenta smiled confidently. "Well, you kicked our butts on the way up, but we're pretty reckless on the descent. Lots of jumping and sliding."

"Yeah, well, keep the jumping and sliding off to the side of the trail. You almost decapitated us with your loose scree."

"Oh, sorry. We kind of cheated a little. We came to a cliff, and the only way around it was to use the trail a little. That's probably how it happened. Does that mean we're disqualified, Keeper?"

"Not DQ'd, just penalized. I'm first, Danci second, Minnie third, and you two are tied for last."

Forrest won Bass Mountain and Quartz. The three girls came in one, two, three on Red Pine, and they got a big head start on Crane Peak and won again.

That night at the awards dinner, the membership was treated to an accounting of the climb, the scree, the penalty, and the order of finish. Keep America got a crampon glued onto a wooden base for her trophy.

Day four was the fishing derby.

At breakfast, Hiawatha and Kamali took their place at the head of the table. "Keep America," said Hiawatha, "you came up with this idea, so tell us the rules. Kamali and I are not runners or mountain climbers, but we're in for the hundred-dollar fishing derby prize."

"Okay, troopers," said Keep America, "this fishing derby will break the tie for the grand prize between Forrest and me, provided we don't both come in dead last, meaning no fish at all. Here are the rules: no dynamite, no spears or nets, and most importantly, no bait, live or dead. It's spinning gear with lures, wet flies and dry flies, all barbless, so you hardware people with your multiple sets of treble hooks have to remove all but one and de-barb it. I'm really violating my moral code even to allow a treble. For one of you in particular, who shall remain nameless, old habits die hard. One lure that I forbid is the flatfish.

"You can pick from any of the ten lakes on the property. Make sure you go by SUV or Jeep to maximize your time on the water. Also, you don't want to tire yourself out by carrying your big twenty-pounder all the way home. Everybody knows the large population of pike is in the Red Pine chain. Little Red, Middle Red, and Big Red, and don't forget Red Pine River, where the club record was caught. But there are pike elsewhere too, and they are the biggest ones."

Keep America had deliberately left out Brush Lake with its small population of gigantic ones. The devilish aspect of her omission was that she had been cultivating a monster female pike in Brush Lake for years. The fish had her own little environment in an obscure underwater cavern. The big ones like her seek out the best places and own them, killing and eating all the ambitious youngsters who dare to offer a challenge. A couple of times over the years, Keep America would toss a secret fly she tied herself, and catch the big girl on the first cast every time. She would boat it, measure it, and return it to water in a matter of seconds. The idea was, when the fish exceeded the club record by a significant amount, like an inch or two, she would harvest it, weigh it (with witnesses), measure it, and record it with the International Game Fish Association, with all the required photos, of the fish, the angler, the scale used to weigh the fish, and the tackle. It was a big, complicated procedure with lots of pitfalls. Bottom line, Keep America knew where the biggest northern pike ever to exist on the Chippewa Club's property was, and she could catch it on any given day. The question was, should she harvest it for this derby? She decided no. The big thing she needed to do was protect her monster. She would fish Brush Lake right around the underwater cavern, depending on her fellow fishermen's etiquette not to encroach on her space. She would catch another big one, probably the derby winner, and leave "Betsy" to become a world record.

Keep America, Hayowenta, and Forrest fished alone. There were no teams, just boatmates. Minnie and Danci fished together in the same boat. If one of them caught the record fish, Keep America could call it an individual title, but to them, it would be a shared prize.

Hayowenta went right away to Little Red Pine and tossed his bluegill-sized poppers. Little Red Pine was the smallest and shallowest lake and the best for frog imitations. Hayowenta was on the water predawn, and he landed some incredible bass approaching five pounds. "Unbelievable; if I had been fishing for these hogs, I would have caught pike all day long. Today, no pike."

Naturally, Minnie and Danci went together in the same boat. They trolled spoons with lead sinkers. Theory being, the big ones are on the bottom.

Forrest had a favorite spot on Middle Red: The Picnic Rock. He had been landing pretty good-sized Northerns in there his whole life, and one really big one when he was seventeen. The rock was also adjacent to the narrows connecting Middle to Big Red Lake, a rich pike environment. He liked his choice, because of the three distinct waters: Picnic Bay, The Narrows, and Big Red Lake. The premier spot on the big lake was the reed bed. The reeds hid the delta where Magic Stream entered the lake, carrying all manner of creatures with it—minnows, fry, crayfish, frogs—a veritable smorgasbord for big bass and pike.

Keep America was on Brush Lake, where the really big ones were. Not that many of them, though. After tossing an assortment of dry flies along the shore and in shallow water, even trolling one behind the boat, she changed to a streamer on sinking line. That's when the big one hit. She thought it might snap the rod, as it was in a rod holder in the gunwale, with no play in it. She fought the fish for several minutes, figuring that after this, she could go home and read her favorite book for the rest of the day. When she finally saw it, the color was wrong; it had a different shape. Darn! Lake trout! Nobody catches lake trout on Brush. Release her and keep on trolling. No, actually on second thought, kill her and keep her for dinner. Trout is much better than pike, and fewer bones. For a minute there, Keep America thought she was done for the day. Better keep trolling.

Minnie and Danci had their rod in the holder too, and they were enjoying the day as it warmed up. It was Danci's turn to row, so Minnie lay out on the floor of the boat, studying the clouds against the blue of the sky. They talked about new songs to sing and cute boys. All of a sudden, BANG! The rod bent almost double, with the tip actually touching the water. Danci said, "Grab it! Keep the line tight and don't give her any slack." Minnie reeled and reeled, but the fish kept stripping line. When Danci's arms finally got tired, they realized they and the boat were being towed all over the lake by this beast.

"Here, you row," said Danci, "and I'll take the rod."

The fight went on for a half hour, and when the fish came to the boat, the net was too small.

"Here, I'll keep the front half in the net," said Minnie, "and you row to that beach over there. Maybe we can land her that way."

By the time they made land, the pike was exhausted. They rolled her up on the sand and dispatched her with a blow to the head. They always kept a child's baseball bat for that purpose.

"Holy crap! Do you have a measuring tape?"

"Wait a minute. Maybe in my pack. Yes! Here, put that end on her nose."

"Forty-eight inches! Really? What's the one mounted in the Club House? The club record?"

"I think forty-eight."

"Let's go in; our fishing day is over."

The decision to travel by Jeep really paid off because carrying their potential club record by the gills over three miles would dry her out and she would lose weight. Luckily, a beach towel was in the Jeep. They soaked it in lake water and wrapped her up tight.

"Let's take her to the kitchen and put her in the fridge," said Minnie. "When is the weigh-in and judgment?"

"I think Keep America said three o'clock in the Club House," Danci replied. "We can go have a Coke and relax on the beach."

"Maybe we should get started on the world record project first. Let's get the exact length and weight. There's a certificated fish scale in the office. It's approved by the Department of Natural Resources. Keep America says to get a picture of us weighing her with a date time group. Then a photo of us officially measuring it."

"Let's do the measuring right now. I've got the big Nikon with wide angle. You hold the tag end, and I'll hold the reel. I think I can snap the shot one-handed."

After they tried and Minnie looked at the photo, she said, "Didn't work. Too blurry, and we cut the tail off."

"Look! There's a worker," said Danci. "Hey, Maki, can you come over here and help us with something?"

"Sure, whatcha got there?" asked Maki. "Holy crap, that's a biggun!"

"Yeah," said Minnie. "We think it might be a record of some kind. Make sure you get the whole fish. I'll do the focus and zoom setting for you. All you need to do is make sure you're centered and push the black button on top. Good! Now move back a little and get the two of us in there too; just our faces is okay. Now one of each of us alone with the fish. Great! Thanks, Maki."

"That measurement we did out at the lake was a little rushed," said Danci. "Let's measure her again carefully. Straight line from the nose to the very tip of the tail, not up and over the back like some cheaters do."

"Okay, Danci; that looks like forty-nine inches, not forty-eight."

"Yeah, forty-nine and, let's see, looks like a quarter, no maybe three-eighths. Yeah, forty-nine and three-eighths. If she's fat enough, we might have the new club record, and Bobby Singer can take that one of his off the Club House wall and put it back in his cabin, where it belongs."

"Okay, now for the weight. Look how she drapes over both ends of the scale. Get the snapshot. Move it in and sharpen the image as best you can. It's thirty-three. Thirty-three pounds and…three-and-a-half ounces. Can we round that off to four ounces?"

"Let's just submit it the way we see it, and the way the camera shows it. The International Game Fish Association can figure out how to score it. The important thing is to follow every step just the way they say to. One little mistake and they'll disqualify us. Dad told me they're famous for that."

Pretty soon, the rest of the fishermen came in one at a time. First, it was Hayowenta with a twenty-eight incher.

"Right away, when Keep America said pike," Hayowenta explained, "I thought Little Red Lake. I caught a slew of them—I actually lost count—but this was the biggest. There's a ton of them in there, but they're all young. I think there's a big mama that lives off the young ones and keeps them from growing up. No luck getting her today. Anybody else have luck?"

"Minnie and I were the first ones in," said Danci, "and you're second. No telling what the others might come home with, but it doesn't matter."

"What do you mean it doesn't matter? Of course it does. This is a competition."

"Look what we've got in the fridge," said Minnie. "There's a reason we came in early."

"Good, Lord! How big?" asked Hayowenta, peering into the fridge.

"Forty-nine and three-eighths inches," said Minnie. "Thirty-three pounds, three-and-a-half ounces. Go look at Bobby Singer's mount in the Club House. I think we're the new champs. Where's our hundred bucks?"

Forrest came in with Keep America. He had a twenty-nine incher that was really fat. Seven pounds. No factor. Keep America was empty-handed. When she saw the twins' fish, she was glad she hadn't brought in Betsy. What an embarrassment that would have been. Bring in her record project she had worked on for years, only to get beat. Maybe not get beat, but it was too close for comfort.

"Keeper, who's the best taxidermist for our new club record?" asked Danci.

"Justin Ferry in Ishpeming. Freeze it as solid as possible, wrapped in a towel. Make sure you know which is the 'show' side. Justin's not fast, so be patient. You'll love it when it's done."

"Okay, we're done with the pike derby. Time for the Skeet shoot," said Minnie.

"No, it's trap, remember?" said Danci. "Us from sixteen yards and Army Navy from twenty-seven."

"Wait, Danci," said Hayowenta. "Mom and Dad are still out there somewhere. Uh, oh, I think they might have gone to Red Pine River, where Bobby Singer caught the club record. Don't count on the hundred bucks yet. Look, here they come! And he's got a pretty big fish."

Hiawatha was in high spirits. "We did well. My pike is thirty-one inches, and so is this nice steelhead your mom caught."

Danci breathed easier. "Sorry, Dad. Minnie's was forty-nine and three-eighths. We're hoping for a club record. Thanks for the steelhead, though. Now we can choose either yours or Keeper's laker. Are you shooting?"

"Well, as a former club champion many years ago, I certainly am," Hiawatha replied. "I'll shoot with the military, and Kamali will be with you."

"Good. Put your fish in the cooler with ours. That way, we can go straight to the trap field. You all have your guns in your Jeeps, right?"

"Right!"

Don's Field was named in memory of a heroic member who had been a fireman, and a very good shooter. When they arrived, Forrest and Hayowenta started the generator, checked to be sure the trap was fully loaded with clay pigeons, and fired one off to see if it was working.

"All systems go!" announced Danci.

Keep America and Kamali were confused. "Wait, Danci, The two of us have only shot skeet. We're totally out of our element. You have to tell us how it's done."

"First of all, you're not out of your element," said Danci. "There's one house dead center, not two off to the sides. You're still shooting one twenty-five box of shells per game, and you shoot from five stations, not eight. The targets are the same clays you've been shooting your whole life, so when you add it all up, it's a little less complicated, just different angles than you're used to. I'll stand behind you and supervise. One practice round apiece for you rookies, okay, guys?"

"Sure, more if they want," said Forrest.

Both women were lifelong shotgunners. Kamali was a hunter, being married to Hiawatha, and Keep America was target shooting only.

They both had a twenty-gauge Browning Citori. A nice gun.

Keep America hit ten out of twenty-five, and Kamali hit thirteen. Ironically, they both hit their first one. Not bad for their first time out.

Hiawatha ran the game. "Do you ladies want to go first or second? We can't mix because you would be in front of us—a bad idea."

"First."

"Let's put the twins starting out on stations one and two and the sisters on four and five. Five shots from each station; then you move. Keeper, that means you shoot your five at station five, and then move to one. Okay, here we go. Minnie, call for your bird."

"Pull!"

It was a hit.

In the end, the girls averaged seventeen, and the guys nineteen.

"Pretty even, with the handicap system. Let's keep the game the same next time, if there ever is one."

Danci, who did most of the rowing, and got a sunburn, was bushed. Actually, they were all ready for bed.

Hiawatha got them organized for the next day. "Let's try to get an early start tomorrow. We're camping at the little island that protected us in the fire. We need to pay respects and give thanks to the spirits there. Everyone meets at the Magic Lake boathouse at ten, with all their stuff. I've got an axe and a bow saw. We only need one of each. Bring your normal personal camping stuff. Light and batteries, canteen, tent, bag, knife, soap, matches, T.P., towel. I don't have to tell you. We need to reserve three boats for seven people since we've got stuff. I don't think that's selfish, especially with our equipment and supplies. I'm thinking two nights is plenty, especially with people as obnoxious as you. Just kidding. The beautiful thing is, we can stay longer and survive off nature, once we run out of ice, unless someone is willing to make a run to the kitchen. Oh my God, what softies we are! My Ojibwa ancestors would burn me at the stake, really."

Next morning, they were all present and accounted for. Hiawatha and Kamali in boat one with Bonnie; Forrest and Hayowenta in boat two; Minnie, Danci, and Keep America in boat three with Birdie.

Danci was adamant. "I'm not trolling. We've got too much fish as it is. I hope they got plenty of hot dogs from the kitchen. Now I'm kicking myself. I should have been part of that process. If they don't have chocolate chip cookies, I'm going to kill somebody!"

It was a smooth day on Magic Lake. It was oriented in such a fashion as to be vulnerable to the west wind. Hiawatha trolled, took a look at his catch, and returned it to the water.

On arrival, they set up camp immediately, in the woodsman's tradition. Work before pleasure. Hayowenta brought his bow and arrows and set up a target, just for fun. The girls gathered firewood. Not just kindling, but full-sized deadfall. Nice and dry. Nobody ever came out here, much less camped, so it was plentiful.

Minnie was restless. "So what's going on? Did we come out here to die of boredom?"

Hiawatha was patient.

"Do what your ancestors did. Live in the present. Carve something. Read one of your books. Practice your instrument. Go sit somewhere and memorize the different bird calls. Weave a basket. Go row across the lake and get in touch with the plants and animals around it."

So, day one on the island was part rest from the pressure of the pike derby, part getting organized, part exploration. Minnie brought her fins and diving mask. She tried looking for treasure around the island's shore. She thought someone might have dropped a knife or flashlight while embarking or disembarking. Trouble was, nobody ever came out here on purpose. They might use it as a toilet (no sign of that), or picnic spot or swimming hole. The little sand beach was really pretty, and oriented southwest for good sunbathing. Minnie always wondered where all the sand came from in the UP. Sand beaches, sand-bottomed lakes, sand dunes, sand roads instead of dirt roads. Hiawatha gave her a lesson in geological history.

"This is all part of the Laurentian Shield, which is Precambrian rock filled with minerals and metals, like gold, silver, and copper. It used to be much higher in elevation, like a mountain range—like the Rockies even. In the last ice age, a huge ice sheet formed in Canada. The Laurentide Ice Sheet. It ground all those mountains down to what they are now, rounded hills covered in forest. All that grinding created sand, just like sanding down wood creates sawdust. That's what we're standing on, and that's what covers millions of square miles in Canada and northern USA—mineral sawdust, you might say.

Hayowenta headed for his now-empty boat. "Speaking of minerals, Forrest and I are going gold-panning on Magic Stream like we did as kids. We've got only one fool's gold nugget. I'm trying to keep him from making me cut it in half. We need a second nugget so both of us can keep one."

"Did you ever get real gold?" Danci asked.

"Just some dust, and a couple of little flakes. They say the Algonquins got it all centuries ago. See you around sundown."

During his spare time at home, Hayowenta invented a miniature sluice box and pump about a tenth the size of a real one so they could dredge down a little into the streambed and give themselves a better chance. It worked off a small, twelve-volt lawn mower battery and a small eight-hundred-gallon-per-hour bilge pump he found at a boating supply store. The whole thing, including the foldable aluminum hopper he built from scratch, weighed eight pounds and fit in a modified backpack. This time, they went to the deeper pockets, just downstream of eddies; one dove down with the hose, and the other was on the surface inspecting the miner's carpet for gold. After a couple of hours running the equipment, Forrest came to the surface with a rock.

"What do you think of this? I couldn't really see that well because of all the silt I was stirring up. Let me take this mask off so I can see too."

"Well," said Hayowenta, "it's definitely quartz. About the size of a lemon."

"Turn it over."

"Wow! That's a very bright vein, and large too. I know gold likes quartz. Let's take it back for Hiawatha to see. Maybe we'll be making another trip to the assayer's office."

They switched roles, and Forrest worked a new pocket with no success. "Let's call it quits. I want to find out about our quartz."

Back at the island, Hiawatha was reading *Ojibwe Stories from the Upper Berens River*. Minnie was weaving a basket from dried reeds she had found. Danci was practicing with Forrest's bow and arrow. Kamali and Keep America were playing gin rummy.

Hayowenta jumped out of the boat and tied it off while Forrest waded to shore. "Dad, you should see what we found. Show it to him, Forrest."

"Oh," said Hiawatha once it was handed to him. "Yeah, that's a nice one. Could be worth real money, depending on the gold content. Actually, natural nuggets like this and the pure gold ones sell for more than the actual gold price per ounce, because of the aesthetic value. Keep that in your safest place, and take it to Waltz and Waltz in Joliette when we get home. Some of the big ones like that get into the thousands."

Keep America and Kamali came over. "It's pretty," said Kamali. "Too big for a pendant, though; paperweight, maybe?"

Keep America was ready to start prepping for dinner. "Can you boys clean and scale the lake trout? We need to start the fire too, so the potatoes can cook in the coals. Danci, pack them in mud, Ojibwa style. I'm saving the hot dogs for lunch tomorrow. There's two steaks and pasta salad from the kitchen, and chicken breasts and ground beef. I'll organize all this for two dinners, three breakfasts, and three lunches. What's in that cooler of yours, boys?"

"Beer and wine," said Forrest.

"Tell her everything, Forrest," Hayowenta added.

"And whiskey (not much.)"

Keep America was definitely in charge. Hiawatha might be chief, but she was ogimiqwe (boss) in the kitchen.

"Okay then, time for cocktails. Beer for the guys, wine for the girls. Soda for Hiawatha and the twins."

Pretty soon, there was fish broiled over the fire, then steaks and potatoes with a ready-made Caesar salad that had been created in the club kitchen. Dessert was blueberry pie, made by Dana, the chef.

"Know why the pie's so good?" asked Keep America. "Fresh-picked berries from the Denney Flats, where our aboriginal ancestors harvested them more than five thousand years ago. They're the original wild ones, intense concentrated flavor, but the seeds stick between your teeth. Also, she only uses pure butter for the crust."

After the dishes were washed and the garbage buried as far from the camp as possible, which wasn't far, considering the size of the island, Keep America had an announcement to make.

"Let's tell stories. Who wants to recall our last visit, during the fire? Forrest, what do you remember?"

"I remember my arms burning like hell from the paddling. I know you put Hayowenta and me in the bow, for power, but that was ridiculous. It's got to be over three miles from Dooley Point, and we never took a break. What a relief to get here, though. I was thinking, "at least we have a chance, now.""

"Hayowenta, how about you?"

"No problem. Just another day on the lake for me! Just kidding! I was scared and exhausted and falling behind. I had to dig down and find something more than my physical strength. I prayed to all the forebears and Gitche Manitou and the Christian God and Jesus too. Throw them all in the mix at a time like that. That's what I say. We made it, didn't we? I mean we could have settled for just floating on the water and hoping for the best, but these canoes are birch bark and there were embers everywhere. Much better to be safely on land with the protection of the Spirits."

Danci spoke for the twins and joined in on the spiritual thing. "Did anybody but me and Minnie get a special feeling that night? When we were on the water, we were trembling with fear, and choking on tears, but once we hit this island, we felt totally protected. Daddy had us on ember lookout duty. We would call them out, and he would come over to stamp them out, but they extinguished as soon as they hit the ground, and it was very dry. It was like the island put them out for us. And another thing. The wind was howling everywhere you looked on the lake. You could see whitecaps on the black water, but on our island it was a slight breeze. What about you, Daddy?"

"First off, I kicked myself for letting my guard down. It's incomprehensible that my famous senses would be dulled somehow. I blame it on exhaustion and a deep dream-filled sleep. Once we were embarked and on the move, I started feeling more comfortable, and once we were on the island, I knew we were safe and protected.

"I don't know if these powers have always been here, and that's what attracted Gaston Julia and Thomas Edison, or if their presence and knowledge of further dimensions stirred it up, but it's ironic, isn't it? Back in the Edison days, most of the members called it Julia Island on Lake Edison. You can find old maps with this lake labeled as either Magic Lake or Lake Edison. Now it's pretty much back to the original Magic name. A few old timers still use Edison."

"I know we're not much on the New Age spiritual stuff," said Keep America, "but please humor me. Let's all get in a circle in the lotus position. That's with your legs crossed like so. And we'll have Hiawatha lead us in chanting. Make sure it's the ones we know, please, Hy."

Chapter 17
Departure

Tuesday, September 3, 2013 was the day after Labor Day. That morning, Matthias Aho, the patrol chief at the Chippewa Club called the Joliette County Sheriff.

"Dan, because of the holiday I waited an extra day to tell you this, but we need your help at the club. We have a party of seven who went camping last week. They never returned. It was supposed to be a three-day, two-night campout. On day four, we sent a unit out to the campsite and found it apparently abandoned. We've been on our own search and rescue with no success. There are some strange aspects of the situation that could suggest a crime. Can you meet me at my office today to help evaluate the scene?"

"I would be happy to. I would suggest we include Detective Erno Leppinen in the group. He's my most effective analyst, and my greatest asset in situations like this. His instincts and his attention to detail are very refined. We're lucky to have him at all. New York City would be a more appropriate department, but he's a Yooper and he's going to stay one. We call him Ernie."

"Thanks, Dan. When do you think you can get out here?"

"Give me an hour and a half. That will leave us with plenty of sunlight left for the analysis."

"Good, that will give me time to have the boat shop put the whaler on the water on Magic Lake."

They drove out separately, Matthias in his Jeep and Dan in his Police Utility SUV, with Ernie for analysis and a deputy for the grunt work.

Stopping at the boathouse, Matt started his narrative. "Here's where they would have embarked from. We inspected the remaining four Adirondack boats that they left here, just in case they were in them for whatever reason, and then chose the three they used. No evidence here, besides the usual lures and plastic water bottles. Hop in the whaler, guys; let's go see."

Matt pointed out the island as they approached. "You probably won't be needing crime scene tape. There's about thirty club members on the property, and I briefed them to stay away. Zero threat of contamination by people. Those boats in the house are padlocked, and I took the oars back to the compound on day one."

"I definitely will tape off the campsite portion at a bare minimum, just to cover my ass. Can you imagine if something came up at trial? 'Sheriff Leppinen, are you testifying that you did not secure the crime scene at the time of your inspection?'"

"I see what you mean. Forgive me for telling you how to do your job."

They disembarked at the little beach.

"You can see how tiny this place is. There's the flat area on the south end, where the tents are still set up. There's the food area several yards away. Typical Yooper caution, force of habit, when it comes to bears, even though the threat is minimal out here. All their stuff is perfectly normal-looking. The tents set up and staked, with their sleeping bags unrolled, screens zipped shut, ready for bedtime. The personal effects all in logical places. Electric lanterns in each tent. Fire in the pit burnt down to charcoal dust, but not doused. Look; the ashes are still light and fluffy. At first, it seemed like an unusual thing to me. Yoopers, especially Chippewa Club members, never leave a campfire without dousing. When you think about it, though, even that makes sense. It's just another sign that nobody was planning to leave. Look at the kitchen and dining utensils all washed and stacked neatly for the next meal. No sign of struggle, no blood, no evidence of intruders or strangers, and their three boats are all carefully secured with clove hitches to nice, stout tree trunks. You would expect them to emerge from the undergrowth, proud of their stealthy trick."

Ernie was examining the area closest to the firepit. "What do you suppose these scorched spots are?"

"What are you talking about?"

"Look at these burned-looking places on the ground. They're arranged in a circle, see?"

"Yeah, good eyes, Ernie; can you tell what made them?"

"Thing about them is they're not identical. Not even similar in shape except they're all about two feet square, roughly, but they're spaced out equally, almost perfect. All seven of them."

"Deputy, bring your evidence kit over here and take a sample from each of these burn spots. Number them and take photos to go with each one. This is the first thing I've seen today that doesn't look completely normal. Ernie, are you satisfied we haven't missed anything?"

"Yes, sir! We've photo-documented every square inch of this place. I took inside and outside shots of all the tents and their contents. We took casts of any tracks that are clear enough to print, and we got high-quality images of the treads. If we had suspicious clothing or gear, we could swipe it for DNA, but I don't see anything unusual. As far as the strange spots go, they're not really burned. More like overheated, or stained, even. See, the grass blades aren't broken down or changed to ash. It's more like when a dog pees on your lawn and makes it yellow, only these are more brownish black."

"Okay, if you're done, we can go. Matt, do you have anything else for us?"

"Not unless you think diving for bodies will pay off, which is really grasping at straws. This is the most perplexing experience I've ever had. They didn't leave by boat, at least not the ones they came in. They're not here. No signs of violence. What could it be—a suicide pact? All seven of them drowned? How long before bloated bodies sink again, Dan?"

"You do have a point, Matt. I'll get the dive team out here tomorrow. It's the only area we haven't eliminated. Underwater. Even if we don't find a body, or bodies, we might uncover a piece of evidence or two."

Ernie waved them over to the firepit as they were heading for the whaler. "Sheriff, I found two more."

"Two more what?"

"Brown spots. Come and take a look."

The Sheriff walked over to where Ernie was pointing.

"See here?" said Ernie. "They're long and thin, and I swear this one near me is the perfect silhouette of a dog laying on its side. See that? There's the four legs and the head with its ears, even a tail at the other end."

Chapter 18
Extra! Extra!

N EXT MORNING, SEPTEMBER 4, IT was all over the news.

SEVEN CHIPPEWA CLUB MEMBERS MISSING!

Somebody from the club, a member or employee, had brought the story to the *Joliette Mining Journal*. Luckily, the club manager got the word to the Green family in Chicago and other relatives of the missing members when they first disappeared, before the sheriff got involved or it hit the national news. So the Greens came up immediately and got involved in organizing the search and rescue with Matt's patrol.

The TV news loved this kind of situation, with all the mystery and emotion involved. A new version of the old news adage: "If it bleeds, it leads," this was more like "Corner the mother, ask her how she feels, and get footage of her anguish." Tears, the modern version of blood for the press. The reporters were at a disadvantage, though, with the club being private property. They were relegated to standing around outside the club guardhouse with cameras and mikes, relaying to the viewing public what they didn't know yet, and what "unnamed sources" had revealed. The coverage resembled the average school shooting story. They ran footage of the same scene, the guardhouse, and traffic at the gate all day long, and a reporter repeating over and over that there was no new information. Then the news about scorched spots on the earth broke and the story exploded. It made the front page of *The New York Times* above the fold and was the lead story on *The Today Show*, featuring NASA's top expert, who used his official terminology for UFOs: "anomalous phenomenon."

Sheriff Dan gave his first press conference. Since the relatives had been notified, he released the names and ages of the missing, and the name of Lake Edison. The reporters all had maps of the club property and found the lake right away.

"My map says Magic Lake, and Joe's older one says Lake Edison."

Matt had the answer. "Over the years, it's changed names back and forth. Different members prefer one over the other."

"Sheriff, where is the island on this map? What's the name of it?"

"It's that very small spot you see in the north center of the lake. It has no name that I know of. It's just a very small island that people rarely visit. It has a little crescent-shaped beach, where we found the boats tethered, and a flat area where we found the tents. There was a firepit where they had cooked their meals. It's what you would call a primitive campsite. In questioning the club membership currently in attendance, we couldn't find anybody who had ever been ashore there."

Matt started to feel guilty that he hadn't had a meeting with the members, especially now that the story was viral nationwide. He called them into the Club House and filled them in on all the details he knew. Among the members was James Russel McMillion. During the question and answer period, he raised a question.

"Why do you keep saying the island has no name?"

"Because, in my research, interviewing members and studying maps all the way back to the founding in 1889, I've never seen or heard of a name."

"There's another body of knowledge in the culture of this club, Mr. Leppinen," James Russel replied, "and it goes back seven generations. It's the oral history. First, you have to know that Lake Edison was named for one of the founders, Thomas Edison. I don't need to familiarize you with him. He was a founding member of the club. During the latter part of his life, he made the acquaintance of a young mathematician named Gaston Julia. The two of them made a habit over the years of camping on that little island, where they could explore their scientific theories, including such subjects as parallel universes and multiple dimensions. They named it Julia Island, just between themselves. The word got out, of course, and for a generation or two, everybody called it that: Julia Island. Over time, the name of such an insignificant site got lost. Great Daddy McMillion knew it, though, and passed it on to me. The most significant experience in my life, to this day, was when I was seventeen and I camped out there by myself, all alone. Do you remember when in your life the realization hit you that you weren't something special—that you were insignificant in the grand scheme of things? I was lying on my back, looking up at the cosmos and searching for the few obvious constellations I knew, when I was struck by a force that transformed me from human existence into the realm of universal consciousness. I traveled into the far reaches of the universe. I gained the realization that I was eternally connected to all parts of the multiverse at all times, and that my body was a temporary form, one of my many forms. I received the blessing of immortality. And guess where I landed? Julia Island! Gaston Julia's other Julia Island. The one in the Julia set, and the Mandelbrot set. The one they calculated all those years ago.

"The twins felt it too. Many years later, when they were little and I took them to revisit the island, we spent two days and a night. In the morning, right out of nowhere, they asked me, 'Uncle Russ, when we're on Julia Island, are we there, or is it here, or is it both?'

"That's what I've been trying to figure out ever since."

Made in the USA
Columbia, SC
27 August 2021